Prai

"Exceptionally well written from beginning to end, *Mr. Green Jeans* is all the more impressive when considering that it is author Chris McGee's debut venture as an eco-novelist. *Mr. Green Jeans* is very highly recommended, especially to the attention of environmental activists, and will make an enduringly popular addition to community library General Fiction collections."

—John Taylor, *Midwest Book Review*

"If you're stuck in a mid-life slump, this, well, maybe won"t solve everything, but it will get you thinking."

—*The Daily Climate*

"An entertaining, thought-provoking romp that will have anyone who thinks about their impact on the planet reconsidering their choices, big and small."

—Douglas Fischer, Director, Environmental Health Sciences

"*Mr. Green Jeans* gives voice to the frustrations that beleaguer the minds of those who can't escape that whisper of planetary responsibility."

—Brien Durham, Educator

MR. GREEN JEANS

By Chris S. McGee

Harvard Square Editions
New York
2016

Mr. Green Jeans

Copyright © 2016 Chris S. McGee

None of the material contained herein may be
reproduced or stored without permission of the author
under International and Pan-American
Copyright Conventions.

ISBN 978-1-941861-13-4
Printed in the United States of America

Published in the United States by
Harvard Square Editions
www.harvardsquareeditions.org

*This book is a work of fiction. References to real people, events,
establishments, organizations, or locales are intended only to
provide a sense of authenticity, and are used fictitiously. All
other characters, and all incidents and dialogue, are drawn from
the author's imagination and are not to be construed as real.*

This book is dedicated to my mother, who celebrated the discoveries I made in the woods as a little boy, and to my lovely wife, Lynn who has given me peace, support and the freedom to be who I want to be. It makes all the difference.

Chapter One

"SOMETIMES YOU JUST have to start something and then polish it as you go." My dad had always said that, and now I was going to put it to the test. A test he probably wouldn't have condoned but might have applauded with the heart of the latent rebel I had always pictured him to be. He died when I was twelve, right in front of me, of a heart attack, and thirty-eight years later, I wonder and long for what it might have been like to have a father. That night, he was in my thoughts more than usual because I was about to do something really stupid. I was sitting in my rusted, almost worn-out pickup on an outer road of 1-70 in rural Missouri. Home was twenty miles away. It's the middle of the night with a steady spring rain falling, I took the last drag of my organic cigarette, one of my many shortcomings.

Lake, my wife of unconditional love, didn't know I was out here. I was supposed to be camping by myself on a long-needed spiritual quest to regain some youth and vision. She bought it; it wasn't hard. We both used to be avid backpackers, and she thought I was hitting some middle-aged wall of confusion. She encouraged me. A kiss goodbye, and I was off. That was ten hours ago. My camp was set up in the Mark Twain National Forest, one hundred and fifty thousand acres of deciduous woods crisscrossed with bluff-lined creeks and dotted with caves. I picked a day with rain likely, no moon, and I wasn't disappointed. More camouflage for me.

I was frustrated, confused, pissed off and just about ready to take a gun to my head, because I just didn't care anymore. Maybe there was reincarnation, spirit guides, or elementals at work, or maybe I had just a plain ole solid connection to the Earth, because I spent my childhood on the ground watching the ants and all that the forest floor calls their home. I learned much about the world in my youth crawling around in the dirt and uncovering what lay under a rock or a rotting piece of wood. Now I saw a world with humans as the ants, but with no sustainability model. My passion might have escaped me for most of my life, but desperation has been my constant companion, a reminder that there is something integral missing in my existence.

The time had come for me to sound a 'wake-up call' to the self-serving bureaucracy I despise so. The corporations and the unknowing masses had been destroying this planet for a long time. The big boys know that oversight and enforcement of the flawed game rules will have no whiplash of any measurable degree. These fools continually change our way of life with little regard for the permanent effects of their mindless greed. The animals live in fear, the people buy their bread with their corporate bread, and the earth suffers every second of every day.

I've seen it, felt it, been a contributor for so long, and that's why I was here on this dark rainy night, parked off the side of a one-lane blacktop. The gun to my head had flirted with my being over the past year. Lying down for the night, my thoughts often ended there before sleep overtook. I was just so tired and about to give up if I didn't just say, "Screw it! I'm doing something about this!" Being angry all the time, sucked.

Rain splattered through my half-opened pickup window, and my hands were starting to sweat. I was wearing black pants, a black hoodie and black shoes, all purchased at the thrift store two weeks ago for cash. The outer road to the freeway where I was parked was deserted, and the stand of trees that block my truck from the interstate was in full growth. I put out my cigarette in the ashtray. I hate people who throw their butts on the ground. It's been determined that enough cigarette butts are littered throughout the world each day to reach the moon. A butt litterer is something I've never been. You can bet a butt litterer does a bunch of dis-connected crap each day. This type of dialogue runs through my head every day.

Looking in my rear-view mirror, a bead of perspiration dropped off my nose. The last few years, I've looked in the mirror and seen my father. I look so much like him. High cheekbones, brown hair with a generous peppering of gray, and green eyes.

Closing the door quietly, even though no one was around for miles, I pulled off the lid of the plastic tub in the truck bed. I grabbed a can of spray paint from the tub and put it into the pocket of my hoodie. Then, I pulled out the only other thing in the tub, a chainsaw. It was new. Orange. Paid in cash. No money trail. Maybe a little overly cautious, but anything I could do to lessen a possible arrest, seemed like a smart choice. I've been watching the human species destroy our immutable connection to the earth since I could reason. Tonight's action was stupid at best, and would make no difference, but my heart was alive as I crossed the road with my new chainsaw and stepped into the tree line.

Passing through mostly silver maple and red cedar, I spotted them. Ugly, out of place, the signs needed to be gone. I'd cursed every day I drove past them on the way to work. The first advertised 'VASECTOMY REVERSAL', the second 'LIVE FREE—BOX-MART, exit 143'. I'd leave 'SENSATIONS ADULT EMPORIUM' for later. Billboards can ruin a perfectly nice drive down the roads of America, and these two were going to their graves.

Semis screamed by, and the mass of humanity flowed down the interstate twenty yards from my shelter of saplings, high grass and a smattering of Missouri wildflowers. No moon and a good rain had the driver's eyes on the road. Interstate I-70 is the first paved channel coast-to-coast in America. A lot of animals took their last breath on this highway. I'd stopped many times on this constant petrol stream to help a wayward box turtle avoid a certain fatal trek.

Crouching, I pulled the chainsaw. Not a hesitation, it started like it was an extension of my gut. Letting out a long breath, I moved from the stand of trees and brush and hurried through the rain to my first target. Four, six-by-six, treated posts cemented into the ground crossed with two-by-fours forming the lines that the four pieces of plywood were screwed to. A piece of crap billboard that someone had been making money on for decades. The offspring of the billboard's owner awaited this piece of the American pie as their inheritance. It was on a slope, and after cutting the third post, physics went to work on number four. The sign began to slowly wane. Saw to last post, and before a complete cut, she snapped. Boom! "VASECTOMY REVERSAL is down!" There were too many of us bipeds sucking the life from this planet without some fool going back to get his semen streaming again.

Drenched, I walked back into the tree line carrying the chainsaw and up over a slight rise to the 'BOX-MART' sign. I was three years sober from 'BOX-MART'. This megastore's grip on every community has the same effect that corporate agriculture has on the almost-extinct family farm. It took three pulls on the chainsaw and the 'BOX-MART BUY MORE CHINESE CRAP, SAVE CHILD LABOR' piece-of-crap billboard was on its way to terra firma. These were sorry-ass signs compared to the monoliths of steel rising forty feet in the air that started sprouting up a few decades ago along this stretch of I-70 in the Heartland. After cutting three posts of the 'BOX-MART' sign, the rain was just a sprinkle and headlights exposed me as I made the final cut. All four posts cut, and 'BOX-MART' didn't even waver. There was some irony. The ground under the sign didn't have much of a slope, so I picked the side that seemed higher and put all my weight against the billboard. It didn't budge. I probably hadn't fully cut through one of the posts. I took a running go at it, slamming my wet mass at full force against the plywood. One of the posts caught my knee and sharp shooting pain ran up my leg. Down went 'BOX-MART' with me on top.

"Owwww!" I shouted, holding my throbbing appendage and about to throw up. The cold sweat came. I lay for a good two minutes on top of the plywood 'Mart' part of the sign. My knee wasn't broken, but I was going to have a painful time walking, and one hell of bruise. Yet, there was one last step. I took the can of spray paint out of my pocket: high-gloss, lime green. Giving the can a hardy, thirty-second shake, I wrote 'Mr. Green Jeans' across the billboard in large letters. I listened to the interstate traffic whiz by and wondered if anyone would even notice. It didn't matter right now. I was satisfied with my conquest. Me, Jack Creek, some middle-aged nobody had taken action! A few billboards, what a laugh. Many would say I was a fool, but there are a few who would give me a standing ovation. I'd take any audience I could get. Our window to change our ways as a species was quickly closing. Tick-tock.

Snapping out of my contemplation, which now happens as a constant stream, I realized I needed to get out of here. Almost forgetting the chainsaw, I limped to the truck. Branches scraped my face, and it would be one more thing I'd have to explain about to Lake when I returned home tomorrow. Back in the truck, I lit a smoke and cracked the window. It was 3:20 a.m. My knee was throbbing and I was soaked.

No pain, no gain. The outer road was still vacant. I took the exit ramp onto 1-70. I'd drive by my accomplishment tomorrow, as I now headed west of the crime scene. Ten minutes later, I exited 1-70 and followed a two-lane, blacktop north for five miles through the countryside, and then left a mile and half down a gravel track to the parking area for the Mark Twain trailhead. Pulling into the vacant parking area and turning off the engine, I sat. The rain had stopped, and the sound of the oak and maple leaves dripping combined with the fresh smell of a wet earth was helping me to relax. I rested my head against the back window of the truck's cab. Nothing. Nothing happened. No one had followed me. I was a two-bit outlaw now. A smile grew on my face, and I exited my steadfast chariot. Hard to explain the feeling, but it was good, and it was mine. Grabbing the flashlight and chainsaw from the truck bed, I limped down the forest trail to my campsite.

It was almost 4:00 a.m. when I spotted my forest-green tent. Unzipping the tent's door, I grabbed a small bag of trail mix and found a good back rest against an old cedar set on the edge of a hundred-foot, limestone bluff that formed a horseshoe canyon around a pristine valley. The sky had cleared, and the stars had begun their sparkle dance. Sitting on a bed of pine needles against the old twisted cedar, I ate a few handfuls of nuts and raisins and stared at the twinkles above. Closing my eyes, my mind wandered off into the night's events. No action, no change. A single person sometimes has little chance to be heard, and this was my first shout. Weak I knew. Nothing that was going to change anything, and nothing to do with the big problems that filled my thoughts, wake or sleep. I was either going to mess up my whole life, or become a half-assed legend, Mr. Green Jeans, 'Cowboy Steward of the Planet'. More than likely, I was going screw my life up if I continued, but right now, I didn't care. Do something or shut up, I thought. I can't take living a life of mediocrity anymore, rather be dead.

I woke to the sound of a male cardinal's peep coming from the branches above my head. It was just before dawn. I took it as a message of 'thanks', as I looked up into the tree to view the bold red figure aware of my presence. I had to get home and see Lake. For the first time in a long time, I didn't feel angry.

Chapter Two

ON THE WAY BACK HOME, I wondered if my vandalism would make the news. Maybe Mr. Green Jeans needed to tip the reporters off? It was Sunday, and Lake and I usually take our two dogs, both rescues, out on a run. Barney was the big one, part Lab, German Shepard, and maybe some Corky, funny looking dog. The other one, Pearl, is cattle dog and part coyote. She was our-ten-year-old reservation dog we'd rescued before leaving our teaching gigs on the Navajo Nation. Moving back to the Midwest to be closer to my mother, we bought a hundred-and-five-year-old farmhouse in the country, fifteen miles from my mother, and our work in Manchester. A Rockwell picture we couldn't replace for any less than five times that cost in the Southwest. It sat on five acres of Black Walnut and Oak. Life was good in that way, and now I was potentially screwing that up. Pulling into the long driveway off the gravel road, I went over my story, trying to figure out how I would explain my injuries.

Lake and I had met later in life after both finishing our first and second round of marriages, and we were ready for what it meant to be partners. After much good effort, eventually we were rewarded with the trophy. We were deeply in love, and never did we question that this was it for the rest of it. Of course, certainty is the fool's game, but this was as good as either of us had ever had it, and we were going to make this one last. So far, it had been as easy as spreading jam on toast. Our politics, the need for independence, and the understanding that all life is connected, were as aligned as either of us had ever known in another person.

As I opened the truck door, out of the house bounded Barney. "What are you doing big boy!" I said, very happy to be with my family again.

"Hi, baby!" Lake said coming off the porch. She was just shy of six feet, had a thin-frame, long dark brown hair, and a contagious smile.

"Hey, babe!" I replied, pulling my pack from the truck bed.

"Want me to grab this tub?" She asked.

"No, no, just leave that there," I responded, hoping I didn't sound too suspicious.

"Any insight into the meaning of existence?" she asked following me onto the porch.

"I'm looking at it," I said, turning to look her in the eyes.

"Sounds like you did learn something out there."

"Still want to go on our walk?"

"Jack, what did you do to your leg!?" Lake asked, staring at a dried streak of blood running from my knee and down into my boot.

"I'm all right, just took a spill down a ravine. Let's take our walk, I'll clean it up when we get home," I responded, opening the front door and calling for Pearl.

"Baby, let me clean you up first."

"Would Jerimiah Johnson stop and tend to every scratch he got? There was that cougar though?"

"Oh, I hope you made friends with him. Pearl, come on!"

Pearl slowly made her way out the door and then had to be picked up and put in Lake's Subaru; she was terrified of cars, but loved the majority of our destinations. Barney was already anxiously awaiting the opening of the door to the back seat. Once in, she lay panting in anticipation of the upcoming smells, and piddle, and poop fest.

Walking through the cottonwoods along the muddy Missouri River, Barney checked out every spot Pearl identified. Pearl was the reservation dog. Up until she was given a home with us, she'd run wild, eating garbage and anything she found just to stay alive. The life of most reservation dogs is horrific, to put it mildly, especially if they're female. Her nose was finely tuned. Barney was there to just double check Pearl's smells and serve as an assistant if they found anything to chase. We didn't allow the dogs to pursue even a rabbit for more than a few yards. We understood that the natural world was not to be used as a playground for our domestic animals. House cats are the biggest killers of indigenous wildlife in any western nation. Our cat, Smokey Joe was given supervised outings in the yard. He was as well balanced and as happy as any cat.

"So, you didn't get too wet out there?" asked Lake as we strolled on a wide dirt path under the towering cottonwoods.

"Nope, that rainfly did the job; glad I sealed it before I left. I just decided to take a night hike; it's beautiful out there," I answered with my second lie.

"We need to take a road trip. Get a little taste of the Southwest again," Lake said, throwing a stick for Barney. We'd both spent a good deal of our lives in Arizona and New Mexico and missed it every day.

"Sounds great. Maybe this summer?"

"Yeah. Let's really do it this time, okay?"

Loading the kids in the car after the walk, I decided to drive into Manchester and pick up some lunch at our favorite restaurant, Main Squeeze, the only vegetarian restaurant for a hundred mile radius in central Missouri. It was exceptional food, but the real reason to take the detour was it would allow me to drive past last night's crime scene and see if Lake would notice the absence of the billboards.

With our lunch sitting in a brown paper bag on Lake's lap, I took the ramp to I-70. Only three more miles of freeway till last night's event. I hoped she would notice.

"Ego-driven bunch of mothers, aren't we?' I said hitting I-70.

"What?" Lake was already eating a bite of her vegan sesame seed cookie.

"Nothing. Just a comment on our adolescent species," I responded as we topped the hill where the billboards once stood. I blurted out stupid comments like that all the time now. No rhyme or reason, they just popped into my head, with no connection to what we were currently doing or even talking about.

"Oh! Oh! Oh!, they're gone!" exclaimed Lake as she spit out some cookie onto the dashboard.

"What's gone?" the third lie.

"The billboards! They're just lying there on the ground, no more 'VASECTOMY REVERSAL' or 'BOX-MART'. You didn't see that?"

"I took them out last night." I couldn't believe I had said that so matter of fact.

"Was that after you saw the cougar?" she responded as she often did, offering a beginning for another fictional story we would tell back and forth on just about any topic. Especially when we took long road trips, passing through a small town we would make up a fictional account of the town's history.

"The cougar and I ended up sleeping together. No, this was earlier. No big deal, hooked up a chain to the truck and pulled 'em down."

"No one saw you?" she played along.

"Oh yeah, there were about six cops chasing me, but we went off road and I lost them after I leaped a creek in the truck. Sorry, I forgot to mention that," I continued, knowing that could have happened, except I would have rammed the truck into the creek, started to run, been tackled, handcuffed, thrown behind bars, lost my teaching credentials and really changed things forever. I looked into the rear-view mirror and saw the gentle curve of the empty hilltop. It looked nice.

"You know San Paulo, Brazil, something like the second or third largest city in the world took down all their billboards. San Paulo's mayor said it was visual pollution," I inserted to help my eventual reveal.

"I hate billboard signs. Two down on our drive, I swear someone took them out," Lake replied chewing her third bite.

"You want to have sex when we get home?" I asked, realizing that I was still on my outlaw's high.

"Aren't you a little tiger today?"

"I'd prefer large, male king of the pride, savage beast."

"Of course you would."

"So?"

"Yes, I think I can fit that in. You need to shower and clean that nasty blood streak first."

"Don't get too excited." We gave each other a familiar glance as we sped down the freeway. The day was good, no need to ruin it with the small fact of the signs. I could walk away now, if I wanted to.

"Mimosas!" Lake said as she rose from the bed.

"Sounds good. Hey, that was great. Thank you."

"Thank you, tiger." She was off to the fridge.

I lay in bed and petted our seventeen-pound, Russian Blue, Smokey Joe. Maybe I would just keep my secret and carry on with life knowing at least I'd done one small 'rage against the machine' thing before I died.

Chapter Three

WEEKS PASSED, and I was starting to feel like my old self again. I didn't like it. The rush of my first conquest was wearing off quickly. I was getting angry again. As I lay dormant, the destruction of the planet continued, and taking down billboards wasn't going to change that, but it still felt good. There was never any recognition of my feat in the news. It was Friday afternoon, and I sat at my desk finalizing next week's lesson plans, having a hard time focusing. I kept drifting back to my days as a river guide in the Grand Canyon. I was in my twenties. Life was easy and beautiful. Being in the Canyon, away from society, can make you feel awfully good.

I started as the groover. The groover is the guy who put up and took down the toilets at each camp and collected all the trash. Some trips lasted twenty days and that's a lot of fecal material. I'd bag the trips' sewer contents and lock them up in air-tight ammo containers. These would all be located in my raft stationed at the back of the pack each day. I was in effect the sanitation engineer for the mobile sewer system, all trash included. My last two years, I was lead dog as I proved dependable, capable and consciousness to the guests. A few of which I got to know rather well and still talk to today. They were mostly rich folks on these trips, and the rafting company went all out with the food and drink. The isolation and spiritual freedom of the canyon just squeezed the love and peace out of a person. If it didn't, then it was hard to know what would. The Grand Canyon is a remarkable awe-inspiring place, and you know you are there every moment. Not too many places like that left.

After setting up camp on a gravel bar, the Colorado gently flowing by, we'd start the dinner prep. Politics and 'what-if' conversations would erupt. People would just let go and speak as though the canyon was their church. I naturally followed suit, many times as though I was campaigning for the presidency.

"If I was president, I'd put aside Alaska, most of the Southwest and any migration path for the hundreds of species of birds that fly across the US every year. Free-range cattle and sheep would have to compete equally with environmentalists for lease of public land. Timber and mining would soon end, replaced with renewable sources and the jobs would not be less, but more. We would have a million small organic farms that would be supported by the government. No jobs lost, a better planet...." Da da da, I would go on and on.

There would be great applause, and in a week or so, everybody would be back home, living in the system again. Conviction evaporated outside of the walls of the canyon.

I thought I had the answers, but I was old enough even then to know that all I could do was raise a ruckus if I was to be heard. Money had never led me. In the history of the world, few people without the gold were able to rise against the system and change the system. Gandhi, Martin Luther King and John Muir were my favorites, and I knew I'd never be anything like these men. In fact, I was on the track to becoming a menace to society. Maybe if I continued my antics, news coverage would follow, and maybe people would be interested, look at themselves, and change. Farfetched most likely, but I felt committed to this line of action. I had to do something before I left this world besides teaching the generations of tomorrow. That just wasn't enough anymore. I was getting burned out anyway, after twenty three years in a myriad of schools over four states. The profession had changed. Teaching was sometimes just a small part of the job, depending on the school's population and the district's goals. So many dysfunctional families still having kids and so many school districts concerned with only irrelevant test scores. I was tired of being the parent, the cop, and the occasional teacher.

Now that the high of my sabotage was gone, I missed the rush. I felt no remorse. My ideology on this quest was to never hurt a living thing, just create a stir of conversation. It was simple, and I never imagined I'd be challenged on this aspect of my creed. Vandalism seemed a necessary evil and would quickly land me in jail. But…breaking out of another self-imposed dialogue, I raised myself from my desk as I heard my name called out.

"Mr. Creek?"

"Hey Sarah, what can I do for you?" I looked over to see one of my senior art students, texting on her phone as she talked to me.

"You said today that if you don't know nature, you won't know art?"

"Yep. What's your question?" I replied, gathering up my things.

"I don't understand it." She looked at me, putting away her phone in the front pocket of her jeans.

"You're quite talented, Sarah. Your use of color blows me away. Tell you what, this weekend, take two hikes, just spend a few hours outside in the woods. When I see you Monday, let me know if anything sparked."

"Okay. Have a good weekend, Mr. Creek."

"You, too. Thanks for asking."

"Thanks for answering," Sarah said over her shoulder as she left my classroom.

It was nice to have one of my students stop by after school, the rarity of it always raised hopes. But now, it was time for chapter two. The Mother is in pain. I packed my bag and told myself I'd finish the lesson plans at home. I needed to get out of there.

Picking up a pizza at Shakespeare's, a locally owned pizzeria, I headed down the freeway to the country, and home. Another exhausting week had come to an end. Today, I attempted teaching my high school students how to let go of convention and paint something abstract. I wanted them to think outside the box and experience their own uniqueness through an assignment that had no rules of composition. Fifty minutes with just paint and a nine-by-twelve-inch piece of Masonite board. Some got it, but many held tight to what they'd been told was good and what wasn't. A few just sat there. This lack of courage I saw as a reflection of what society had become; the uniformity sweeping across our nation seemed to be getting more pervasive all the time.

Pulling up to the house I let out a long breath. I needed to get out of my head. I needed action. As I stepped onto the porch, I saw something hanging on the doorknob.

"This is good," I said out loud. In a plastic bag on the doorknob hung a pamphlet explaining the virtues of giving your life over to Jesus Christ. *Three Reasons for Jesus* was the booklet's title. Whoever dropped this off wasn't aware that pushing religion was one of my triggers. Well, it would make a good coaster.

As I opened the front door, Pearl and Barney greeted me in their customary, overly gregarious celebration of jumping, wagging and doing circles. Smokey Joe was there rubbing up against my leg.

"Hey guys! What's going on? It's the weekend!"

They followed me to the kitchen, as I deposited the pizza in the oven, turning it on warm. There were ten Boulevard pale ales in the fridge from a twelve pack I'd purchased last weekend. I grabbed one.

"Okay, okay, let's go out." The kids crowded me as I opened the door to our backyard sanctuary. Forty-foot Walnut trees stood proud over a good deal of our five-acre property. The dogs rushed out the door first. The cat waited his turn and walked out with me. Smokey Joe never went far. In fact, today as I sat to soak up the beautiful spring afternoon in a rocker on the deck, he jumped in my lap. Most of our property was wooded and bordered by conservation land on two sides. The county gravel road flanked the front. The west side, a dirt driveway through the trees, ran back to our friend's, Todd and Barb's, house. Todd worked with the blind, and Barb taught physics at a junior college. They were great neighbors, and we had spent many evenings around a backyard fire talking late into the night. Taking a sip of pale ale, I began to drift off again into my den of mindless jumble about the planet's imminent demise. Couldn't seem to stop the chatter in my head, my heart was hurting.

"Anybody home!?"

Lake deposited her two bags on the dining room table and walked out on the porch.

"Hey baby."

"Hey love." She leaned down, and we gave each other a quick peck.

"How was the day?" she inquired sitting in the rocker next to me as Barney and Pearl arrived to greet their favorite person on the planet.

"Not bad, but that new kid, Doug? Wiped red paint on Shasha and ruined her new T-shirt. Had to call his parents who don't have a dime to their name and get them to up the money for a new shirt. Doug will probably get slapped around tonight."

"What are you going to do, ya know? It's just so messed up out there for a lot of people," Lake said, walking down the steps with the dogs.

"Yeah, what are you going to do?" I replied, rubbing my hand across Smokey Joe. We'd both seen so much of it, we'd learned to pass over it quickly and try not to take things home with us that we had no control over. Right? We always took things home with us. We still had a pulse.

"Oh, Barb and Todd wanted to know if we wanted to get together tonight for a fire? I already said yes," Lake called from the yard.

"Sounds good," I yelled back.

Barb and Todd's house sat behind ours through woods. It was always fun to walk to their driveway under the greening canopy of branches from hundreds of trees. They had an interesting U-shaped house. On the backside of the house, a large, slate patio spilled over the inside of the U and looked out over the Missouri River Valley. A glass-topped table and wrought-iron chairs with rusted, orange-colored cushions gave each settler a fabulous view. Worth a fortune if they ever decided to sell.

"So, summer's around the corner. You guys going anywhere this year?" Todd asked as he popped another pizza roll in his mouth. Todd was a big guy, a little overweight, but he carried it well. He was as jovial a person as you'd ever meet.

"Maybe."

"The Southwest, right?" Barb asked.

"Yeah. Hope this will be the year. But if we don't, we're definitely getting a goat," Lake said and looked over at me.

"A goat!" Barb responded with a laugh. Barb was a small, pretty woman with the heart of a dove.

"To mow the grass!" Lake said with an enthusiastic giggle that transferred to all of us.

"Don't ask me to take care of your goat when you're gone." Todd responded.

"Todd's scared of goats, maybe just bovines in general," Barb said.

"I am not. I just don't like animals that don't respond to the human voice in a productive manner."

"You're scared of bovines, man?"

"Jack, give me some support here," Todd said. "You're scared of things, too. Maybe not living things, but there's stuff out there that scares you, and I wouldn't bring it on you right now."

"True that. I'm not going to get into a pissing contest with you, but a goat, buddy?"

"Look, they're an unknown variable."

"You might get racked," Barb inserted.

"Among other things, honey. At least their poop is in pellet form, right?" Todd said in defense.

The night ran past the midnight hour, and as Lake and I walked their drive back to our place, I couldn't help myself. "Baby, you know those signs?"

"Yeah, there was a truck up there today; 'BOX-MART' will back up by tomorrow. Woo-hoo! The machine keeps rolling!"

"Baby, I chain sawed them down. I'm serious." I felt relief and then an immediate impending danger. There was a long silence. It lasted too long.

"Excuse me?" Lake stopped, stood and just stared at me. Right in the eyes. There's potential for a major problem when she does that.

"You serious? When you went camping on your mini vision quest, you were really taking down billboards?"

"Yeah."

Another long silence.

I followed her as she walked on. "So? You pissed?" I said in my strong, scared voice, knowing that most relationships might be troubled by one of the parties taking down large billboards without any prior consultation.

Lake stopped and grabbed me taking her lips and sealing them on my open mouth. Five minutes later, we arose from the grass. Whoever says a quickie is over-rated, needs to qualify each and every second. We hadn't had sex like that for a few years.

"What are we doing next?"

"What!?" I stood dumbfounded.

"What are we doing next, Jack?"

"Next? What the hell are you talking about? There's no next. It did feel damn good though. You're not pissed?"

"Nope. I want in on this. Just one more time." She was squeezing my hand.

"Let's just talk about it in the morning."

"Fine, but tell me what it was like. I want to know everything, how long you thought this out, what it was like being out there. Jack! I don't believe it! Baby! What were you thinking?!"

"I wasn't thinking so much as I was doing. It helps when you do things like that."

"Wow, my husband took down 'BOX-MART'. That's freaking cool."

"Don't forget the 'VASECTOMY REVERSAL'."

"That sign was just embarrassing. Good choice."

"Are you serious?"

"Uh-huh."

As we walked the rest of the way home the fireflies lit the trees, and the bullfrogs were singing their guttural mating song from the pond on the conservation land. The nature is thick in the Midwest, so thick that at times you feel like you're woven into it, which in truth we all are. Then the mosquitoes start to feed, and you realize that it's not just a spiritual connectedness but a very physical one, too.

Chapter Four

SATURDAY MORNING, it was raining. Opening my eyes and looking out the window, I realized there would be no gardening today. I rolled over, and Lake was gone. She never left the bed before me on a Saturday. Pulling on jeans and a 'No Army Since 1948 – Costa Rica' T-shirt, I went downstairs to find her sitting at our primitive harvest table in the dining room, which was invaded by a jungle of tropicals and cacti in pots of varying sizes and colors, leaving very little table space. She had a big of mug of coffee and was writing on a legal pad between a Christmas cactus and 20-year-old aloe.

"Hey sleepy, coffee's made, and I'll get some breakfast in a little bit."

"What are you doing up?" I responded.

"A list, a very special list of possible targets," she replied, not looking up.

"You're kidding me?"

"I like Mr. Green Jeans, even though it leaves me out. But it will make people think there's just one guy. Good cover from the cops. How about just, 'Green Jeans'? Anyway, we can discuss that later. Here's my list of possible targets. Okay…" Lake enthusiastically spilled.

"Whoa, wait a minute. I think we need to talk about this some more," I interrupted, as I went to the kitchen for my first cup of Joe.

"What's there to talk about? We get caught we go to jail, maybe. We definitely lose our teaching jobs. So, we just can't get caught. There's really not much else to talk about, except possible targets and risk management. We are both so pissed off with the way the world is going and the devastation of the planet. We don't have kids, so, what the hell!? I'm tired Jack, we're both tired of not doing anything and feeling helpless.

Let's rock, baby!" She was on a roll. Lake was a double Leo, both moon and sun. When she took off on something, there was no stopping her.

"Let me tell you, as a recent veteran of this business, you start to think that getting away with it once is all you got in your cards. I do not want to see you hauled away. It was stupid crazy what I did." I hurried back into the dining room.

"Recent veteran? Are you serious? Maybe I should call you Billboard Clyde."

"And you're Billboard Bonnie?"

"Yep."

"You really are serious, aren't you?" I now sat directly across from her. Pearl laid her head on my lap.

"Did you know Ted Danson and one of his friends, who later became one of the founders of Earth First, were responsible for taking down five hundred or more billboards between Flagstaff and the Grand Canyon while they were students at Flagstaff High?"

"Yeah, I'm the one that told you that," I replied, wondering if I should have just kept my deed a secret.

"Well, two billboards are significant, and I still can't believe you did that, but I'm game for a few more." She pushed her list across the table to him.

'TESTICLE FESTIVAL MUMFORD MISSOURI JUNE 13-15', and 'SAUCY TIME ADULT SUPER CENTER', and 'GUNS AMMO AND LIQUOR EXIT 231', and the list ran onto the next page.

"Yeah, those are good ones, but baby, come on, let's slow down," I said with all the seriousness I could muster while at the same time looking at her with desire and huge respect. I was done, ready to cash it all in and go for it. The earth is hurting, and we were the reason. I had a semblance of a plan I'd been going over for years. Taking down some billboards was just a warm-up exercise.

"Were you going to slow down? Were you ever going to tell me? Lake countered.

"I'm glad I told you, it was killing me."

"You getting gun shy?" she asked with compassion.

"I don't know. You know I sometimes don't think things out too much, I just act." I'm an Aries, and we're infamous for getting a ball rolling and then backing off.

"Pick a few signs." Lake nudged the pad closer to me.

"So we're going after just two billboards? No more, and then we're done?" I asked, trying to get a grip on this atypical Sunday morning conversation with my wife.

"I don't know, probably, just want to get my beak wet," she replied as she got up for another cup of coffee.

"Okay. Pearl, your parents are becoming outlaws, sweetheart." I petted her head as she closed her eyes.

"Green Jeans can't die!" shouted Lake from the kitchen.

Coming out of the kitchen, Lake petted my head and began pacing around the dining room. "We're just getting started, baby."

She put down her coffee and walked to the staircase, then turned and looked at me. On the third step, she let the robe slip off, poised in her birthday suit. I stood like a soldier in front of a superior.

"Can you help me make the bed, sweetheart?" she said as she continued up the stairs. What was going on? Take down a few billboards and your eco-activist wife makes other dreams come true? I wasn't going to question it. I followed her up the stairs.

Chapter Five

A WEEK LATER, Saturday morning 2:00 a.m. It was dark, midnight-blue dark. We had waited for the new moon. Armed with the tools of the trade, we made our way through the thick brush. Having chosen the I-70 corridor again, placement of the signs was critical. Ones that were too close to the road were off limits. The other criteria for a possible hit included surrounding foliage enough to offer cover at a moment's notice, a place to park on an outer road that was not visible to any homes or businesses, and in the event of crisis, if we had to leave our vehicle, well, then we were screwed. There weren't many places where billboards sat along I-70 in Missouri that didn't have something else close by. This was tricky business.

"Owwww," Lake whispered, as she followed me through a thick stand of eight-foot river birch, one snapping back and slapping her in the face.

"You okay?"

"Yeah, I'm tough. You don't worry about me mister." Lake rubbed her face where the branch had hit her.

"We can turn back right now."

"No, I'm doing this."

I turned, and we continued until we could see the sign from the trees. We'd chosen 'SAUCY TIME ADULT SUPER STORE' as our first prey. This sign was especially embarrassing when family and friends came to visit, and we were driving them back from the airport in Kansas City. 'WELCOME TO MISSOURI' was hard enough sometimes. It would be a pretty drive if there were no billboards at all. Old barns and stretches of woods and hills dotted the landscape, but even one billboard can ruin a beautiful landscape. Visual pollution was low on the list of societal concerns. For a short but significant stretch, I-70 was dotted with 'NUDE DANCING', 'SECRET FANTASIES', 'PORNO EXTRAVAGANZA', and the list went on. Lake called it pornography alley. Unfortunately, the only one we could take down was this one, which had wooden posts. All the rest broadcasted high above the ground on the galvanized columns of the New World.

"Okay, we're going to start with the posts on each end and then work our way in. We stop after each cut and inspect the sign, we don't want to get squished. As soon as we know which way it's going to fall, we cut the remaining posts. You understand?"

"Got it," she said with a head bob. She was holding the idling new orange chain saw and I had a used one I'd purchased again with cash at a thrift store. With two saws we'd be able to work quicker and thus have less chance of being caught. I could tell she was scared, and I didn't want her to know I was, too.

"You're doing great." It was a whole different story with her out here with me. I wasn't sure if I liked it, but of course, I did because I had a partner and lover wrapped up in one, at least tonight.

With chainsaws running, we cut through the first two ends and stopped. I checked for any obvious lean. It was definitely going down on the side we were cutting from. I motioned for us to switch sides. Positioning ourselves on the two inner posts, I gave the nod to start cutting. Halfway through the cuts the sign began to bend. I grabbed Lake's shoulder and pulled her back as the posts cracked and the sign crashed to the ground.

"Oh my God!" she shouted in a whisper.

Lake stood in awe. With the chainsaws idling but still in hand, I indicated it was time for the last step. Lake followed my lead, as I began to cut across the downed sign, making it impossible to salvage. A minute later, the billboard was in pieces. I then took the green spray paint, and in large, capital letters wrote 'MR. GREEN JEANS WAS HERE!' across the cut-up pieces of plywood. In total, the whole job took no more than five minutes. Lake pulled out a camera and took a picture with flash.

"What are doing!?" I yelled.

"I'm going to start a scrapbook."

"No, you're not. Let's go." We both ran through the woods and jumped in the truck.

"Jack, that was incredible!" Lake screamed as the truck picked up speed on the outer road.

"Yeah, try to match that rush," I stated, as I checked the rear-view mirror.

"Oh my God! I'm shaking!"

"No more pictures baby."

"I know, I completely forgot about the flash," She said apologetically.

"No, we can't have any evidence anywhere. No more pictures," I stated as fact.

"Okay Clyde," Lake agreed with a smile. She was on cloud something or other. We both were. Now, on to the next piece of visual pollution, 'TESTICAL FESTIVAL'. Which in reality was just that, a festival that celebrated the eating of cow testes. Animal agriculture is 40% - 50% of our greenhouse emissions, more than transportation and that's outside of the immense cruelty millions the animals are inflicted with each year. It becomes so easy to find targets these days, it is as though we are born into blanket of abuse, and the easy way out is to pull up the covers and pretend it's not going on.

The last sign offered much better parking. The last two posts on 'TESTICAL FESTIVAL MUMFORD MISSOURI' were encased in a metal skin. It wasn't too thick, only meant to serve as protection from the moisture. I thought the chainsaw would rip through it without any problem. I motioned for Lake to move away. As I placed the saw against the metal it instantly kicked back and flew within inches of my face and I fell back on the ground with the chainsaw still in hand.

"Let's go," Lake said.

"No." I got the saw started again and held tight. Once through the thin metal sleeve, the posts went like butter. Boom! Down went TESTICLE FESTIVAL. I handed Lake the spray paint and she did the honors of signing. I then finished by cutting the plywood into pieces.

"You go baby!" Lake was doing some kind of war dance. Her father had been full Greek and on her mother's side, there were stories her great-great grandmother had been full Iroquois. Both her parents had passed. She hadn't talked to her sister in ten years. This dance had more to do than just the downed sign.

"Let's get out of here!"

Back at home, we sat on the deck and stared off into trees. It was just an hour before sunrise and a few birds could be heard beginning their morning conversations.

"We just changed our lives didn't we?" she asked.

"Pretty much. I mean we can't tell anyone, but there's a certain something that's going on" I replied.

"I feel the somethin. We should wear gloves from now on," Lake said as she felt herself taking on a persona she'd never known.

"We should," I replied, taking a deep breath.

"Owwwwwwwwww!" I let out my best wolf call.

"Owwwwwwwwww!" Lake let one go too.

An owl replied in the distance with his own call. We were in it now. Together.

Chapter Six

LAKE WAS DOING YOGA in front of the TV. The local 6:00 a.m. Monday early news was reviewing the weekend's stories. I sat in our red, thrift-store, 50's armchair drinking coffee and trying to concentrate on the news. I wasn't having much luck. Lake's turquoise tights and her one-size-too-small T-shirt was proving to be too great a distraction. We'd be married twelve years and my attraction to her had only increased. Summer break was two weeks away, and we'd be able to spend every day together.

I forced myself to look back at the TV. "Baby! Look at the TV!" I shouted.

She was doing a downward dog and raised her head to see a shot of the downed 'SAUCY TIME ADULT SUPER STORE' billboard. A young correspondent started his report.

"We're on I-70 west of Manchester about nine miles. This billboard and one other were vandalized this weekend. The police have no leads at this point. However, the vandal or vandals left a tag. 'Mr. Green Jeans.' If you have any information regarding this crime, please call 'Crimestoppers' at 1-800-NOCRIME. Your identity will be kept confidential. This is John Savannas, back to you Sheri, what a story huh?"

"John, wasn't Mr. Green Jeans Captain Kangaroo's sidekick?" Sheri asked.

"Well, Sheri, that's before my time, but I don't think this is the same Mr. Green Jeans. It also looks like there might be two more billboards connected to Mr. Green Jeans. Three weeks ago, two other signs were cut down just outside of Manchester on I-70. Both those signs have since been repaired and are back up. Police say a chainsaw was used."

"Okay, John, thank you. Seems Mr. Green Jeans doesn't like billboards. We'll keep you updated on this unusual act of vandalism. Now, let's turn to the weather…"

Lake and I stared at each other, mouths open and eyes wide.

"They said Mr. Green Jeans four or five times! Far out!" Lake yelled as she started a sun salutation.

"I'm going to hide the chainsaws." I was on my feet and heading to the back door.

"What?! Where?" Lake followed me.

"In that hole on the bluff face."

"Baby, there's no way they can link this to us."

"I agree. But I'll feel better if those saws aren't in the shed." I was out the door.

"All right, I'll help, let's do this quick. We have to get school." Lake hurried after me.

On the back of our five acres, was a twenty-foot rock outcropping. On its face was a dead-end, dry cave. It extended about ten feet back into the rock and was big enough for one person to climb into comfortably. I climbed in the hole and Lake handed me the chainsaws. We filled the front of the opening with some dead branches and headed back up the hill to the house.

On our drive to work together, we sat in silence for the first few minutes. We had started to carpool when our schedules coincided to lower our carbon footprint, and found that it was actually kind of fun to take the twenty-minute drive together each morning.

"You think they'll look for fingerprints?" Lake asked as she moved into the passing lane to get around a pickup truck that had its back window covered in one of those stick-on, American flags, a bald eagle imposed over the flag giving the finger with its talon and the words 'Jihad This'.

"We'll wear gloves from now on, or just remember to wipe them down," I said, looking up at the truck's driver; a middle-aged man looking older than he probably was, smoking a cigarette staring down at me from his brand new, cherry-red, 4x4, long-bed Ford. Lake had six bumper stickers of the environmental ilk pasted on her Subaru. It was like two worlds passing each other. It happened daily all over this country. It was difficult, at first, moving back to Missouri. Lake had never been here before, and I had never intended to move back. My mother was happy, though, and that sealed the deal. It was also much cheaper to live here and being teachers, we wouldn't have to be chained to a mortgage as we would have been in the Southwest, where we couldn't touch the prices on anything decent. The overall consciousness of the Midwest challenged us, but there were significant pockets of people we could relate to, and we had some extra money to travel at least once every two years. Two years earlier, it was Costa Rica. This year it was either our five acres, long summer days in the yard and garden or the great Southwest. Unless we were arrested.

"I have an idea!" I said, as Lake pulled into Boone High School.

"Tell me tonight, okay." Lake was visibly shaken from the newscast.

"Okay. Love you," I replied, hoping out of the Subaru, knowing that I sometimes didn't let things settle before I was off onto something else.

"Love you too, baby." And she was off to her school, just a mile away.

Walking into Boone High School, I noticed my gate going down the halls had new buoyancy to it. A little bad-ass trot if you will.

"Mr. Creek, what's up?" De-Shawn, a seventeen-year-old kid whose father had been in prison since he was five, laid out a hand for some skin as he passed.

"Hey De-Shawn, how's it going, man?" I locked my fingers into his for a quick shake.

"Did an abstract last night, Mr. Creek."

"No kidding, I'd like to see it."

"My grandma said it was real good. I called it 'Life on the Curb'."

"You got it going on, dude. I like that title," I replied with a genuine smile and looked into his eyes.

"See you in class, Mr. Creek." De-Shawn continued down the hall to his first-hour class.

This is the only reason I keep teaching. The relationships I make with the students were my strong suit. I wasn't much on dotting i's or crossing the t's. I figured so many of these kids came from such awful homes where neglect and often other of forms of abuse happened daily, that there was no way school was going to be a place of success, unless someone showed them they cared. It wasn't always easy to break their shell; these kids didn't trust anybody, especially not a middle-aged white guy. Some of my colleagues ran a tight ship in their rooms, and these kids on the borderline quickly became disengaged and fell behind. I figured if a kid started to feel good about himself, then he would produce. If he didn't he would shut down. If he dropped out, society wouldn't be kind to him. What was the good in that? I stayed low to the ground at Boone High and most days ate lunch alone. I didn't speak up at faculty meetings when inside it was killing me not to say something. I knew that if I did voice an opinion, then I was in it. And I wasn't about to take on what I considered a broken public education system. That devotion would only end in despair. No, I would go on making a difference one child at a time and one billboard at a time.

When the final bell rang that afternoon, I was anxious for Lake to pick me up. I sat outside on the school's front steps and pondered my new idea for Mr. Green Jeans' exploits.

Lake liked her job and was very good at it. Her Special Ed. classroom was the talk of the district. She taught students who were mentally and often physically handicapped. She focused on life skills, like doing the dishes, laundry, cooking, going out into the community and volunteering at the food bank. Her kids weren't going to learn to read and write, they would never have the capacity for that, but some might live somewhere outside their parents' home someday. Simple life skills would serve them more than anything else they could be taught.

I heard her before I saw her driving into the parking lot. Windows were down and she was rocking out to one our favorite musicians, Van Morrison. Old school. This was a good sign.

"Main Squeeze?" Lake asked as I got into the car.

"Love it," I replied, dropping my book bag at my feet.

"Good day?' I asked.

"Debra pooped all over herself in the cafeteria, Charlie stole all the markers off my desk again, but the rest of them had a good day."

"Sounds like about a 7.5."

"So?" Lake looked over at me.

"So?" I replied.

"How you feeling?" asked Lake

"Got a little skip to my step today."

"Do ya?"

"Yes, I do. And you?"

"I'm hopping a bit," She said with a snicker.

We found a table at the window. As we waited for our food to arrive, I revealed my new plan for 'Mr. Green Jeans'.

Chapter Seven

"I LOVE IT!" Lake burst out, getting the attention of the tables in close proximity, as she took another bite of her Buddha Delight, an organic tofu, rice, guacamole, cheese and red-bean burrito.

"Cool, 'cause I'm thinking we can capture a lot more attention doing this than the other. A more peaceful warrior approach," I responded, having already finished my Chakra rice bowl and now diving into an enormous soy brownie. For us, being vegetarians, vegans-in-training, was as important as anything we did in life. If we couldn't kill it ourselves, then we weren't going to eat it. Fish was my exception. I'd have a fillet of wild salmon or tilapia occasionally. My actual title was really fish-eating vegetarian. We still wore leather shoes and still hadn't weaned ourselves totally off plastic. Still hooked up on the grid. And on and on. It's hard to be a hundred percent at anything. We'd hopefully get there before we died. If our species intended to continue living on this planet, what we consumed and how much we consumed was integral.

"So, I'm going to draw up some ideas and get the lumber this week." I shoved another piece of the brownie in my mouth.

"I think a few should say, 'LOVE IT OR KISS IT GOODBYE.'"

I counted the words in my head. "That's totally doable. I like it. To the point."

On the drive home, we passed the new 'BOX-MART' billboard. It had attached lights now. Now it was 'BOX-MART 24/7'. That backfired.

"Need to blow those lights out," Lake said as we passed the sign.

"In due time, Bonnie," I said with a laugh, realizing she was really on board here.

"Whatever you say, Clyde," Lake responded with a new voice meant to sound sultry and hard-edged at the same time. And it was.

"Wow, baby. I should have started this a long time ago."

"Your timing is perfect. Now. Let's get home, Clyde. I think your gun might need polishing."

"I think you're right." I pushed on the accelerator. I felt like I was in a dream, living someone else's life. Being a school night, we were both usually too tired to fall into bed together to do anything other than sleep. But we had just been injected with a vial of superhero glucose. We knew this unknown ride could get bumpy soon, but right now, we were trying to stay in the moment.

The rest of the school week went well, I didn't even have to break up one fight. Although there were fights that week; there were fights every week. What would you expect with thirty-two hundred kids in one building? No chance at community with those numbers. Public School Inc. One more week until summer break.

On my way home for a sequestered weekend, I stopped by a local hardware store. Unknown to me, Lake was already at home, setting up saw horses for our new project. I picked up some cheap, drywall screws, and found three gallons of brightly colored, high-gloss enamel for sale on the return table. I paid cash. On the drive home, I gave in to my more practical side and began looking at the future. Getting caught was the only red flag for me. Get caught and then was it worth it? Absolutely not. Option one: Stop right now. Option two: Don't get caught. I pushed the cassette tape into my fifteen-year-old, forty-dollar stereo, working on one speaker. Morrison belted out 'Bright Side of the Road'. I turned onto the county gravel road that led home, hoping Lake would not be far behind me.

Pulling up to the house, I saw her Subaru. Another strange phenomenon, she never beat me home.

"Hey baby!" Lake yelled from the shed. 'Long live Mr. Green Jeans!'

"Long live Mr. Green Jeans! What are you doing beating me home?" I shouted, getting out the truck.

"I'm committed. Did you get the paint?" Lake laughed, walking up to the truck followed by Barney and Pearl, tails wagging.

"Let's see, Orange, green, and black, all high gloss," I answered; looking in the truck bed.

"Excellent. Barb and Todd are coming over tonight," Lake stated.

"Oh, I wanted to get started on the signs."

"It'll be at least two hours before they get here."

"All right, that should work. Good day today, baby?"

"It's Friday, and I'm sticking to that. With one week to go, I can do anything at this point."

"I hear that. Let me go change, and we'll get started."

"Well, come on!" Lake picked up the paint from the truck bed and walked across the yard to the shed.

The shed was one of our favorite places. It was maybe fifteen feet deep by twenty feet across. The whole thing sagged towards the west. It must have been there eighty years or more and was sided in oak, barn wood with a dirt floor. It doubled as my summer art studio.

I had already cut up quarter-inch plywood into 2 x 3-foot squares earlier that week, so we were ready to paint. "Okay, what do you say to an orange background with green and black letters?" I asked opening the orange.

"Green background for Mr. Green Jeans. Let's always do green backgrounds, we have to get a consistency going if we plan to be recognized."

"When did you become a marketing genius?"

"You know so little about me." Lake was smiling as she dipped her brush into the bright green enamel.

"I wish I could tell you all my secrets, but ahh I'd have to…."

"I am freaking out, just so you know. But in a good way," Lake interrupted not looking up.

"Me too."

"So if this gets us attention in a more positive way, we're done with billboards right?" Lake asked spreading the paint on thick.

"That's the plan, yeah."

"It's going to work. I feel it."

"Yeah, I think so too. So, with thirty boards and stakes cut. One of your ideas is 'LOVE IT - OR -KISS IT GOODBYE'. That leaves twenty six boards."

"One should say THINK, I think." Lake was getting giddy.

"CONNECT, gotta have that one." We were having the perfect storm.

"What about, WAKE THE HELL UP!" Lake exclaimed.

"You know I love it, but cussing isn't going to garner us the type of support we want," I responded.

"Okay, you're right. I just get so frustrated that there are so many people out there that don't even believe we're responsible for Climate Change!"

"I know, it baffles me all the time."

Thirty minutes later, all our boards were bright green.

"Let's get cleaned up." Lake flicked her brush at me and a stream of dots splattered across me, from my pants up onto my face.

"That was stupid," I said, wondering if I should respond in kind.

"Really?"

"I explain later how stupid that was."

"I'm shaking."

"Good."

After we both showered, I was in charge of cleaning off our table and chairs on the deck. Lake was in the kitchen making some guacamole. Todd and Barb never knocked anymore, they just came in.

"One week you lazy bums, where are you?!" Todd shouted as he gently kicked the door closed.

"In here suckers!" Lake yelled from the kitchen.

It was a mosquito-ridden night. We sat on the deck, talking and laughing. Bug spray was everyone's best friend. A few libations, and talk became loose.

"I'm sick of this government! They say they're going to do this and then don't. They do the opposite. Then it's done. And there you go, wake, rise and see what they did today." Todd was on a roll, and the rest of us fell into step.

"Brother, you speak the truth. So, what's to be done?" I spoke and then looked at Lake. Lake acknowledged me with a little wink.

"I don't know. Run for office, leave the country, and become an expat, buy a big swash of land say goodbye to the rest. I don't know, it's just sad to see our voices slipping away. Sure, that's what thousands of generations said before us, who knows? All I know is, they're not making any more of it, land that is, and there isn't a place on this earth where the corporations haven't had their hands into it. I don't freaking know anymore. I'll tell you one thing, I like those Green Jeans people," Todd finished and petted Pearl, who seemed to be offering Todd some condolence.

"Oh, they're great!" Bard added.

"You really think so?" Lake asked.

"They got balls, I'll tell you that. And they're here, in the Midwest, one of the most conservative places in the country. Go Green Jeans!" Todd said, filling his plate with more chips and guacamole.

"Baby?" I looked across the table at Lake, who sat with her feet up in her chair, cradling a sleeping Smokey Joe.

"Go ahead." She flipped her hand, she was peaceful.

"Okay, here it is guys. We're Mr. Green Jeans."

"Right, and I'm the Lone Ranger," Todd countered.

"He's serious, Todd." Barb was looking right at me.

"No way! You guys took down those billboards?" Todd needed a few more details, and he sat back in his chair and just stared at us.

"Saucy Time?!" Barb was grabbing Lake's arm.

"Saucy Time down," Lake said with fresh pride.

"My fellow fools, this is some crazy far-out boom-baa stuff, right now. What?! You did what?!" Todd was on his feet, and he wasn't a small man. He towered six five with a carriage of two fifty.

I was twenty again and righteous and on my feet, too. "We had some free time on our hands, what can I say?"

"Unbelievable! Barb, our best friends and neighbors are Green Jeans!" Todd began a dance that looked more like he needed to go to the bathroom badly.

"We know climate change is here, and the world we now know is soon to disappear. We're on the literal cusp of 'game over'. You feel me?"

"I'll feel ya, man," Todd added, holding his hand up for a good slap.

"Yeah, we want to spread the word and use any means we can to make a spectacle of ourselves. I mean…"

"Whoa, what are you talking about? You're going to do more? Todd asked, now still.

"It's the ninth inning ladies and gentlemen, and there are no extra innings," Lake responded.

"It started when we invented corporations," Barb added.

"Wait! What are you guys talking about?" Todd was incredulous.

"Hard to say. Come with us on the next run," Lake responded, Smokey Joe still in her lap, although awake now after Todd's dance.

"Next run? What is that? Run? Jack? What's she talking about?" Todd still hadn't moved.

"We are going to put a strip of signs just across the river on I-70. Come on. Be in on this and then be done. It's a high," I said, wondering if I should have kept my mouth shut.

"I'm in! Sign us up!" Todd said, spinning on a dime and starting his dance again.

"Todd! Todd, we'll talk about this tomorrow," Barb said, feeling uncomfortable and grabbing Lake's hand.

"I can do it once. Come on, Barb," Todd continued his jig on our deck.

"I'll call you tomorrow, sweetheart," Barb said, hugging Lake at the front door. Embraces all around.

"I'll give 'em some Green Jeans, man," Todd stated squeezing me in tight bear hug.

We watched them walk off to their driveway and disappear into the trees. I looked at Lake.

"Maybe we should have kept quiet?" Lake suggested.

"Maybe, maybe," I responded.

"We're about to enter Maybe Land," Lake inserted.

"No, Maybe Land is all there ever was," I took her hand, and we sat on the front porch and listened to tree frogs talk to each other.

Chapter Eight

THERE'S NOT A TEACHER LIVING who doesn't give thanks for summer. The last week passed quickly, and school was now officially out for the summer. Barb and Lake talked to each other every day on the phone. Barb was on board; she just needed to think about it awhile before committing. When, where and how were the constant topics. Todd and I hadn't spoken to each other since the night Lake and I had asked them to join us. I wasn't worried. If anything was really bothering Todd, Barb would have told Lake.

"Honey, Barb and Todd are going to be here in thirty minutes!" Lake yelled down into our unfinished basement. I was making a mess of a painting in my makeshift art studio next to the washer and dryer. It was so hard to concentrate with all this going on. Summer freedom was waving its flag, and at the same time, we were pushing the limits of our sanity. We had it pretty good here and the potential to screw that up would get more likely, the longer we kept this up.

"Okay!" I yelled back.

"Yep, Game on!" Lake replied from the stairwell.

Cheese Enchiladas topped with fresh onions from our garden sat on the table in a glass baking dish before the four of us. We passed an incredible salad with everything from broccoli to sunflower seeds around the table.

"This looks great," said Todd, showing obvious signs of unsettledness.

"This is my all-time favorite meal," I added, wondering who was going to break the ice first.

"Thank you and you, Enchiladas." Lake dipped the spatula under the first two cheesy gooey delights. This was anything but a vegan dinner, at least the cheese was from a local farm where the cows lived in a pasture and were treated with dignity.

After everyone had been served, Lake and Barb raised their water glasses as though it had been rehearsed.

"Here's to Mr. Green Jeans, and may his creations inspire a deeper connectedness amongst the human species." Barb clinked her glass with Lake's. Todd and I fell in and completed the toast circuit.

"Now this next operation..." I started.

Todd got up from the table. His anxiety was almost tactile. "I'm just going to grab a beer from the fridge," he said turning for the kitchen.

Todd's nerves were working their way right into me. I had a feeling his initial excitement might wane. When Todd settled back down, Lake began. "We have thirty-two signs now, with stakes attached. We need to get all those signs placed in one night, and then sit back and watch and see what kind of response we get."

"Our biggest danger is obviously getting the signs in the ground. We do it on the next new moon, which is tomorrow," Lake continued like she was reading a script.

"What are we doing?" Todd couldn't hold it back any longer.

"What?" Barb looked at him, surprised and at the same time expecting it.

"We get caught doing this, and we really mess up our lives." Todd exhaled and sat back in his chair as a bead of sweat rolled off his brow. "Look, I'm all for shaking up the system. I guess I just don't know if I want to take the risk. I'm scared to death right now, if you want to know the truth."

"I'm scared too, man. I started this, and I never even planned to let Lake in on it. I certainly didn't want you guys knowing. I still say we do it, though. This time, we're not destroying anything. It's completely peaceful. But Todd, if you want out right now, I completely understand and respect the decision." I looked at him for a response.

There was a moment of silence at the table. Barb and Lake exchanged glances. I looked out the window. Todd sat motionless except for various facial expressions that showed the battle was raging. Todd would be a horrible poker player. He rose and paced around the dining room.

"Okay, I'm really scared about this. But fear to the wind! I got one life to live and I'm tired of living in the shadows!"

"You sure?" Barb asked.

Todd nodded.

It was on.

Chapter Nine

ANOTHER NEW MOON. The mosquitoes were feasting on anything with a pulse. Lake and I pulled into the Missouri Bottoms conservation parking area first, and quickly began getting the signs out from under the tarp in the bed of my pickup. This conservation area was hardly ever used except by quail, deer and duck hunters. The hunting season had ended a while ago, so over the next few months, this place would only see the occasional hiker and poacher. It was the flood plain for the Missouri River and it was occasionally under water. Barb and Todd pulled alongside of us a minute later and parked. Todd, wearing a fake beard and dressed in black overalls, got out. Lake and I just smiled.

"That's my Todd," Barb said with her hands above her head.

"My name's Woodrow, until we get back home," Todd replied, giving us a humorous reprieve from what we were about to do.

Todd and I each strapped eleven signs a piece on our backs. I had already tied the signs in bundles with some webbing, and we used the extra length on each end to tie around our waist. It was uncomfortable, but there was no way we could loosely carry that many signs at one time. Lake and Barb each strapped on five signs apiece.

"Time check." Todd was looking at his watch.

"2:32." Lake read her dad's wristwatch. It was one of the only items Lake had of her father's. He had died a few years ago, and this watch meant that he was here with her.

"Gloves?" I looked to see that everyone had on a pair.

"We meet back here at no later than 3:02. Everyone understand?" Todd said, looking at his watch.

"Got it, Jed."

'Woodrow. Okay, let's head out. Good luck guys."

He and Barb hiked off down a trail that ran parallel to the highway. Lake and I headed the opposite direction on the same trail. The trail was only visible from the highway in pieces. Most of it was hidden by thick stands of willows and river birch. This was the Missouri River bottoms. This land had been farmed up until the turn of the century. Then the conservation department bought it and turned it into wetlands, its original state a hundred years ago. We had picked this spot because it had a long stretch with no billboards, and the placement of our signs would easily be seen.

"Owww!" Todd cried out as his face swiped a wild raspberry bush. The bush caught his fake beard and yanked it off his face.

"Owwww! Crap!" he'd used spirit glue to adhere it. The beard still attached to the bush recoiled hitting Barb.

"Owww!" Barb shouted.

"Sorry, grab the beard." Todd continued through the tree line until he was within twenty feet of the interstate. The traffic rushed by at eighty miles an hour. Mainly trucker traffic at this hour.

"This one is first, baby." A quarter mile in the other direction, Lake and I were preparing to plant our signs. We had the signs on the ground and were laying them out in the correct order.

Lake took the first three 'LOVE', 'HER' and 'OR'. I grabbed 'KISS', 'US' and 'GOODBYE'. The ground was still wet from yesterday's rain, and the signs slid into soil with little effort.

Back in the other direction, Todd stumbled through the brush so he could lay out his signs. Not bringing flashlights for obvious reasons, it was difficult to see from one step to the next. "Oh no! What the hell did I step in!?" Todd took a few quick steps away from the squish and crackle his left foot had just made. "I just stepped on a dead animal."

"Oh, the stink!" Barb followed making sure to stay clear of the spot Todd had just been through.

"Let's get this thing done." Todd untied his bundle and starting laying down the signs. Barb got her signs untied and together they placed them in the correct order. Todd shoved down his first sign. The smell was soaked into his boot and lower pant leg and letting off a horrible odor. Fifteen feet away from the highway now and with no cover, the traffic roared by, the wind coming off the semis. The berm the conservation department had built to keep the water contained when the Missouri River flooded the wetlands served as a perfect display for our signs.

"Okay, baby, we're done," Lake said, raising her hand for a high five.

"Done." I slapped her hand, and we were off and back into the woods lining the interstate.

"What time is it?" I asked, turning to Lake. I didn't wear a watch, I hated watches.

"2:56."

"Perfect," I said increasing my pace to the truck.

When we arrived back at the parking lot it was 3:05, and we were alone. We didn't hear Barb or Todd approaching.

"I'm going to go look for them."

"Okay, if you're gone more than five minutes I'm coming after you," Lake said, looking around the pitch dark parking area.

"Give me six or seven minutes," I said and turned onto the trail.

A few minutes of hiking down the trail, I heard someone talking by the freeway.

"Look at this, Joe!" I heard the shout coming through the thick stand of willows separating me from the highway. Quietly creeping into the trees, I made out a semi stopped on the shoulder with its headlights on. A man holding a flashlight was directing the beam across the top of the berm.

"Now is...the...time...to...." Joe, a full-bellied, long haul trucker was flashing his light from one sign to the next and reading them out loud to his partner, who stood by truck. Where were Todd and Barb?

"There's another one up here! It says Wake!"

"Come on and take your poop, we need to get going. The truck's burning money every second," said a chunky man in his sixties.

"All right, all right." Joe found a spot and squatted and emitted a series of farts that could easily be heard above the drone of late night traffic.

Barb and Todd were lying flat on their stomachs just over the other side of the berm. They looked at each other and smiled with panic in their eyes. The sound of Joe emptying his bowels fit with a diet of truck stop greasy specials. I held still and listened for any sounds of my friends. I knew they must be hunkered down somewhere very close.

Joe finished and I could hear him walking back to the truck. When I heard the truck door slam and the semi pulling out, I started along the berm following the signs.

"Todd, Barb!"

"Woodrow! Over here!" Todd emerged, just down from where I was walking. He was holding his last two signs. Barb popped up from the other side of the berm.

"Barb, head on back, Lake's by the parking lot, we'll be right behind you." She headed through the trees as I caught up to Todd.

"That was too close, amigo," Todd said, shoving the last sign onto the ground.

"What stinks?" I asked.

"That'd be me," Todd stated.

"Ohhhh man. Okay, that's the last of your signs?" I asked, putting some space between us.

"Yep, let's go." Back into the woods and onto the trail. I was feeling extremely anxious and wanted to get out of there as fast as possible. Passing Todd on the trail, I felt my stomach start to turn over. "Whoa. You smell like a dead possum."

"I'm aware of that," he said.

At the parking lot, Lake and Barb were in the vehicles and ready to roll. Not saying another word, Todd and I got into our respective rides and drove home.

It was 3:30 when we pulled up to our house. Barb kept their car running and stuck her head out the window from our shared drive.

"We'll be back in as soon as we get possum boy cleaned up? I mean I can't sleep. Can you?" Barb spoke to Lake as I checked the pickup bed for any evidence of the crime.

"Ouuuuuuuuuuu, Jack said it was bad, but… Wow!" Lake stepped back from their car laughing.

"Thank you. I know that," Todd said from the passenger seat.

"I still love my little possum boy. So, you guys up for an early breakfast and then a drive by?" Barb asked.

"I'm not going to sleep until I see it. Jack, you're staying up, right?" Lake asked.

"Yeah. I'm kinda freaking out too much to sleep," I responded.

"We're all freaking out. See you in a bit, honey. Tomato sauce works well," Lake suggested.

"Barb, can we go?" Barb smiled and rolled down all the windows in the car and drove off to their house in the woods.

Two hours later, all clean and finished with breakfast, we headed out. The sun was just cresting, and the signs were positioned to catch the early morning light. Todd still smelled unfavorably, but nothing like it had been. All the windows in Lake's Subaru were rolled down. A few miles down the freeway, we crossed the mighty Missouri, and there they were. The low hanging fog was lifting off the river bottom, and the high gloss green background of thirty two 2x3 signs were gleaning their message. Staked out five feet apart, covering 160 feet or more of real estate. They were easy to see. Success. Lake read our message out loud as we passed.

'NOW IS THE MOMENT TO WAKE UP! THE MOTHER IS IN PAIN! TIME TO DO SOMETHING ABOUT IT! BE GOOD TO OUR MOTHER! LOVE HER OR KISS US GOODBYE! MR. GREEN JEANS.'

"Wooooooooooooooo!!!" Todd yelled from the backseat.

"We did it!! I feel absolutely incredible right now." This was getting addictive.

"We have to make another pass," Barb said, kissing Todd. Lake grabbed my hand and squeezed. We looked at each other and had one of those moments you can only have when you rage against the machine. Pure magic.

I turned off at the next exit and crossed the interstate. For the next hour we drove back and forth passing our hard work six times. It never got old.

Chapter Ten

"OH YEAH, BABY! Get in here!" I yelled from the couch in the parlor. We called it the parlor because our house used to be a brothel eighty years ago, at least that was the story we had heard from some of the old timers. Where I sat now sipping my coffee and watching the TV, once sat another man awaiting a bit of company and negotiating the price of companionship while drinking a corn whiskey.

"Baby, hurry up!"

"What?" Lake bounded into the room with a wash towel in one hand and coffee in the other.

I pointed to the television. The morning local news was on. It was Monday, two days after our third strike.

"We're coming to you from the shoulder of I-70 westbound, just across the Missouri River. It seems the 'Mr. Green Jeans' has struck again."

"They said 'Mr. Green Jeans'!" I shouted.

"Wooooooooo-hooooo!" Lake stood transfixed to the TV.

"Some thirty plus signs have been staked out along the highway here." An attractive young reporter looked into the camera.

We watched the camera pan across the stretch of signs. 'NOW IS THE MOMENT TO WAKE UP! THE MOTHER IS IN PAIN'...a few more young willows...'TIME TO DO SOMETHING ABOUT IT'...large, lone river birch...'BE GOOD TO OUR MOTHER!...tall grass, and a few wild flowers... 'LOVE HER OR KISS US GOODBYE   MR. GREEN JEANS'. The shot went back to the young reporter.

"Well, there you have it. Seems we have some concerned citizens giving a voice to the planet. This is Anne Brewer, reporting live from I-70 west. Back to you, Tom."

"Anne, is there any idea as to who Mr. Green Jeans is?" Tom asked from the news desk.

"Authorities told me they checked tire tracks in the Darrell Bottoms Conservation area parking lot, but that was a dead end as the amount of time and money to actually follow up on that was virtually impossible and would by no means show any conclusive evidence at this point. Other than that the perpetrators left no evidence of their presence two nights ago."

"Why were the signs left up until Monday?" It was a slow news day, and Tom needed to soak this for thirty more seconds.

"Public Works is nine to five Monday through Friday, unless there's an emergency. Seems Mr. Green Jeans might have planned it this way to get as much exposure as possible, Tom." Anne smiled at the camera. She was about twenty-five, with rosy cheeks and shoulder-length, blond hair. She had the look of someone who might be going places.

"So there you have it. Mr. Green Jeans, whoever he or they are, started with taking billboards down, and makes them. This is Anne Brewer, reporting live from I-70 west."

"Wow, I love her!" I exclaimed relaxing back on the couch sipping on my three-quarter coffee, one-quarter hazelnut creamer in an oversized mug. I looked over at Lake, who now took a seat in one of our many recycled chairs from the Salvation Army or a local garage sale.

"Did you record that?" Lake asked.

"I don't know how to use the DVR."

"What? I want to watch that again."

"Go online," I said.

"Oh yeah, Jack! We made the news again, baby!"

"A little news piece about us! What do you know?" I replied, doing a little parlor dance.

"I'm starting to freak out again," Lake said, getting up and needing to walk around.

"That reporter is our go-to gal." I was excited. Second week of summer break, and we were on our way to folk hero land.

"Our go-to gal?" Lake looked over at me, completely confused.

"She's smart, pretty and I bet she's hungry to move on to bigger and better things." I had a gleam in my eye.

"What are you talking about?"

"I'm talking about someone we can use to get the message out."

"What? Are we going to go see her and let her know we're Mr. Green Jeans!?" Lake was still pacing back and forth across our homes' hundred-year-old oak floors, and I was already off to future plans.

"No, we call her anonymously from a payphone and let her know that she's our 'go-to gal.' You know, let her know that she's going to have the exclusive rights to Mr. Green Jeans!" I was on my way to give Lake a big hug.

"Step back, mister. You've shown me reservations already with all this and now you're ready to be the next Greenpeace or Earth First. Slow down, Bubba. A payphone? Where's a payphone?" Lake always took longer to let something settle than me, which was often a good thing.

"I'm calling Barb." Lake was on her way to the phone.

"No." I was right behind her.

She turned to look at me.

"You can't call on the cell or the landline," I said. "We have to pay attention now. If we want this to work, we have to stay alive. No risk taking, baby."

"Jack, you got to tell me where you're at right now." Lake knew when she saw a bomb being built.

"Okay, I know its summer, and that totally frees up our mind and all. I do have a way of getting ahead of myself, and yeah, that's where I am right now. But Honey, I'm jazzed, that was fabulous! You know how many people just saw that?!"

"A lot," she stated, with a good deal of pride, but obvious confusion as to what I had in mind.

"Right. Look, I don't know what to do necessarily, but let's get the groove going. We just have to keep a tight ship."

"I'll put a note on their door," Lake said.

"No, no note."

"You're paranoid."

"Fine, but we need to be paranoid."

"That's if we're going to continue to do this," she stated and went into the kitchen. I stood there and took a deep breath. It was that time, and I knew it. No guts, no glory. I only hoped Lake wasn't backing out now, because I knew I couldn't do this alone anymore, unless I was alone. And I didn't want to be alone.

Chapter Eleven

I THOUGHT ABOUT FOLLOWING HER into the kitchen, but decided to let it rest for a while, which meant maybe till the end of the day.

As a boy, I collected box turtles, snakes, toads and frogs to show my mother and then, after she gave me a supportive comment, released them. I loved the woods, the outdoors, from the ants, which I would lay on the ground and watch at length, coming and going out of their underground mansions, to the overall connected feeling I would get just being in the natural world. I was beholden at a young age to the earth. For whatever reason, I understood that everything is connected. Years later, returning to visit my mother from Arizona, I remember walking back into those woods behind her house. It had changed. It wasn't development; no new houses had been built. The small stand of woods was only a few acres with a small creek flowing through it, but there were no crawdads, no frogs, and no water bugs flitting across the creek's surface. My little creek was dying and I didn't know why. I remembered sitting on the limestone boulder that seemed so huge to me as a kid. I used sit there and close my eyes and just be. I did that again then, and if I had let myself, I would have cried. Decades of feeling and knowing the importance of connectedness with the natural world, and my stream was dying. I didn't know what to do but be angry and start to blame everyone and everything I could think of. All of that and more had finally caught up to me and now I was here. Some middle-aged guy trying to shout out to the world. Who was I fooling? The corporate machine was so much bigger than I could even imagine. But to hell with it. Mr. Green Jeans was here now. I set my coffee down, got up from my memory and looked to Lake in the kitchen.

"Hey baby, I'm going to take the kids out for a walk. You want to go?"

"No, I'm going to hang out here," Lake replied from the kitchen.

"Okay, see ya."

"Be careful."

I picked up my small backpack I always kept supplied with water, trash bags, flashlight, a few energy bars and some other goodies and was off.

"Come on guys!"

Barney followed Pearl out the door, and I took up the rear. The day couldn't have been better. Most people were at work. I counted twelve more Mondays before we would have to report back. About seventy degrees with a slight breeze, the leaves on the trees barely moved. Everything was close to being in full foliage. I needed to get out here and get my mind clear. Being in nature always helps me find some peace. It was beginning to storm upstairs. Pearl let out bark at the edge of the bluff at the back of our property. I hurried to see what it was.

"Get back, get back now!" I yelled, as Barney too came to see Pearl's discovery. It was a black timber rattler coiled up and ready to strike. It had been sunning itself before Pearl showed up to introduce herself. Both the dogs backed up as I got a little closer.

"Hey baby. You're scared aren't you? We'll be on our way. You just settle back into the sun," I said as the four-foot black beauty shook its rattle at me. I was just a few feet from the snake, but I knew that I was safe. The old myth of a rattler striking its body length was just that, a myth. I couldn't count the times I'd stopped on a gravel road in Arizona, and removed a rattlesnake from the road with nothing more than a stick to gently pick up the snake and place it back in the desert. I knew there were many people who would just as soon run it over, and feel like they had made a contribution to the safety of mankind. It was rare to see a rattler in Missouri, and I took it to be a sign. In Indian medicine, the snake represents transmutation. There was something that I needed to transmute from myself to reach wholeness with the Great Spirit, and Mr. Green Jeans was my trans-mutter. Probably delusional, but that was really where I had lived my entire life, imagining what this world could be like.

"Thank you, baby," I said to the snake.

"Okay, my furry mates. Let's go see the cave."

Slowly making my way down a steep ravine holding onto young oaks, exposed roots and whatever else I could balance myself with, the three of us made it to the cave's entrance. I was the last one down. The cave was called Muir Cave, named after John Muir, founder of the Sierra Club. Although he'd never been here, the cave couldn't have a better name. Muir had to be about my biggest hero. The man was responsible for beginning the conservation movement in America. To me, Muir's accomplishments were the height of success. Fat cats and Hollywood stars were apples and oranges to Muir. Muir had a reason far outside of himself for doing the things he did in life. Muir was connected to nature's fabric and fought his entire life to preserve the wilderness, not only because it is an integral part of us, but it was the right thing to do for the rest of earth's life that had no voice in their future.

It was a huge cave, now under the protection and ownership of the Conservation Department. The cave had been fenced off and closed to the public for over twenty years to protect the gray bat. The stream flowing from the cave emptied two hundred yards away into the Missouri River. Lewis and Clark had stopped here on their epic adventure. Before the Core of Engineers got their hands on the river and channeled it for hundreds of miles, the river's original spread probably reached close to the mouth of the cave. It had surely been a stopping place for settlers, explorers and many tribes of Native Americans over the last 2000 years. I was trespassing each time I came down here, but I loved the place and had appointed myself the cave's steward. People often referred to The Missouri Conservation Department as the 'Hunting and Fishing Club of Missouri'. America kills more of its wildlife through the 'sport' of hunting than any other country in the world. Most of the Conservation Department's resources were spent maintaining habitat for the hunters. Very little was spent for those of us who like to hike and softly enjoy the wonders of Mother Nature. None of it was set aside for the animals to have a safe refuge and if it was there would little way to protect that habitat. The conservation department was much like the education, filled with a bunch of good-willing people not able to spread the good will because the money was spent elsewhere.

We reached the cave entrance, a forty-foot high opening. Someone had been here since I last visited. Beer cans, soda bottles and chip bags littered the cave's entrance. "Sorry cave," I said out loud, Pearl sniffed the trash. Barney was yards away still smelling Pearl's last hallucinogenic olfactory spot.

"Okay kids, let's get out some bags and take care of this." I unzipped my pack and took out a few plastic bags. I always carried a few small trash bags when I hiked. I filled up a bag and half and would pick them up on the way out.

"Let's go kiddos."

Crawling under the chain-link fence where erosion from the cave's stream had formed a rut, I turned on my LED headlamp and located the old boardwalk that ran the first six hundred yards into the cave's interior. Decades ago this cave was a commercial operation for tourists. When the three of us reached the end of the broken down boardwalk, the cave was left to its own path. It was so real being here, that sometimes chills ran up my backside. Pearl and Barney would always let me take the lead in the cave. It wasn't someplace they would think to explore, once the darkness encroached.

It was summer. It was a Monday. I was a quarter mile back in the cave with my dogs. Life was good. I turned off the headlamp. Total darkness. I could hear the dogs walking in the stream that ran through the cave, but nothing else. I thought of Lake. I loved that woman liked I loved nature. It was good to be in the cave with my dogs and my wife up above in the old brothel, what more could I ask for? Maybe just a little justice before I died. I turned the light back on.

"Okay guys; let's go a little further than last time." We headed into the bowels of the underground environment, and I wondered what Lake was thinking above.

Chapter Twelve

IT WAS MIDAFTERNOON when I returned. I sat on our back steps and scraped off a combination of mud and guano from my boots. My pants would have to come off, too, before I went inside. Pearl and Barney looked like they belonged in a pigpen. They'd be hosed off and left outside to dry before they came in and took their customary spots on the couch. I'd been gone quite a while, and I expected Lake to be out in the garden or outside somewhere. She wasn't. It was a glorious day, not too hot, gentle breeze below, and the turkey vultures were riding the exchanges above.

"Okay little puddies, come here and let's get that nasty bat poo-poo off you." Leaving the kids outside to dry off in the sun, I entered the house through the back door. I threw my dirty clothes down into the basement. The smell of sandalwood immediately hit my nasal receptors. "Hmmmm?" Jack Johnson played softly from the living room. Something was in the oven, and it smelled delicious. All of these were good signs. Lake was enjoying herself today.

"Hey baby," I called out.

Nothing.

I walked up the stairs in my birthday suit and peeked into our bedroom. The oven timer was ticking away on the table next to the bed where Lake with a pillow between her legs was curled up gently sleeping. Smokey Joe had a little snore going, he was a big cat; big cats snore. I turned and headed into the bathroom, I stunk of guano.

"Hi," Lake whispered from the bed, and I stuck my head back into our bedroom.

"Hi baby. Smells good downstairs. How ya doing?"

"Good baby."

"Good."

"Take your shower, I'll see you downstairs. We need to talk."

"Okay." In the shower, I went over the possibilities of what she was going to tell me. I wouldn't be surprised if she was calling it quits. I mean, what did we think we were doing? We'd just passed the half-century mark. Another ten years of teaching, and we could both retire. People like us didn't do things like this. Kids in their twenties camping out in the national forest did things like this. Angry guys, who live alone with a case of scotch whiskey did this. We should continue to donate money to ASPCA and the Green Peace and leave it at that. But I didn't want to do that. I couldn't do that now.

Toweling off and putting on my paint clothes, I expected to hear the worst, and therefore would need to keep my mind occupied after she told me it was over. Painting would serve that purpose well. I took a deep breath and started to head to the basement.

"Hi babe, have a good time today?" She asked from behind me, as she reached in the fridge and grabbed a container of raspberry yogurt.

"Yeah, we went back into the cave further than we ever have," I responded, standing at the top of the stairs.

"Cool." She was calm.

"Yeah, Barney got scared, but he can't help but follow Pearl, you know?" I said following suit, and went back into the kitchen and grabbed a yogurt too.

"He's a big baby. Let's sit on the deck."

I followed her out the door, we got comfortable in the rockers and after a few suspenseful moments, she spoke.

"Okay. First of all. We're crazy."

"Second that."

"And if we get caught, we're screwed big time."

"Very high probability of being screwed big time if we're caught."

"So, I've been going over it and over it, and here's what I think." She scooped out the last of her yogurt, licked her spoon and set the container down on the deck. One long exhale and she began.

"I propose that we continue to get our message out there through the summer and then re-evaluate sometime in early August before school starts. I do, however, think we need a plan of action, whether or not we accomplish it all. We need to have some direction and logistics to make this effort worthwhile. So, I've written a list of targets, most of them highly visible, which is what we want, and we don't tear down anything anymore. I like your idea of making contact with that girl on the news, and as you have said, we have to use the media to our advantage, and that means the internet too. I have a bunch of ideas written down to that end, also. Bottom-line, I hate saying that phrase, but I said it, I feel alive right now, part of something bigger than me. In short, I feel like I'm just starting to wake up. I don't want to quit. Not yet." She stopped and looked over at me

"Wow."

"Yeah, I know, didn't expect that, did you?"

"No. No, I did not. Let me see your list."

She handed me a spiral notebook. It was an impressive list of targets with ideas for messages in each place. The target list started local and then began expanding across the state. On the margins she had written, "Gather. Protest. Slam the Machine." I closed the notebook, laid it on my lap and looked out into the woods. The Cardinals, Junkos and Blue Jays were beginning to appear for their evening meal at our feeders.

"I think I'll go get a beer, want anything?"

"Just a glass of water, please."

Back on the deck, I could tell Lake was awaiting my response.

"Jack, I know you like to be dramatic, but this is getting ridiculous. Come on, what do you think?"

"First of all, I love you."

"I know that. Come on Jack."

"It's incredible. It blows my master plan to smithereens. Honey, what you're proposing is a movement. You know that?"

"Yeah, it is. It doesn't mean we do it all, it's just possibilities. We can quit anytime. What was your master plan? I didn't even know you had a master plan."

"Yeah, as much of a master plan as I've ever had. All in my head and forever changing. I'm just blown away, because I thought we were probably done."

"Yeah, me too. I got really scared, but our planet is changing every day for the worse, and although I'm very concerned about child and women welfare as well a bunch of other topics, this one is the total game changer for everything."

"Yeah, it is. If we learn how to treat our home with compassion and gratitude, think what it will mean about the way we treat everything else, ya know?"

"Compassion begets compassion," Lake stated.

"Well said, baby."

She laughed. "It's on the list of messages."

"Shall we begin with the first thing on your list?" I stood and started pacing the deck.

"The columns?"

"Da columns."

She lifted her water. I met it with my non-corporate beer.

Clink.

Chapter Thirteen

IT WAS 3:30 A.M. Lake was dressed up as a fairy queen with a Richard Nixon mask. I wore Todd's beard, a blond wig, a bandana like a cowboy and a baseball cap. I also gave myself 30 extra pounds with a pillow stuffed in my sweatshirt. We both wore gloves. Just as I had placed our last sign, Lake lightly shook the ladder. When I looked down at her, she pointed to an obviously drunk college couple coming down the sidewalk on the backside of the columns. I managed to get off the ladder and slide the extension down, trying to wipe it clean of any previous fingerprints. The couple was about to turn the corner and would be in full sight of the signs and us. I laid down the ladder, and we both hurried behind the columns to hide. The couple stopped, but never even noticed the signs. They started kissing and then were down in the grass, rolling around. Just then, a group of frat boys came onto the quad from the opposite side. They, too, were returning from some late-night party and were singing a song that neither Lake nor I had ever heard before, some kind of rap. It was time to leave, and as banditos we made our way across the lawn, leaving the ladder lying at the base of the columns. I wasn't worried about the ladder. It was a forty-year-old ladder purchased years ago at a yard sale. No evidence left.

"Can I speak with Anne Brewer, please?" I was standing at a payphone outside of the Pierpont Store, a rustic little general that served the rural community south of Manchester. Finding a payphone anywhere these days was next to impossible, we'd have to buy some disposable cells soon. It was six o'clock in the morning. I was sure Anne would be at the station.

"Can I tell her who's calling?"

"Just say someone with a lead on a hot story."

"Hold on." My nervous system was a wreck. Lake stood next to me in no better shape.

"Hi, this is Anne."

"Yes, this is Mr. Green Jeans. The columns on the University quad: take a look. We'll be back in touch with you soon." I was about to hang up.

"Wait. Can we meet sometime?" Anne was sharp. I had been right.

"No, not yet anyway." I hadn't rehearsed this part.

"It will be completely confidential, I swear."

"Peace." I hung up.

"That was a rush! She wanted to meet with us." I let go a deep exhale and laid my hand on Lake's shoulder.

"Do you think she's going to go check out the columns?" Lake asked with her mouth wide open.

"Oh yeah. I bet she's on her way there right now."

"We should get the ladder." Lake leaned up against the phone booth.

"No. The ladder will connection to us. Let's get out of here. We've been gone all night. The kids are probably wondering if we're ever coming back." I offered Lake my hand, and we walked to the truck.

We didn't have any human kids, and not by choice. Our efforts to produce a child naturally were unsuccessful, and we never pursued assistance with fertility. We had looked into adopting, but when the cost was so far from what we could afford, we lost hope. If we had been fortunate enough to have a child, we would have never gone beyond one. We both agreed it was completely irresponsible to have more than that. A single human has a big impact on Mother Earth, and human occupancy had far exceeded harmony.

"Okay, wide pan on me with the columns in the background. Slowly take the shot into me, and when I take my arm and make a sweeping motion, I want you to run the shot across the columns in order of the statement and then back to me. How does that sound, Gus?" Anne had only been out of journalism school for a year, but she planned to make as much out of this as possible. She had her eye on one of the big national morning shows as most up-and-comers do. That would be years away, but she was resolute to get there. She hoped Mr. Green Jeans wouldn't slip up, and get caught. This could be one for her portfolio.

"Couldn't have called it any better. I might think about this dandelion as an opening and closing shot though, lots of symbolism here? This is some pretty crazy 60's stuff, you know?" Gus said, as he set up the camera on the tripod. Gus was a veteran of the news business. He was sixty-five, five-foot-eight, proudly displayed a gray ponytail, a few tattoos, all birds, and had been around the world too many times to count. He made the big time when he was just a few years older than Anne was now. He worked Vietnam before, during and after the war. He ran camera for almost all of the big players and was sometimes getting paid by more than one affiliate in a single day. His nickname at the time was 'Ditch' because he often returned to the hotel completely covered in jungle mud. When someone commented on his appearance once, he replied, "Been in the ditches again. Only way to get the shot sometimes." He didn't want to say trenches out of respect for the soldiers. Gus didn't like guns. He'd seen too many and knew what trouble they caused. He had been here in Manchester for ten years, married to a Vietnamese woman for the last thirty years. After almost eight years in Vietnam and another twenty taking jobs anywhere from Tahiti to Afghanistan, he was tired. His wife was tired. During a three-month road trip across the US, they decided on Manchester. Here they lived a peaceful life and got the biggest bang for their buck. It was easy to get a job with the local station. The pay was minimal, but it was a living supplemented with social security. They were comfortable. He recognized the gleam in Anne's eyes; he'd seen it many times. He was happy for her, and also knew that she could very well be the real deal. Time would tell.

"Okay, time to make you shine, darling. Rolling…"

Todd and Barb had come over after work, and the four of us were sitting in the living room around the TV. Lake pressed the play button. We'd already watched it many times, but Todd and Barb hadn't seen it yet.

"As you can see we're standing at the University of Missouri Columns this morning, and behind me is the latest in Mr. Green Jeans' attempt to voice his concerns."

"She's pandering to us. I like it," I stated, glued to the TV, even though this was at least the tenth time we'd seen it.

"Well, let's take a look at what Mr. Green Jeans has to say." Anne swept her hand up as though she was unveiling a new art installment.

The camera panned the columns. These were six, seventy-five-foot-tall, limestone Doric columns that were attached a hundred years ago to the university's main administration building. A fire had left only the columns which now sat prominently on a three-acre, meticulously groomed lawn. The 'quad', as it was called, was surrounded on all four sides by impressive classroom buildings constructed in the late 1800's. It was the heart of the University's campus. This time, the signs were twice the size. We used cardboard and framed them on the back with three pine one-by-twos for strength. Four signs made up the message, white for the words and green for the background. The signs were attached halfway up the columns. A small sign sat at the base of the middle column and read 'Mr. Green Jeans'. The camera focused on each sign long enough to read it and then panned out for a full shot.

IF WE DO NOT CHANGE DIRECTION
WE ARE LIKELY
TO END UP EXACTLY
WHERE WE ARE HEADED

"Hard to argue that point. This is Anne Brewer. If you're coming out to look at the signs, they were taken down this morning. In fact, the university's ground keepers said they used the ladder that was left last night by Mr. Green Jeans himself.

We tried to get a comment from the university's president, but her schedule wouldn't allow one today. Once again, this Anne Brewer reporting on location at the University columns."

"Well?" Lake asked.

Barb and Todd looked at each other seeming to ask the other to speak first.

"You guys are out, right?" I directed the question at both of them.

"I think so." Todd spoke first.

"We just can't risk what would happen if we were caught. We're really sorry. It's a great thing. It's just….." Barb was interrupted by Lake.

"Hey, we completely understand," Lake said, looking at Barb.

"Just don't tell anyone." I was halfway smiling but also dead serious in my expression.

"Please. You know this will always be our secret. We have as much to lose if you talk. It was a blast that night on the freeway though! Balls off to you guys," Todd reassured me.

I stuck out my hand to Todd and he encircled me in a bear hug. Lake hugged Barb, and then we switched. As far as trust went, it couldn't have been any more genuine. They were family. Now a family with secrets. And what family doesn't have secrets?

"Long live Mr. Green Jeans!" Todd said as he and Barb opened the front door, walked down the steps and off the front porch.

As Lake and I waved and watched them walk down the gravel drive, Lake squeezed my hand.

"It's going to be all right." I squeezed her hand back and gave her a kiss on the cheek.

"Shall we watch it again, Clyde?"

I laughed. "Why Bonnie, you just read my mind."

"Why, I'll be." Lake laughed and closed the front door.

Comfortably back on the couch, Lake hit play for the eleventh time.

"My mom would be so proud," I commented.

"She would be devastated," Lake added.

"Wish we hadn't lost the ladder."

"Better that than getting caught. We had to get out of there and carrying a ladder across the lawn could have busted our cover," Lake replied.

"That couple doing the serious groping probably wouldn't have even noticed if we walked by them with the ladder."

"Glad Todd loaned you his beard," Lake said and laughed as she thought how ridiculous we had both looked last night.

"Do you think Todd and Barb are all right, baby?" Lake asked.

"Yeah, I mean there's nothing we can do now, what's done is done. I'll knock 'em off if it looks like they're going to rat us out." I stood at the foot of the stairs.

"You going to bed?" Lake asked.

"Yeah, do some reading. You all right?" I asked.

"I'm doing all right. Are you okay?"

"Yeah, mildly freaking out, but in a good way."

"Me too," She said and walked up and kissed me on the lips.

"Let's take a drive tomorrow, I want to show you this spot I think might work very, very well," I said, walking up the stairs.

"Okay Clyde."

"Night, Bonnie."

"Night, Clyde."

Chapter Fourteen

FOUR DAYS LATER. A full nine weeks left of summer break. We successfully struck again.

OUR TAX DOLLARS
A 30 MILLION DOLLAR TOWN HALL? REALLY?
HOW ABOUT A 1 MILLION DOLLAR FARMERS MARKET?
A NEW CLEAN ENERGY POWER PLANT?
A BIO-DIESEL BUS SYSTEM?
MR. GREEN JEANS!

Two days ago, that was draped across the front of Manchester's brand-spanking-new town hall in the heart of downtown, a block away from the police station. It was much easier than we expected. 4:00 a.m. is a great time for this kind of work, and with two trees flanking the opening to town hall, our job was easy. Wearing full stocking masks, we hoped the cameras wouldn't be able to identify us. We had made the decision to switch to canvas, a little costly, but ease of installation and raising the level of our presentation was important. Lake and I painted the 6 x 24-foot, rolled-out canvas on our lawn at home. Signature-green background with black lettering. I added a few suns and Native American symbols. A call at five a.m. to Anne Brewer from Manchester's last downtown payphone in front of the Quickie Mart on Eleventh and Locust. The story ran the local morning, noon and evening news. Manchester wasn't a big town so it was easy to make the local news. We'd counted on that.

It was now 3:00 a.m., the witching hour, and I was positioning our newly purchased, extension ladder on a monolithic billboard stuck in the earth on the side of I-70. It currently advertised a casino on the banks of the Missouri River, not far from Manchester and garnered it consumers from rural central Missouri.

"Hey babe, as soon I get a hold up here, I'm going to pull up the canvas." I climbed the ladder holding a rope that was attached to our banner.

"Okay. Be careful."

These large monstrosities had their own platform at the base of the billboard, complete with lights for around-the-clock advertising. We positioned the ladder to reach the metal steps built into the steel column. The steps started about fifteen feet up the pole and then made their way up to the platform. This was by far the most dangerous mission we'd attempted so far. The placement of our signs was critical to our success. We had to push the envelope to be noticed. This message would be high and take some work to get down. We wanted as much airtime as we could get.

"Okay, I'm up."

I-70 was alive even at this hour. Cars and trucks streamed by fifteen yards away. I stood on the thin platform and pulled up the rope that was tied to our new canvas message, as Lake directed it from below until it was out of her reach. This billboard was well-lit, and all who passed could easily see me up here. I was Batman tonight, black clothes and a high quality, rubber, Batman mask. I was tempted to wave. Once I had the canvas on the platform with me, I found one of the upper corners and pulled out the caulk gun filled with a tube of Stronger than Nails from my backpack, and squeezed a healthy amount on the canvas. I carefully walked over to the far end of the sign and reached as high as I could and pressed the corner down onto the billboard and held it for twenty seconds, then releasing it. It held! I did the same to the other three corners, and in five minutes, I was done and coming down the ladder. A few cars honked from the interstate. I was in clear view.

"Careful baby, slow down," Lake said, holding the ladder.

"That was a rush!" I said, on the ground, starting to bring down the extension ladder.

Once the ladder was consolidated, we each took an end and ran up the hill to where Lake's Subaru was parked on an outer service road. Securing the ladder on the car rack, we slowly drove off and then descended the ramp onto I-70.

"Baby, that was crazy with you up there."

"You're telling me. Okay, it's coming up."

There it was, once Big Mo Casino, now:

'SUPPORT REAL PLACES OWNED BY REAL PEOPLE'—'SHOP LOCAL'—'SUPPORT LOCAL'—'THIS IS OUR TOWN'—'NOT THEIR TOWN'. 'MR GREEN JEANS'.

"Oh yeah, that's what I'm talking about!"

"You did it, babe!"

"We did it!"

Our canvas didn't completely cover the top or bottom of the Big Mo Casino, but our sign was all you registered when you drove by. It was all lit up and standing proud. The billboard company would have to be called and service men sent out. It would probably be up there until the afternoon.

"I guess I'll call," I said, holding our new cell phone as Lake drove down the freeway.

"We know for sure the phone won't be traced."

"No. But I'll take out the battery when I'm done."

I dialed Anne's personal number she had given me after I had called in the town hall strike.

"Hi Anne, I-70 eastbound between Stadium and Providence, look for the billboard." I paused.

"Mr. Green Jeans?"

"Yeah."

"Really, that was quick. I want to go national with this, just to let you know. You guys think you'll be around for a while?" Anne asked raising from her three down pillow nest.

"Ahhh, yeah."

"I like what you're doing. Any chance I could meet you, no cameras, just a talk?" Anne continued to take advantage of the open line.

She was good. Of course, I'd never been on this end, on either end. All this was new. I was a neophyte, playing a new game, and the rules were one: Don't get caught.

"I don't know. Got to go, Anne." I almost hung up.

"If I say I've been in contact with you, would you stop calling me?" she asked.

"No, I don't think so." Where was this going?

"Can I get a statement, like a mission statement from you…?"

"Get connected or face loss of service." I hung up, took the back off the phone and undid the circuit board and battery. "Oh my God, she wants to go national with this."

"What?!" Lake said, taking the next exit so we could loop around again.

"That's what she said. This is going faster than I anticipated…"

"A little kitty crying can go viral on YouTube in a day. I think this trumps a kitty," Lake interrupted.

"True. Maybe we should lay low for a bit."

"Yeah. Not a bad idea. I like, 'Get connected or face loss of service'."

"Not bad, huh?"

After a short nap that morning, we decided to go into town to shoot some pool at Booches, a Manchester landmark. It was known for its burgers, which neither of us consumed anymore. The atmosphere was just what we needed, though. We got a rack of balls and headed to an empty table. This was an old building and some of the tables needed to be propped up with slivers of wood to keep them level. A few regulars, two old men sitting a stool apart at the bar, were watching a horserace on the box above the bar.

"Hi Folks, what can I get you?" asked a young, good-looking college student coming back to our table as I got the balls racked.

"Large plate of fries for me, please. Bonnie?

"What can I get you, ma'am'?" the college kid asked again.

"I'll have stuffed mushrooms and a glass of water, and please don't call me, ma'am', my name is Bonnie"

"Sorry. Be back in a few minutes, Bonnie?"

Lake was smiling. I was smiling. We were reveling in the moment. Lake broke, and we started a game of eight ball.

The door to Booches swung open and a collection of young college coeds streamed into the bar.

"Turn on channel eight! Mr. Green Jeans is on!" yelled a girl staring at her iPhone. She looked like a cross between Janice Joplin and Snooky.

The bartender switched the channel on the TV, to the disappointment of the two old guys watching the horserace. We laid our sticks on the table and walked up to the bar to watch.

"This is Anne Brewer, reporting live and on location where the latest Mr. Green Jeans message is being taken down."

The shot started with Anne standing on the side of I-70, semis roaring by and blowing her blond hair, a good opening action shot. Gus's idea, it turned out. Then it panned to the billboard. The entire message was shown before two guys in coveralls on the billboard deck pulled on the upper corner of the canvas.

'SUPPORT REAL PLACES OWNED BY REAL PEOPLE'—'SHOP LOCAL'— 'SUPPORT LOCAL'— 'THIS IS OUR TOWN'— 'NOT THEIR TOWN'—'MR GREEN JEANS'.

With a good pull, the canvas was ripped off the sign and Mo River Casino, part of an international chain of small casinos primarily built in small communities, was left with a just few scars. The shot returned to Anne to finish the report.

"In an exclusive conversation with Mr. Green Jeans early this morning, he informed me his mission statement was 'Get connected or face loss of service'. This is Anne Brewer, reporting live from I-70.

"Whoa! How cool is that!?" yelled the girl with the iPhone.

"Very cool, I'm putting that on a T-Shirt!" said a lanky, somewhat long-haired, college student wearing baggy shorts, sandals and a Radio-Head T-shirt. The two old guys raised their glass steins of pilsner hoping the horseraces would be turned back on, but happy for the moment and what was happening.

"I like his message. The corporations are taking over everything, let me tell ya. I've been in the business for 40 years now, and I once bought almost everything I needed here from someone local. Now, 80% is from some damn other place, 'cause the Corps put all my people out of business. And that's the God-fearing truth," said Lloyd, the owner of Booches. He was a thin, well-dressed man in his seventies, who was there every day, scurrying around, either cleaning pool tables, checking the registrar, or conversing with his customers.

"I'm with you Lloyd, these kids are doing something I should have done," replied Frank, one of the ole guys sipping a lite beer.

"You can't climb a ladder anymore, Frank," said Sam, Frank's best friend and three-beer buddy a few days a week.

"Yep, you're right about that, but I can still take some chalk to the sidewalk."

"Not a bad idea, Sam."

"Don't be getting any ideas guys," Lloyd said, laughing.

"To the sidewalks kids!" Frank raised his stein to whole bar.

Sam and Frank, professors now retired from the university, their steins in the air again, shouted, "Long live Mr. Green Jeans!" till Booches' whole population had their drinks up and joined in. Lake and I, of course, took a seat at the bar and became part of celebration.

"You guys think this Mr. Green Jeans has a chance at changing anything?" I asked nudging Lake with my elbow. She smiled and grabbed my leg under the bar. The young college kid placed our fries and mushrooms before us.

"Who knows in this day and age? But that's what this country was built on, speaking your mind and having the right to do so," replied Lloyd, wiping down the bar.

"I'd give him a big old kiss," said iPhone girl.

"So would I, and maybe something more," Lake added.

We all laughed, and the 'Mr. Green Jeans and the Save the World' dialog began and lasted for another two hours with many an, 'I'll buy the next round!'

"We're not driving." Lake grabbed my leg and looked at me with warning eyes."

"No. I'll call Todd," I replied. We rarely went out and had drinks. Today had been special, and it was too hard to resist joining in on the spontaneous celebration.

"Good," Lake responded, leaning against me.

Thirty minutes later, Todd showed up. He was always happy to visit Booches, his very favorite place in Manchester.

"Hey guys, little stuckage problem?" Todd was in a good mood. Having once taken an active role, he felt relaxed in a subordinate accessory role of the getaway driver. I started to get up.

"Whoa, we're not leaving till I have a Guinness." Todd was already on a barstool.

"Okay." We were in no hurry. We were both drinking water.

"Hey Todd, haven't seen you in a while," Lloyd said setting down his Guinness.

"Nope, been laying low, Lloyd."

"Understand that. Beer's on me." Lloyd walked off.

Didn't take Todd too long to down his Guinness, and we were on our way home. We would come back to pick up our car tomorrow. Before we reached 1-70 west, Todd slid into a Taco Bell drive thru. Todd loved Taco Bell. Not a good choice for Lake though. Her move to become a vegan required you to have no oils that weren't cold pressed, and the refined vegetable oil that was used to cook a plethora of ingredients in any fast food joint negated it being a vegan choice. Besides that, there was anything but real food to be had.

"I want super-duper nachos, hold the meat," she muttered from the back seat. A few drinks and one's convictions could be altered. That's why politicians, years ago in small communities, had 'drinks on the house' during Election Day.

It was a food fest on the way home. Someday, maybe there would be a vegan/vegetarian fast food joint. Today had been a good day. A very good day.

Chapter Fifteen

TODD DROVE ME to retrieve our car the next morning. We glided down I-70 in his silver Chrysler 300, a throwback to the gangster cars. Nice ride, and it fit Todd.

"Jack, I've been thinking about your whole mission. You're intent on getting as much attention as possible. I think that the objective should target the most prominent places with the same message. Stop changing the message; it's too much for people to remember. Bush won because he kept saying, "Ya know where I stand," and it stuck in people's minds, grant you, not the ones with any brains, but that's over half the population, unfortunately. What do you think?" Todd looked over at me.

"Same message?" I asked, rolling down the window to take away the new car scent Todd always had applied at the car wash.

"Same message, and then it could grow if it caught on. You'd be known for something specific, and I think that's how it works. I don't know, but that's how they sell products. Everybody's got a jingle from the Sierra Club to Coca-Cola. You guys are selling a concept right? A way of living. You need a jingle." Todd finished and looked over at me again.

"Makes sense, man," I responded, knowing we weren't going to do that. I didn't want to talk to anyone but Lake about Mr. Green Jeans anymore.

Once to Ninth Street in downtown Manchester, we pulled up next to the Subaru. It was before 8:00, and the meter maids hadn't clocked in yet. No ticket.

"Thanks Todd. Jingle. I like it," I said opening the passenger door.

"See you guys this weekend maybe," Todd said through the open passenger window. "Must be nice to have every day be a Saturday. I'm off to see my clients."

I waved. "See ya, man."

"Hey, buddy, you know what you're doing right?"

"Nope, but it feels good."

"Okay. Be careful, brother." Todd drove off.

When I got home, I checked in on Lake. She was sleeping soundly. I went outside with the rest of the family: the two dogs and Smokey Joe. The sun was shining through the walnut trees on the garden's perimeter. Standing in the garden, I picked up the hoe and began to weed our garlic.

The next day, feeling refreshed, we decided against the one slogan approach Todd had suggested. The signature of Mr. Green Jeans was the key. We had too much to say. The earth had too much to say.

"We crash these words hard, and hope for the best," I said as I painted a forest-green background onto a forty-foot piece of canvas rolled out on the lawn.

"This is getting crazy now. St Louis, Kansas City and then maybe Chicago?" Lake said as she painted the other end of the canvas spread out on the grass.

I looked at her. "I know. But if we don't raise our level, we're nothing more than a few graffiti artists."

"I know that a lot people don't understand what's going down in the world, but I'm scared baby, I'm really scared. We've been lucky so far." Lake stopped painting and stood with her brush in hand. I stopped painting, realizing she was questioning this whole thing again. I put my arm around her shoulders. She started to cry. This was not something you can train for, there were no preparation manuals for how to deal with this.

"Baby, I know what we're doing is dangerous and crazy. You take some time off. I got to do this. I got to do this," I said because that's all I could think of saying. I was steadfast now. I held her tight as she cried like one does when they're up against something that could go very wrong at any time.

"Baby, you can't do it alone, not this big of a sign and not this many signs. I'm sorry, I'm crying. I feel terrible!" More tears and a runny nose. "I want you to stop, and I don't want you to stop. I don't want to stop, but I don't know…Jack. I'm just scared, baby. Crap! I'm sorry." Lake slipped to the grass and was crying uncontrollably now. I knelt down and continued to hold her.

"Baby, you lay back awhile. I'll be all right. Don't worry," I said and pulled her close.

"I'm just at a point. It just happened. I was fine earlier today, it just hit. I'm sorry. Just give me some time. We have ten years till retirement, and we'll get four thousand a month between the two of us for life. The house will be paid off. What the hell are we doing?!" Lake muttered between tears and blowing her nose on my sleeve.

"I know, its nuts. But I…"

"But what! What Jack, what!"

"I thought you were fine, what happened, baby?"

"The switch went off. You know, and I know that I do this. I freaked out about moving to Missouri. It almost didn't happen. I freaked out about buying this house the day before we closed. And once again, I am freaking out. I'm sorry."

I held her tighter. I wanted her with me. A small part of me always wondered if this might happen. What then? I could think I was on my own. When you're married and in love, you're never really apart. What one does, the other feels. It could have been me as easily as her. For whatever reason, my pedal wasn't letting up on the gas, and hers was braking. I was more alive right now than I had been in over a decade. However selfish it was, I needed to continue. I hoped she'd return. I needed my 'Bonnie'.

"It's going to be all right."

"No, it's not Jack. It's not going to be all right."

We lay in the grass, and I held her, and she wept. I cried too. This was stupid, and I knew that, but I was done living my old life.

Chapter Sixteen

IT WAS A TWO-HOUR DRIVE from our home to Kansas City. At 7:00 a.m., I was parked in an underground garage at one of JC Nichols most decorative Kansas City's Plaza buildings. The five-by-seven block Plaza, was, to many people, the heart of Kansas City. Shopping, restaurants, coffee shops and art galleries scattered with fountains, sculpture, carriage and gondola rides on the weekends, this was Kansas City at its finest. Lots of people visited here daily.

After making my way up the cement stairs to the roof door, I cut the padlock with bolt cutters, another punishable offense on my growing list. Crouching, I had made my way to the corner of the roof, pulling the canvas behind me. Squatting on the tar roof behind the ornate curvatures of the tower at the east end of the grand entrance to the Plaza, I unrolled the first of today's canvases. Traffic strolled by this corner twenty-four hours a day. A huge fountain of horses sat across the intersection. Kansas City was the city of fountains, second only to Rome, and this was one of its most spectacular. Great visibility here, and there was no doubt the sign would be seen as soon as I began putting it up.

"This is scaryyyyy...be very cool, Jack...very coolll," I said out loud. I was alone. I needed to calm down. I needed to breathe. It was early morning. The traffic was already heavy, and I was sure once I began to drape the canvas over the side of the building it would be noticed. It wouldn't be up that long. I used the stronger than nails caulk again and ran a bead down the top of the banner. This was a short one, only twelve feet long. It took me only a few minutes to get the sign in place. Cars began honking halfway through the hanging. I had to get out of here. The Plaza had its own security force. Pushing down on the last end, hoping the adhesive would work, I ran for the roof door and took two steps at a time down the stairs. I needed to get out here fast. The caulk gun in one hand and the bolt cutters in the other, I swiftly made my way to the car. Depositing the bolt cutter and caulk gun under the passenger seat, I left the garage on foot to get a coffee before I'd go check on the sign. Walking down the sidewalk, with sweat dripping down my face, I got out the cell phone.

"Hello."

"Anne, you make it to Kansas City?"

"I'm just south of downtown."

"You're not far. East end of the Plaza, just across from the horse fountain, you'll see it."

"Minutes away. There's more, right?"

"Yeah, there's a lot more to come." I hung up.

I needed to calm down. With a deep exhale, I entered a coffee shop.

"Double mocha latte' please," I said, as I looked over at the early morning clientele of the high-end coffee shop, Joe's Joe. Leaving a healthy tip, I strolled outside. The Plaza's sidewalks were beginning to show signs of life, as the sales clerks and store owners arrived in anticipation of a good Saturday.

I called Lake.

"Hello?" Lake answered with anticipation.

"First one done."

"Is she there?" Lake asked.

"She's on the way as we speak. I'm going to take a look right now?"

"Be super-duper careful, baby," Lake said.

"Super-duper. I will. I'll see you tonight about seven," I replied. It was good to hear her voice.

"I love you! I'm sorry!" Lake shouted.

"You stop that. I love you too!"

"Bye, baby sweetheart." Lake hung up. I held onto the phone for a moment before I took it apart.

I turned the corner sipping my latte and looked up. There it was.

THE PLANET WILL BE HAPPY TO GET RID OF US IF WE DON'T CHANGE OUR WAYS.
MR. GREEN JEANS

A crowd of two-dozen people already stood looking up at the sign. Some were taking pictures, some laughing, but all were staring. And there she was, Anne, in a green skirt and black blouse, Mr. Green Jean colors. She was sharp, as well as extremely easy on the eyes.

"Gus, lots of shots of the banner, and I want to do some interviews here on the street with the sign in background," Anne said checking her mike.

"Got it, boss lady," Gus said videoing some footage of the banner.

I decided to get closer, even though I needed to get going. I had many other stops before I was done with Kansas City. I was just fascinated with my role in this unfolding story and had a tendency to push boundaries. I had informed Anne I had many targets today, and would call her as I made good each time. I hoped she'd spend the day in Kansas City, because I was going to be busy, and she was essential to Mr. Green Jean's expansion. We had spent some hard-earned money on this run.

I crossed to where the crowd had gathered. I made certain to stay out of any shots. She was in the process of obtaining responses from the onlookers.

"Are you familiar with the Mr. Green Jeans, sir?" Anne asked an older gentleman wearing a fedora, standing next to his wife.

"He might not be, but I saw your stories from Manchester. I like Mr. Green Jeans. Harry could care less," the wife answered for him.

Anne laughed, the husband smiled. I smiled too. I was only a few feet from her. Anne looked around to find her next interview. We met eyes and I immediately turned away. I looked back and she was still staring at me. I looked away again and began to walk off. I wore a fishing cap and a glued on mustache. I looked suspicious and stupid. What was I thinking, sticking on a costume shop mustache?

"Gus, get the camera on that guy walking away!" Anne had a hunch and you always followed a hunch if you were a reporter worth your snuff. I rounded a corner and began running.

"Let's go!" Anne was already in pursuit. Gus followed with the camera rolling. I was running up the sidewalk looking for a place to cut off and return to the car. I looked back, and the camera a few hundred feet away was on me. I dashed into another underground parking garage. They were still in pursuit. Finding the stairwell, I leaped up the steps to the third level. Ripping off my blue nylon jacket, mustache and hat, I stuffed them into a trash can by the door to Macy's. Opening the door, I found myself walking into the women's department, the little girl section no less, I was sweating; bad place to be a middle-aged male sweating. Head down, I crossed the store until I reached the street entrance and looking both ways, exited onto the sidewalk. I was now two blocks from my car. I walked swiftly down the sidewalk to the parking garage. That was close.

Fifteen minutes later and I was on the lawn at the Nelson National Art Gallery, a sloping expanse of one hundred yards that was bordered at the bottom by a four-lane boulevard heading into the Plaza. Anyone driving by had a view of the manicured lawn dotted with sculptures that led up to the Nelson Gallery. It was a breathtaking place, and I walked across the pristine lawn carrying a rolled-up canvas over my shoulder. I stopped midway across. A few people wandered the huge lawn, but no one was close. This time, I wore a hoodie and sunglasses, the Uni bomber look. Another stellar idea. I grabbed one end of the canvas and began unrolling the sixty-by-four-foot banner on the grass. People passing on the road a hundred feet away could easily see me. It took only a few seconds to unroll the canvas and a minute more to hammer down a few spikes so it wouldn't blow away. Once done, I ran like a scared rabbit.

"Dude, drive by the Nelson on your way to work. Mr. Green Jeans is hitting Kansas City. Oh yeah!" said Steve, a young man, on his cell phone as he drove past the Nelson.

> MY IMPACT IS YOUR IMPACT—OUR IMPACT IS OUR FUTURE—WE SCREW UP NOW AND GAME OVER—MR. GREEN JEANS

Reading the banner on the lawn, Steve recited the message into the phone.

Back in the Subaru, and I headed to Westport, considered the hippest place in the city for the late-twenties crowd. It was a cheaper and more alternative choice to the Plaza. Pulling into a spot on the street next to Kelly's Bar, I re-connected the phone and called Anne.

"The sculpture lawn at the Nelson."

"We almost had you back there."

"I don't know what you're talking about." I hung up.

Kelly's Bar in Westport was my third stop and was one of Kansas City's oldest and most famous bars and a landmark to boot. I knew Pat, the owner because my brother and he were good friends. Patrick Kelly was a solid man, one that thought with conviction and always loved a good fight. On the phone last night, I took a big chance and asked to put a banner on his building. Pat didn't hesitate and reassured me that I had his trust. I knew I needed more Pats if this movement of ours was to become more than a flash in the pan. Lake and I couldn't do this alone, that is if Lake was even coming back on board.

"It was just past nine o'clock in the morning, and Kelly's had been opened for two hours. They always opened at seven on Saturdays, and a few patrons were already in attendance. Pat offered me an early-morning brew.

"No, an orange juice would be good, though," I said.

"Ladders leaning up against the building in the alley," Pat said, as he set down a tall flute of orange juice before me and began wiping down the thirty-five-foot-long wood bar.

"Excellent. Thanks," I said as I downed most of the juice in one draw.

"Your brother know about this?" Pat asked, as a regular took a seat a few stools down from me and Pat delivered him his first of Bud Lite draft of the day.

"Nope."

"This is nuts, Jack. Mike would be proud, though, let him know," Pat said, stopping in front of me.

"I haven't talked to him in years," I replied, finishing the last of the orange juice.

"I know. Hope that changes, Jack."

"Yeah. I don't want him getting involved."

"Involved? What, are you considering this for a lifestyle?"

"Thanks, Pat, for the letting me do this. We don't know what we're doing really, we're just doing."

"Your brother always said you'd do something someday, but he didn't predict this."

"I didn't either."

We gave each other a hard handshake, and I was off to plant another banner. Pat went back to wiping the bar. This one would be up all day. Pat wasn't going to let anyone take it down, it was his building and because he liked what I was doing, he was going to support us. It could be good for business too, once Anne arrived.

The ladder was there, and it was still early enough that I had no problem getting on the roof unnoticed. Slinging the sign up on the flat roof, I climbed off the ladder and went to work. I unrolled the new sign and began draping it over the side of the building, pushing the canvas through screws that were in place, thanks to Pat. This one would stay up as long as Pat wanted it, too.

Down the ladder, I returned to the car and took a drive by Kelly's. I paused and saw Pat walking out to look at the banner.

'ENERGY SPENT MAKING BEER BEATS ENERGY SPENT MAKING WAR!
                       MR. GREEN JEANS'

Pat turned, smiled and winked at me. I gave the peace sign and drove off. Number three done, just a few to go.

At the corner of Broadway and McGee Street, a White Castle, the Missouri-bred burger joint, sat empty, and I pulled into the vacant parking lot. I had devoured dozens of White Castle burgers in college before going vegetarian. I can still remember the addictive taste. What is in those burgers is anyone's guess.

"Do you know Kelly's in Westport?" I said on the phone to Anne.

"Yeah."

"Number three is up."

"That was quick."

"Keep your phone on, Anne." I was about to hang up.

"Let's meet today."

"Not today, pretty lady." I hung up and felt like a bandito. 'Pretty lady'! Wasn't that something a bandito would say? This activity was getting all the juices flowing.

Ten minutes later, taking Broadway through downtown Kansas City, I parked a block from the Spring Street Farmer's Market on the Missouri River front. This was a big market, drawing sellers from a radius of hundred miles, and the place was already abuzz. I needed two people to make this work. I carried the rolled-up canvas over my shoulder and tried to fit in as a one of sellers that was setting up a stall for the day. I still wore oversized sunglasses, but replaced the hoodie with a jean jacket and baseball cap that said Organic. The Farmers Market was quickly coming to full bloom, and I had a timetable to keep. Ten thousand people or more would be milling about looking for pesticide-free, organic fruits, vegetables, free-range meats, Amish baked goods, baskets, flowers, soap, anything a small farm or business produced themselves. We'd chosen this spot for its popularity and connection to our message. The final stage of today's plan was about to unfold, if I could find the right participants: I needed to find a couple of people willing to make some quick cash.

I approached a homeless pair sitting together on a public bench probably hoping to have a good day panhandling at the market. "Twenty bucks each, ten now, ten more when you're done?" I proposed.

"You be here when we get done?" asked Dale, a thirty-year-old white guy that looked fifty. He lifted himself off the bench.

"I'll leave the rest under this bench when you're done," I replied, holding the rolled up canvas and a roll of green duct tape.

"Sounds good to me. Dreads, you in?" asked Dale.

"Give me the ten, and watch me," answered an older, black woman, with dreads hanging halfway down her back. She still sat on the bench.

I explained to them what I wanted, then doled out two tens and handed over the canvas and tape. They began unrolling the thirty-by-four-foot banner, painted bright green with large, black lettering. People were stepping out of the way of the banner. The market was just about in full bloom. People passing by began taking notice, and when I saw a young woman take out her phone to take a picture, I knew it was time for me to distance myself from the scene.

"Thank you, guys!" I said walking off.

"Just make sure that money is there," said Dreads, now holding one end of the banner. Dale was at the other. I nodded, and the two were off running with the banner through the market. Time to make another call to Anne.

"Hey there. What do think so far?" I said into my cell phone, as I walked through the busy market.

"We just got to Kelly's," Anne replied.

"Get your shot, because the finale is about to begin. Farmers Market, Fifteen minutes."

"We'll be there in a snap. Thanks, and please let me…"

I hung up and took the phone apart.

Dale and Dreads, two seasoned street people, were smiling as they ran through the market with the thirty-foot banner, weaving their way through the crowd. The market was a large affair with at least four hundred vendors, outside in an open-air park with nicely built covered stalls. The entire market was surrounded by restaurants and bars and was bordered on the West by the Missouri River. It was the place to be in Kansas City on a Saturday morning, in the spring to early Fall.

EAT RIGHT, BUY RIGHT, THE MOTHER IS AT STAKE, KEEP THE GMO'S OUT OF OUR LIVES
MR. GREEN JEANS

I watched as people turned to look, and point and chat with each other. Phones were out. This newest message was already on its way across the web.

"Oh yeah!!!!!" Dreads was yelling, as she ran the front of the sign through the crowds. "Mr. Green Jeans is heeah!!!!! Mother is hurting! Give her some love! Come on people, give her some love!!!" Dale was having a hard time keeping up with her, even though he was younger. They seemed to be having a good time and did a few more circuits of the market before ending up on the grandstand, which was empty this early in the morning. The band booked to play later hadn't even begun to set up yet. As instructed, they began taping the banner across the stage's apron. Across the market grounds, I saw the television van pull up and double park. Out hopped Anne and Gus. Gus quickly got his camera and began shooting. Anne saw the sign and motioned for Gus to follow her. She caught up to my accomplices as they climbed off the stage.

"Excuse me, can I get a few words with you guys?" Anne asked as she cornered Dale against the stage.

"We got a payment to collect sister. Come on Dale," Dreads said from a few feet away.

"Sorry. We kinda need to get out of here. The popo, you know?" Dale said, as he followed Dreads off to park bench.

Anne and Gus stayed in pursuit. I had already set the money under the bench and made my way into the crowd. From a good vantage point, I saw the two pick up the money. Anne and Gus were on them like bad upholstery.

"So, who paid you?" Anne asked.

"Lady, back off unless you serving some more of the same," Dreads responded as she folded the money neatly and put into her breast pocket. Dale searched the crowd for any police.

"I'll double it, if I can ask you a few questions." Anne was already taking out her billfold.

"Okay. We got time for a few words I think. Dale?" Dreads asked.

"Let's make it quick," Dale responded.

"What does he look like?" Anne asked.

"Whoa, honey-child. Let's see the green." Dreads, a big woman, was not one to argue with.

Anne pulled out some ones and a five.

"Oh no honey, we need to see a few tens," Dreads added.

"About four of them," Dale stated, still scanning the market for any possible trouble.

Gus added to the pot, and Anne handed over forty dollars.

"White guy, forty-, fifty-something maybe, pretty good looks, brown hair, okay build, and if you like white bread like me, he'd do well," Dreads answered.

"What was he wearing?" she asked.

"Jean jacket, green cap and some huge-ass sunglasses," Dreads answered, folding the money.

"Can you scan the crowd and try to pick him out?" Gus asked from behind the camera.

"No," Dale answered.

"Unless you got more paper presidents?" Dreads said, holding out her hand. I'd already lost the glasses and jacket anticipating a description and was now trying to find a good vantage point for today's premiere attraction, which should be on the way anytime now.

"What do think he was trying to do here today?" Anne asked always wanting to get the street view.

"Have a voice, isn't what we all want? Ain't nothing special, except this dude was focused. You could see that, huh, Dale?"

Yeah. We need to go, Dreads," Dale responded.

"Okay, thanks," Anne said, as Dreads and Dale were off to have a real good Saturday afternoon.

Anne's phone began ringing. "Hello?"

"Hi Anne."

"Where are you?"

"Right behind you."

I watched from the security of a coffee shop, I had to laugh, as Anne turned around hoping I was just behind her. She motioned to Gus to start shooting the crowd.

"Come on Anne, I'm not really behind you. There's something coming up in just a few minutes," I said as I checked the clock on the wall of the coffee shop.

"You're going to hear it first. I suggest you find a place for Gus, so you can get a good vantage point of the sky."

"We need to talk."

"You better hurry for a good shot." I hung up the phone and took it apart again.

"Gus, he said you need a good shot of the sky. Something is going to happen," Anne said, grabbing the tripod from Gus and following him as he walked away from stalls. Everyone heard it. As the sound grew louder, Gus focused on the horizon where the noise seemed to be coming from. The crowd began looking up and then not more than a few hundred feet above, a single propeller plane appeared trailing a banner and flew directly over the market.

THE FATE OF THE SPECIES IS IN YOUR HANDS—BUY ORGANIC—BUY FAIR TRADE—BUY BACK OUR PLANET

MR. GREEN JEANS

As the plane took another sweep over the market, it had the attention of the entire crowd. A few thousand heads craned up to read Mr. Green Jean's latest. And then, something unexpected happened, one of those serendipitous moments. The crowd broke out in applause and then cheers, whistles and a few affirming exclamations.

I watched through the window of the coffee shop, where I could still have an overhead view. People were spilling out of the establishments that encircled the market to see what all the commotion was about. The plane, as promised, made two more passes over the crowd and then one more for good measure. The pilot responding to the standing ovation dipped his wings to give the customary aeronautics, 'Hi.' Even after the plane had left, the market was humming, applause was still breaking out in pockets, and it seemed everyone had a smile on their face.

"This is some good stuff," Gus said as he panned the crowd.

"Response footage?" Anne asked.

"Absolutely." Gus was grinning and thinking of groovy days of decades past.

On the two-hour drive home from Kansas City, I could hardly contain myself. By the time I pulled into our driveway, my face actually hurt from holding my smile so long. The light was on in the upstairs window, and I could hear Barney. Then, Pearl began to bark when I turned off the car. One more hour, and the late evening news would air. I hoped they had edited the piece in the news van on the way home, so it would be ready to run at ten o'clock. Reaching the front porch, the door opened and out bounded the dogs to see their papa. Bonnie had an expression of relief on her face; her Clyde had made it home safely.

Chapter Seventeen

"THAT WAS A GREAT PIECE last night, Anne!" I said, leaning up against the Subaru. We'd driven fifteen minutes from home to avoid any tracing of our phone to the location of our house. Probably ridiculous. It wasn't like there was really anyone after us, but once again better safe than sorry.

"Thank you," Anne said. "Tune into the national news tonight. I think you'll be impressed." She had just sent off ten minutes of her best footage from all the stories she had done to date on Mr. Green Jeans. NBC's nightly news said they were interested and might want to run a piece. She wasn't sure how much they would use, but any coverage was good coverage to help her climb the ladder and build the resume.

"What are you talking about?" I said, about to wet my pants.

"You might be going national. Can I call you Lucky?"

"Lucky?"

"You were wearing a Lucky Charms T-Shirt yesterday, weren't you?" Anne asked.

"A lucky charms T-shirt?" I responded, hoping I wouldn't emit a wet fart.

"The pilot you hired told me that."

"Little investigative reporting. I suppose I'll have to retire that Lucky Charms T-shirt," I replied, tapping on the car window and giving Lake a wide mouth expression.

"So, what's next?" Anne asked as she motioned to Gus across the newsroom to come over and pick up the other line.

"I'll call you when the time's right. You serious about the national news? I mean, all I'm doing is putting up some signs."

"How many people are doing that in this country like you are? Zero. Greenpeace will do a banner every once and awhile, but they're not consistent and they're an organization. I don't know who you are, but you're a lot more interesting. You caught their attention. Look, anything can happen between now and tonight, but I'd tune in if I were you. Can I confirm our agreement about being your exclusive contact?"

"Anne, I'm yours as long as you treat this with respect. It's not about me."

"We need to meet sometime." Anne was looking at Gus, who was now listening on another phone.

"I know. I'm planning on that," I responded.

"Good, I promise all will be confidential."

I'd done a little research, too, and discovered who the older guy running the camera was. Impressive list of accomplishments. "Okay. I'll check out the news tonight. Tell Gus hi." I hung up.

Back in the car and air conditioning, Lake was listening to NPR's 'Car Talk'. It was 95 degrees with 90% humidity outside. It's why they call Missouri, Misery sometimes. For two months a year it could be a hot, sticky mess outside or that is what it used to be like. Nowadays, anywhere you went in this world, there's no telling what the weather might be. People who still don't believe in climate change can kiss my green ass. "Oh, that might be a good sign," I said as I closed the passenger door.

"What?"

"Just thinking out loud. What if Mr. Green Jeans had a sign saying "Kiss my green ass if you don't believe we're playing a part in Climate Change?"

"Like it. So tell me! What did she say?!"

'You're not going to believe this!" I sat dripping in sweat from standing outside for a few minutes. Lake turned down the radio and looked at me.

"Can you say national news?!"

"No way!?"

"Yes way, baby! Yes, way!" I grabbed her iced mocha and took a long draw through the straw.

"What did she say…?"

"Let's go get some breakfast, and I'll tell you every word."

That night Todd and Barb were over. We all positioned ourselves in the parlor, and I turned on the TV. The broadcast opened with: "Tonight we have an interesting story coming from the heartland, Missouri to be exact. With the Green movement struggling to get legislation passed on climate change, this is a piece you don't want to miss." There was a moment of silence as Todd, Barb, Lake and I all sat and looked at each other with dropped-mouth expressions. The story was saved for the end of the broadcast; it ran for 48 seconds. In a montage, it showed every banner we had displayed since Anne had come on board. The report closed with newscaster saying, "Along with Mr. Green Jeans, we here at NBC, also say Go Green, goodnight and God bless."

"That was bomber!" Todd said, shaking his head back and forth.

Lake and I were speechless and immobile. Less than two months ago, I was taking down the VASECTOMY REVERSAL sign, and now the national evening news was on our side. Millions just saw that, millions.

"We just received an endorsement, didn't we? Oh my God!" I said still staring at the screen.

"Anyone for ice-cream downtown?" Barb asked.

"Yeah, that sounds great," Todd agreed. Lake was still sitting stunned in her chair.

"Lake? Earth to Lake?" Todd nudged Lake's arm awakening her from the broadcast.

"Yeah, I'll have pistachio mint," Lake responded, getting up from the sofa in a trance and heading for the front door.

"Dude, you just blew your woman away. You blew me away, too." Todd patted my shoulder. I grabbed my keys and caught up with Lake by the car.

"You all right?" I put my arm around her waist.

"I love you baby. I'm back," Lake said, and took the keys from me and got in her car.

"Baby, are you sure?"

"Jack, if I died tomorrow after doing what you did today, I'd be a happy woman. I'm ready, just believe me."

Green pistachio mint ran down the front of Lake's white, Mexican blouse, as the four of us walked the sidewalks in downtown Manchester. In fact, all four of us had green pistachio mint ice cream. It was only appropriate to eat green ice cream right now. Four green cones, four green people taking the stroll of a lifetime. We knew something no one else in the world knew but us, besides Pat Kelly, and he was as tight-lipped as Fort Knox.

At local news station, Anne walked with two plastic cups of champagne to the back of the newsroom where Gus sat at his computer. He was uploading all the Mr. Green Jeans banner pics on the station's site.

"What have you been up to hippie man?" Anne asked, offering some bubbly to Gus which he gladly took and gulped.

"Check this out." Gus rolled his chair back from the monitor.

"What are you doing?" Anne asked, with a worried voice.

"Getting it out there, more exposure, more movement, more stuff happens," Gus responded, finishing off his champagne.

"What!? Those pictures are property of the station."

"Hang loose sister, hopefully it will help their cause."

"Their cause?" Anne was getting fired up.

"Yeah, their cause, really all our cause, if we want to be an intelligent species."

"Next time, pass this stuff by me first. We have the exclusive rights, Gus."

"We're a team, my bad, little news fairy," Gus replied, not wanting to get into this, but realizing he might have a little monster on his hands.

"Don't get smart, Gus."

Gus kept his mouth shut as Anne walked away. She didn't like to lose control, and if it had been some young buck instead of Gus, she would have gone off on him. Gus knew that.

"Hey Lucky Charms girl!" Gus called out.

Anne stopped in place but didn't turn around.

"Cheers!" Gus held up his empty cup.

Anne didn't turn around to face Gus, but paused in place, held up her cup and gave a weak, "Cheers," back and then continued on her retreat. Gus smiled, he wasn't going to take any crap from some egotistical, twenty-three-year old. He also wasn't going to let her get under his skin. Her drama was her drama; he wanted no part of it. Mr. Green Jeans needed support, not exploitation.

Chapter Eighteen

ONE WEEK LATER, Lake and I checked into our 7th-floor-balcony room at the Sheraton on the St Louis waterfront. Our room overlooked the Gateway Arch, and the park that surrounded it. The Mississippi River offered a spectacular backdrop. This is where Lewis and Clark began their Westward passage expedition. This is where the majority of all early pioneers, left civilization behind to make their claim on a new life in the West. This is where Lake and I hoped to carry out our greatest crash to date.

It was the Fourth of July weekend and St Louis was readying itself for its largest annual celebration, the VP Fair, or Veiled Prophet Fair. It had originally begun in 1878 as a means of bringing the town back together after a bloody union strike. It was organized by the society of the veiled prophets, a collection of the cities debutantes. They celebrated it for a few years and then laid it to rest until 1981 when a local businessman restarted the fair. Today, it is one of America's largest birthday parties. Over a million people attend the fair each year. It was among the top three Fourth-of-July venues in the entire country. Big name bands, vendors, art, crafts, produce market, speakers, educational and informational tents, beer gardens and street players. It was going to be the perfect place to launch the Mr. Green Jean's Creed.

"Ready baby?" I turned off the light in the bathroom.

"Come here, babe," Lake said, looking out the window onto the park below the Arch.

"See those guys hanging out on the far end over there?"

"The homeless people?" I pointed.

"Probably." Lake tried to count how many there were.

"You sure you're cool asking them?" I asked.

"I'm good baby. High noon, like everything else, right? Hit 'em with everything at once," Lake responded.

"Yep." I gave her a slap on the butt and headed for the door.

"Wait, let me take a pee first."

"Of course, what was I thinking?" Lake gave me a face as she entered the bathroom. I often commented on her peeing. It seemed just before we were about to do anything she needed to pee first, sex in particular. It was now a running exchange between us.

Out on the plaza vendors were setting up for hopeful sales. A few hundred city workers along with volunteers were making the final adjustments, setting up stages, hanging banners, positioning toilets, trash cans and recycling containers. Bike police were out in force and a few news and radio station crews had arrived and were setting up their equipment to run live broadcasts. It was six o'clock in the morning. The crowds would be arriving soon. We had thought this one out; it was definitely going to be a notch up from Kansas City. So far, it hadn't been too expensive to live the life of an eco-steward. That changed here. This escapade was costly. I had called Anne last night and knew that she was going to be on the lookout for me. She might already be here; the place was filling up quickly. My identity had been compromised in Kansas City; I was no longer a complete mystery. Middle-aged white bread, I couldn't give away any more clues.

"Be careful out there," I said to Lake, as we walked through the lobby and out to the street.

"Yeah, love you." Lake pecked me on the cheek before stepping off the curb in front of the hotel.

"Love you too," I called out, as I, too, left the hotel grounds and ventured out into the unknown. I was going to scout some vendors. Lake's job was to approach the group of homeless people she had spied from our seventh floor window.

Anne and Gus had arrived and were set up on a grassy hill in the middle of the festival. They had an outstanding view in every direction. The park area around the arch was huge; a steady stream visitors rolled in, hoping to get the best seats for the free concerts. The first band would begin at nine this morning, a local blues group called Confluence. The festival didn't end until Sunday morning when a big breakfast was served, compliments of the city.

"Hi guys!" Lake addressed seven fairly well-kept-but-obviously-homeless guys, ranging in age from twenty to seventy.

"Hi there sweetie, what can we do for ya?" one of the older guys replied, as he passed his smoke to one of his comrades and approached Lake.

"A proposition, gentlemen. How would you like to pass out some flyers, twenty dollars each?" Lake felt a slight tremble run through her.

"Religious crappola?" asked the older guy now within a few inches of her, invading her personal space.

"What does it matter, I'm in," said the youngest of the men standing up from his seat on the lip of a concrete planter.

"It's some information about our planet, no religion, no business advertisements, just the earth gentlemen," Lake responded stepping back.

"How many, how long we have to do it for, and when do we get paid?" asked the older guy, who was ripe. It was hard to keep a pleasant scent living on the street in a Missouri summer.

"One hour tops. However many you can pass out. We start at high noon and you're paid before you begin."

"You come to us?" another asked.

"I'll be here at eleven forty five with the flyers," Lake replied.

"How do you know we just won't take off with the money?" asked the older guy.

"I don't. But we all have to live with our decisions don't we? See you gentlemen soon and if you know anybody else, have them come too." Lake walked off feeling that had gone fairly well. She went off in search of me with anticipation, beginning to hatch a migration of butterflies in her stomach.

On the other end of the park, closer to the Arch, I passed the Muddy River Barbeque stall, a local favorite in St. Louis. Before going vegetarian, I had enjoyed my share of ribs. I now only occasionally had some salmon. Fish would soon go as the industry was decimating our oceans. I couldn't take part in that. Paul McCarthy had said he believed the greatest change we could make as a species would be to become vegetarian. He believed it was a pathway to peace. I often thought about this, and believed, too, that the ripple effect of people no longer eating animals would give the world a big face lift in ways I couldn't even fathom.

I stopped at the 'Got Vegan' food truck, just a few yards off from the Muddy River Barbeque stall. "What? You want me to sell all your T-shirts and keep the money? What the does the shirt say?" asked the slender Hispanic woman preparing vegan buffalo wings.

"It's nothing dirty or religious and I'm not trying advertise a business, but it might get some airtime for your business. I'll be back before noon, you can take a look then."

"Okay, sounds interesting." She smiled and began taking an order from the next person in line. There were some good, fake meat products out there, crazy thing was, all of them cost more than meat. A lot more. Of course, they weren't subsidized by the government.

I strolled off to the next vendor, Sandy's Caramel Corn.

"Hey good looking, what are you doing after the fair?" said a sultry voice from behind me.

I turned, and a tall thin beauty with long blond hair wearing a St Louis Cardinals baseball cap and huge shades was smiling at me.

I didn't register her at first. Lake was in disguise, and all I could think looking at her was that she needed to wear this get-up again when we got home. She looked good. "Jeez, you scared me, how did it go?"

"Went fine. I think most of them will show up. How's it going over here?" Lake asked, smiling at me. I was wearing a ponytail wig under a John Deere cap and sporting a pair of Ray-bans. I could tell she liked the ponytail.

"Pretty good, some yes's, some no's. This is wild isn't it?"

"Oh yeah, this is wild." Lake was still smiling.

"You sure you're all right?" I said, holding Lake's hand.

"I'm doing good, baby. Thanks for asking."

"We can't stop now," I said, immediately, wishing I'd kept my mouth shut.

"Jack, stop worrying about me. I don't want to hear another word, I will let you…"

"Oh no!" I exclaimed, grabbing Lake's shoulders, turning her a hundred and eighty degrees.

"What are you doing!?"

"Anne's right over there! Walk with me, I'll show you." I led the way until we were concealed in the crowd.

"Slowly turn and look about two o'clock on the grassy mound over there. See them?" I whispered, although not necessary.

"Uh-huh" Lake whispered back.

"Yep," I responded, watching Anne and Gus scan the crowd. Gus even had a pair of binoculars around his neck.

"It's on, baby!" Lake squeezed my arm.

"It sure is!" I agreed.

Chapter Nineteen

THE FAIR WAS NOW BUMPER-TO-BUMPER, butt-to-butt. It was about eighty-five degrees with a slight breeze from the west, not bad for July fourth in the Midwest. Minty Crow was to appear on stage a little after noon. She was a native Missourian, born and raised in St Louis. She had attended the University of Missouri at the same time as me. I'd met her once at a Fraternity party in the early eighties, the only one I ever attended. I was the first in my family to not belong to the Greek family. There was no way she would remember me, but I didn't count on that. I made my way to the security rails in front of the stage. Knowing it was a long shot, I got the attention of a muscle-bound security guard.

"Hi, my name is Jonathan Muir, an old friend of Minty's from school. I tried to call her, but she's not picking up. Could you give her this letter? It would mean a lot." I handed him a white envelope along with a hundred dollar bill and crossed my fingers. The guard took the envelope and the hundred-dollar bill and gave me the once over. On the outside of the envelope in large green letters was MR. GREEN JEANS. This is what I hoped would elicit a response, if the letter was given to her. Lake and I knew she was a greenie. The guard disappeared up the stairs and onto the stage's right wing with envelope still in his hand.

"Okay, time to get moving," I said to myself and headed towards the Sheraton entrance on the far side of the Arch. When I entered our room, Lake was already dressed and ready to go. She wore a green jumpsuit and was loading seven boxes of flyers onto a dolly. I changed quickly and loaded up the T-shirts on another dolly. Wearing matching hats that said Muir Delivery, matching green coveralls and still sporting our wigs, we entered an empty elevator and pressed Lobby. The elevator was wall-to-wall mirrors, and looking at ourselves, we did our best Guido impressions. "What are you lookin' at?" Lake silently asked the universe for safe passage as the doors opened to the lobby, which was packed with people all here for the fair. We rolled our dollies across the marble floor, and once outside, went our separate ways. It was all business now.

The men and now women were waiting for Lake, the original number had almost doubled. Lake sliced open the boxes with an X-acto knife and began handing out stacks of bright green, legal-sized flyers with 'The Declaration of Dependence' printed in bold ink.

"Okay folks, pass them out till they're gone. As promised, a twenty for each of you up front." Lake passed out the twenties, 240 dollars in total.

"Last thing, if you can say, "Go Green," when you hand them out, we'd really appreciate it. Thanks, you're doing something that's important for us all. The power of words will forever continue to change our world."

"This is pretty good wordage here, you wrote this?" asked one of the new guys adjusting his backpack and reading the top flyer on his stack.

"No, the man I love wrote that. Cheers guys, I need to scram, mum's the word where you got these, okay?" Lake looked over the motley crew and turned to leave.

"This is Mr. Green Jeans, isn't it?" said the same guy reading the flyer.

Lake looked back and gave an affirming smile and then disappeared into the crowd, leaving the dolly behind. She felt a new layer of herself had just appeared or re-appeared. Whatever the case was, she liked the feeling she was having right now. It was like she was really doing something that made sense and was worthwhile. She took a moment to look over the crowd. People of all ages and ethnicities were eating, drinking, roaming, laughing and generally having a good time. Across the park she could see Minty Crow's roadies setting up the stage. She wondered if my letter would make it to Minty before the concert. Even if it did, it was doubtful she would acknowledge it.

I was opening the last box of T-shirts. Grabbing one and handing it the woman at the 'Got Vegan' food truck. I waited for her reply.

"Ya gotta be kidding me?" she said looking the T-shirt.

"Nope."

"I'll sell these and give the money to a local animal shelter."

"That would be great," I said and walked off leaving her with my last box of shirts and abandoning the dolly a few yards off. I was done. I hoped Lake hadn't run into any problems. I looked over at the grassy hill and saw no sign of Gus or Anne. Walking back to the hotel, I saw one of the homeless guys handing out the flyers. Printed on bright green cardstock, they'd cost us a small fortune. For a teacher, that is.

"Excuse me." Someone tapped me on the shoulder. I turned and was handed a flyer.

"Go green, Sir, go green." A man about my age wearing a full-head paisley bandana smiled, as he turned to say the same thing to another person. It was working.

In the hotel, the concierge gave me an inquisitive stare and began to walk toward me. Fortunately, he was intercepted by an elderly woman asking him for directions to the lobby restrooms. I quickly continued to the elevator, and once in, pushed seven. I let out an audible exhale as the doors closed. I was safe. Or so I told myself. Favors asked, services paid for, lots of money spent, for two school teachers. How would it play out? We'd have to wait and see.

Chapter Twenty

As I entered the room, I heard the shower going. I stripped off the green coveralls, left on the ponytail wig and joined my baby.

"Who are you?" Lake said, pretending to be surprised.

"Maintenance, ma'am'."

"What do you maintain?"

"Our guests."

"Oh. I don't know if we paid for this service."

"Complements of the Sheraton, ma'am'."

"Don't call me ma'am' call me….."

We shouted, hollered and danced in the shower and made love in between. Ten minutes later, toweled off and in comfy clothes, it was time to watch the show.

I opened the French doors, and we walked out onto our small balcony that overlooked the festival. The Arch glistened in the sun, a myriad of smells wafted up into our nostrils, and the hum of a few hundred thousand people or more milling about gave us both pause.

'Wow," was all I could think of saying.

"Yeah, wow," Lake said, too.

"I'm going to get some ice; will you get the binoculars out of the suitcase?"

"I will, handsome."

"Thank you, beautiful."

"Hurry now, I hate not to have a glass of champagne in my hand when the show begins," Lake said, looking out on the festival as I hurried out the door with the ice bucket. I shook my head in disbelief as I walked down the hallway to the ice machine. Life was good today, very good. And with some universe luck, it was about to get better. Minutes later, we were sipping on some mid-range champagne, seven stories above the festival and watching the stage.

"Are you ready St. Louis for Minty Crow – our hometown girl!?" The concert organizer yelled into the mike. You could have heard his voice five blocks away. The crowd responded with the appropriate measure of volume and then some more.

Perched in our bird nest we held hands and silently prayed. Minty Crow made her way front and center.

"Hello Missoura!!!!!! How ya doing today?!!!" Minty shouted from the stage to the massive crowd in front of her. The audience erupted into a sirocco of screams, clapping, cheers and general love for the music they all had listened to for the last twenty-five years. Even for Minty Crow, this never got old.

"As you know this is my town, St Louey!" Another eruption. "Today, something very special might happen and if it does I have something to read to you."

Lake and I immediately turned to each other completely awestruck.

"In the meantime, let's rock St Louis!" The band started and Minty began with 'Maybe Angels'.

"I think she got the Declaration," I said, turning and smiling at Lake.

"I think you're right. What time is it?" Lake asked.

"Twelve twenty-three."

"Okay, cross your fingers. This is wild baby, wwwwiiiild!"

"It's cosmic. Look down there. They're still passing out flyers!" I peered over the railing and saw a few dedicated guys still at it.

"I see Anne. She's talking to one of my guys," Lake said, looking through the binoculars.

"Let me see." Lake handed me the binoculars.

Sure enough, Gus was taping and Anne was talking to the man in his sixties wearing an old corduroy jacket and holding a handful of green flyers.

"No worries," I said, putting down the binoculars.

"No worries, I'm happy to agree. I think we covered our tracks pretty well. Besides, we haven't done anybody or anything any harm, that's our saving grace," Lake stated, and began to sing along with Minty.

Thirty minutes passed, and we wondered if our finale was going to happen. Minty Crow had taken an extended break between songs. Her drummer still played. The audience was impatient and had started to chant, 'Minty, Minty' Once again, we heard, before we saw. This time there were two loud birds in the sky, flying a few hundred feet above the Mississippi River, coming toward the arch. Minty came downstage and looked up. The huge mass of fairgoers began to look to the sky. The double-plane fly-by was just seconds out, directly over the confluence of the Missouri and Mississippi, the reason St. Louis was built where it was. America's two greatest and unfortunately most polluted arteries met just north of the arch.

The first bi-plane passed behind the Arch streaming a banner which said 'HI YA'LL! YOU READY TO GET BUSY?' This plane made two more passes, and then disappeared. A second plane appeared. The crowd was pointing. Minty, and now her entire band stood downstage and all were looking up.

This plane did dives, rolls, twists, turns and acrobatics like a Cirque du Soleil show in the sky. Through the whole routine, it trailed a green stream of smoke. Its first smoke message done, it flew off. What remained, hung in the sky:

THE GREEN DECLARATION OF DEPENDENCE

The second plane reappeared. It began its script.

IT IS THAT TIME MY PEOPLE

Finishing that line the plane entered another patch of clear sky and wrote out,

MR

...then dove off as the second plane took its place and streamed

GREEN JEANS

And was off.

As both planes disappeared into the horizon, the crowd hushed. Then, a murmur began to bubble, followed by a full-out cacophony of yells, hoots and cheers exploding. Minty addressed the audience.

"Okay folks, folks!" She was laughing and smiling. "Let me share some words with you all." The audience silenced, and she continued. "I received an envelope from Mr. Green Jeans just before coming on stage. It sounded familiar for some reason and then someone told me this act had made national news just a week ago. I opened the envelope and inside was this; she held up the green flyer. The Green Declaration of Dependence. I read it. Ya'll know I'm a greenie, so this caught my attention. So without further ado, "The Green Declaration of Dependence."

> We the species; with the ability to change our environment like no other species, must be fully aware and committed to the balance necessary to continue the life of our species and every species, for this is the energy that is us and all else. It will be the duty of each human to exercise a low-carbon footprint on the planet. We will act, as steward to all of earth's flora and fauna, knowing that they are us, and we are them. We will commit to the freedom, liberty and happiness of all creatures great and small, and live according to the earth's immutable laws that connect us all as one. To be unconnected to the life around us and within us, is to admit the ignorance of our inherent gift as caretakers of the planet, from which we derive our existence and spirit. This ignorance will result in the extinction of our species. Only through our knowing of the Dependence on Mother Earth, will we obtain peace within and throughout and continue to exist. Tread softly, take

no more than what is necessary, and give back what you have been shared. With this, we declare to stand forthright as the lighthouse keepers of our true mother, the Earth.

Mr. Green Jeans

"There ya go folks, it doesn't get much clearer than that. I say we celebrate our union, my fellow Missourians. Long life to Mr. Green Jeans and Planet Earth! Whoever you are, Mr. Green Jeans. That's my new declaration. Go Green or go home! 1..2..3..!" The band played their instruments and Minty began to rock out again.

"What the...?" I sat with a stunned expression on my face.

"I don't know, I don't know...I just don't know what that was, baby... Baby, those were some beautiful words. Cheers, my dear Lucky Charms man." We both rose and embraced. We were stunned, simply stunned.

"Whoa, look baby, there's somebody, there's somebody else... they're wearing our T-shirts! Wooo-hooo!" It was like spotting cardinals after a heavy snow. There was a bright green dot here and there and another one over there, and another.... The front side of the T-Shirt said MR. GREEN JEANS and on the back was the entire Green Declaration of Dependence.

Chapter Twenty-One

AFTER THE SPECTACLE, we left the hotel and searched out a vegetarian restaurant to have an excellent early dinner. All through our meal, we kept breaking out in laughs. Screw tomorrow, we rocked it out in St. Louis, period. We feel asleep early that night.

'HOMEGROWN GREEN' was Sunday's St. Louis Post Dispatch front-page headline. The thick Sunday edition sat in the passenger seat. I was sipping on Quickie Mart bitter coffee in my reusable coffee mug. This coffee came from a field sprayed with toxins, then picked with cheap labor, given another dose of poisons and fumigated on its way to America. It was hard to find a clean cup of coffee. After filling up the Subaru, I reluctantly filled my cup, coffee was part of life and we hadn't packed the grinder and French press. Once again, no subsidies for the small guys doing the right thing, growing organic beans. Go figure? This was a microcosm of why we were out here. Lake was sound asleep in back seat, which she never did in the car.

It was 6:00 a.m. and picking up the paper and keeping my eyes on the road at the same time, I looked at the cover picture. A wide shot showed a plane passing behind the Arch having just smoked the 'The Green Declaration of Dependence'. It filled the top two thirds with the bottom third of the picture showing the crowd looking up, dots of green T-shirts scattered throughout. It was an excellent shot. I looked to see who snapped it: Gus Hobart. He was good. That shot was like a ripe seed.

The story went on to describe yesterday's events and ended with the Green Declaration itself. It could not have been better press. The timing was perfect. Climate change, economic short-sightedness, corporate rule. Rome had to fall again. Change was on the horizon, there was no way around it. An evolutionary ecological revolution was what our species had to engage in sooner than later. There was no choice left; there really had never been a choice. Unfortunately, we weren't dealing with a rational species.

With Lake still asleep, I pulled off the highway onto a rural exit ramp and made the call we had been dreading. Up to this point, our identity was unknown, as far as we knew. With this call, that was going to change somewhat. Everything creates a ripple in the pond and Mr. Green Jeans had thrown more than a pebble into the pond this time.

"Okay. You promise me, it's only you and Gus?" I asked, standing outside and looking through the window at Lake, still asleep in the back seat.

"Yes. You have my word."

"Okay, okay. We'll see you soon." I hung up and knocked on the back window. Lake stirred, and I showed her the phone. Her eyes widened, and she opened the back door.

"Well?" Lake asked, walking onto the shoulder.

"Two-thirty at Cedar Creek," I responded.

"Sounds like a plan. You sure about this?" Lake asked.

"Are you sure?" I asked back.

"No, not sure at all. But baby, something seems so right about it. We'd be fools to stop now. We're officially crazy. But if our identities stay safe and the confidentiality of our relationship is honored, we're going to be fine. We're not hurting anyone," Lake said, doing some yoga stretches on the exit ramp. She was beautiful. Her long frame stretched with her feet on the medians gravel and her hands outstretched on the grass lining the median, she lifted a leg and let out a breath.

"In China, we'd already be in jail eating maggot-ridden biscuits off the floor and wiping diarrhea off our legs," I responded, finishing the horrible coffee.

"Gross," Lake said, not looking up and unsurprised at my graphic description.

"I'm just saying. The path is about to get bumpy, I think."

"Bring it on. I'm a certified Special Ed. Teacher in five states," Lake replied, lifting her other leg.

"I hear that. Okay, let's do it, Bonnie," I said, getting back in the car.

"We really did it, didn't we?" Lake said, pinching my shoulder as she got into the passenger seat.

"We did baby. I mean Minty Crow read our declaration to tens of thousands of people, and then the news picked it up. It was perfect. We definitely have some momentum now."

"Yes, we do."

Back on the highway, we'd look at each other, make faces and break into one laugh after another. She cranked the tunes, selecting a little Buffalo Springfield, 'For what it's Worth'. Perfect tune. For the next ninety miles we relished our St. Louis victory.

Two hours later, we pulled to a stop at the end of a dirt road. There was no one else there. We were just thirty miles south of Manchester. This was where I spent most of my weekends as a teenager. On most Fridays after school, I would load my backpack into the 66 Mustang my father had driven and then given to me, and head to the woods. Sometimes with a friend, but often by myself. There were forty square miles of national forest to explore. I knew all the hollows, the caves and every bend in the creek. We'd chosen Cedar Creek, because it had recently been earmarked for timber removal, not because it offered a quick getaway, it didn't. Roads gouged through this forest. The loss of habitat was completely unnecessary, but it was easier to just continue down the same old path, until the bottom line didn't show a profit anymore. The current arrogance and ignorance was like a man carrying a sack of potatoes with a hole in it.

"You okay?" Lake asked, as I turned off the car and looked at the old bridge, which now just had a few boards across it for foot traffic.

"Yeah. I just get so pissed off when I think what might happen to this place."

"Well, that's why we're doing what we're doing, baby."

Donning paper bags with holes cut out for our eyes and mouth and a pair of sunglasses, we opened the hatch, and Lake got out a canvas car cover. Just as we finished draping the car, Anne, as agreed, drove up in something other than a news vehicle. An early-nineties, white Toyota 4x4 pickup pulled to stop beside us, and Anne rolled down the window.

"Mr. Green Jeans?"

"That be us."

"Oh, us? Gus, let's park," Anne said, smiling.

From the driver's seat, Gus looked over at us and winked.

"Hi," Anne said, as she stepped out of the truck. Boy, she was a looker. I knew looks were an asset in the news business. All you had to do was click to any of the talking head shows. It seemed over half the announcers had walked off a fashion shoot. She wore running shoes and shorts. Normally that would do, but the ground was soft today. She could expect to trash them fairly soon.

"I'm Anne, and this is Gus. Thank you for meeting us."

"You're welcome. Shall we walk?" I said, putting on a daypack.

"Oh, well… sure. Gus, you up to it?"

"Sweetheart, I was born in the woods. Vermont," Gus stated.

"Beautiful country, and the greenest state in the union," I responded, shaking both their hands.

"This is Bonnie."

"Hi," Lake said, and we headed to the old bridge crossing Cedar Creek.

"No cameras," I said, and looked at Gus.

"Sorry, habit." Gus removed the camera from around his neck and put it the cab of his truck.

"Okay then, we're off. You guys ever been here before?" I asked.

"No. Didn't even know this place was here," Anne said, and she carefully placed one foot in front of another and tried not to look down at the creek, which was thirty feet down. The bridge was once able to accommodate cars. Now it was just a few 2x6 treated lengths of wood spanning the creek.

"How far are we planning on going?" Anne asked.

"Just twenty to thirty minutes. It's well worth the walk."

The trail snaked up and down past enormous ancient oaks, through clear-running streams with the heartening sound of frogs jumping in as we passed. A loud flapping of wings, and a group of wild turkeys took flight as we walked through a meadow of tall grass and wild raspberry bushes. Thirty minutes later the trail hit the edge of a horseshoe bluff known as Devil's Backbone. The trail ran along the edge of the U-shaped bluff, and looking across to the other side of the bluff line, you realized it would take the good part of a few hours to reach the far side. What lay in the middle surrounded by the creek's path below the bluff line was what I held in my heart from the first time I saw it, some thirty-five years ago. I'd seen this place in every season. There was a late 1800's two-story farmhouse sitting on a hill in the middle of the greenest grass field you could imagine. A dirt road wound its way down into this pristine valley ringed on three sides by the bluff and creek. An incredible turn-of-the-century, large, red barn sat off from the house. I'd never seen anyone living there. But it was always well kept. This was the postcard I wanted to walk into someday.

"Let's stop here. What do think Anne?" I asked, sweeping my hand across the view.

"That I'm glad we stopped. I'm really not much of a nature girl, and I think these new tennies are shot," Anne said, as she found a seat on a rock outcropping looking down over the valley.

"I could live here and never leave," Gus said, taking it all in.

"Apple anyone?" said Lake, unzipping the pack on my back.

It was time for our first interview.

Chapter Twenty-Two

"WHY ARE YOU DOING THIS?" A steady wind came up over the bluff where we sat. Anne held a small microphone to the crude mouth opening of my paper bag. Since putting on these bags before the walk, mine had developed a wet line of sweat across my forehead.

"Because I am this rock, that tree, those clouds. Because we want to do our part. These are dire times for our planet. There is no doubt in our minds, that if we as a species don't start to live in harmony with the planet, then we will perish and it won't be pretty. Many will suffer. Hell, many are suffering and dying now because of our insatiable appetite for more and more. What we do in one place on the planet, affects the entire planet. Nations are not islands; we are all in this together. I don't need to tell you how many species have gone extinct because of humans. I don't need to tell you how many more go each month. Climate change is real and if you don't believe we're responsible, then you can kiss my green bottom."

"Right on," Gus said, with a smile on his face.

Anne gave Gus a look that said, "Shut up." Then, she continued, "What are your future plans?"

"We'll let you know."

"Do you guys even know what you're doing next?" Anne asked.

"We know," Lake responded, sitting against a green-and-yellow-lichen-covered, limestone boulder. She didn't like Anne, I could tell from her tone.

"But you're not going to let us know now?" Anne asked again.

"Not now," I answered.

"Anne, if I may offer a suggestion," Gus said, hoping Anne realized she was on a big learning curve here.

"Sure," Anne said with sarcasm, turning off the recorder.

"You're creating characters for our viewers. The more the public can relate to these guys, the more momentum they will have, and the more stories you get to do. So, ask questions about what they eat, do for fun, favorite books, why Green Jeans etc…?"

"Thank you, Gus. I got it. Okay." Anne was obviously annoyed. She didn't like to be challenged. She also was in a hurry to get this interview over with. Not only weren't her designer tennis shoes white anymore, she was getting bitten by mosquitoes.

"I like organic frosted flakes, going on long walks with our dogs, and I just finished reading *Siddhartha* by Hermann Hesse for the third time," I said, winking through my eyehole at Gus.

"Okay…" Anne said.

"I like beans and wild rice and the vegan delights at Main Squeeze," Lake said, interrupting Anne, "holding hands with Clyde, and I'm currently reading *Lucky You*, by Carl Hiaasen."

"Great book, funny," Gus commented.

"That part with turtles…" Lake added.

"Yeah, I loved that…." Gus started, and then was interrupted by Anne.

"Why the name Green Jeans?" Anne asked.

"It just came to me. No relation to Captain Kangaroo. Although, I loved that show as a kid," I responded.

"Bonnie, what's it like being a married couple doing this?"

"Who said we're married?" Lake responded.

"Wedding rings on both your hands," Anne said, pointing to Lake's.

"Any comment?" Anne waited. Neither of us said a thing.

"Okay, so you're not planning to stop, even knowing that if you get caught, you're possibly going to jail."

Lake took the lead. "If we stop, then we were just a flash in the pan."

"So, stopping is not an option?" Anne asked.

"It's always an option," I responded.

The interview went on for another ten minutes. The whole purpose was to put a persona to Mr. Green Jeans, create an identity that would bring in more followers. It was marketing, plain and simple. Gus was right on track.

Back at the vehicles, we said our goodbyes. Lake hugged Gus as was her custom when there was a connection with someone. I said we'd be in touch and shook Anne's hand. Without any video, Anne knew she would have to get creative with some footage from previous exploits and do some sort of narrative over it. Gus would have some great ideas, but she was upset at him like a daughter gets with a parent after being corrected in public.

After watching them drive out of sight, we tore off our paper bags and gave each other a good hard look.

"Whoa!" Lake said.

"Yeah, buddy!"

"Shall we celebrate?" she asked.

"Want to take another hike?"

"You read my mind."

Arriving at home and unpacking the Subaru before going into the house, we heard Pearl and Barney crying inside as though they'd been locked up for months. Barb and Todd had agreed to feed them and let them out for potty breaks, but they knew when their real parents had arrived. They were beside themselves. As I opened the front door, Barney jumped up and about knocked me off the porch. Pearl squeezed by and made her way to Lake.

On the dining room table, was a stack of Minty Crow CDs and a DVD entitled 'A Trip to the St Louis Arch'. We hadn't told Barb or Todd where we were going, but as it turned out, all you had to do was watch the news or read a paper. The phone rang. Lake picked it up.

"Hello. Oh, hi Lillian. Yes, we had a wonderful time. Yeah, we saw it all. It was amazing. Yes, thank you…okay, I'll put him on." Lake handed the phone to me with a wink.

"Hi Mom. What? …No, we didn't do that. Yes, I'm sure… Yeah, we had fun. Tomorrow night?" I looked at Lake. She nodded. "Ok, sure we can be there. Five o'clock. Okay. Bye, Mom." I hung up the phone.

"Dinner?" Lake asked.

"Yeah, tomorrow. She asked me if we were the ones who did that stuff in St Louis."

"No way."

"She's always been concerned that I'd do something stupid someday."

"She cannot find out," Lake said, looking directly at me.

"No, she can't."

"Good luck with that," Lake smiled.

At the local news station, there was a buzz of activity. Everyone who worked there was beginning to realize this ongoing story with Mr. Green Jeans, was the biggest thing to hit the station in a long time. Anne was downloading the audio from the interview, and Gus was going through all the video they had collected over the last few months. Gus knew this story would have airtime, but unless the exploits continued, it would die. He was behind us. He even admired us.

"Gus, we've got two hours to get this in the can. Have you cut any footage yet?" Anne asked, as she listened to the interview on headphones.

"Not yet grasshopper, I want to look at all of it first."

"Don't call me grasshopper anymore," Anne said, still concentrating on the audio.

"Okay, would you prefer pupa or larva instead?" Gus countered.

"Whatever, fossil head."

"Not bad," Gus replied. He didn't need this job, and he wasn't about to take any crap from her. He did love this story though. It would be a great way to end his career.

Chapter Twenty-Three

MY MOTHER WAS A SWEETHEART. She had been living alone for the past thirty-seven years after my dad died. He had been a lawyer, the good type. Sometimes he'd take a case for a sack of potatoes, if he felt the person had been wronged. He never made much money, but had the respect of the community for being fair and honest. I always thought it was the system that had led to his early death.

My mom was eighty-seven years old, collected social security, and the house was paid for. She got around pretty well and had just renewed her driver's license for another five years. She was just a few inches over five feet; her weight was well suited to her frame; and she walked daily at Manchester's public fitness center.

"I want you to come in and find me on the floor dead. That way there will be no hassle. You cremate me; the plot next to your father is already paid for. You sell the house and all the stuff in it, and carry on," Lillian said, taking a bite of pizza. We always had frozen pizza when we ate at her house.

"Mom, stop that okay."

"I will not. Now, how's your summer going?" Lillian asked, looking at both of us.

"Good, just doing some gardening, Jack has been painting and…" Lake was interrupted.

"You two just don't lose those jobs. People are losing their jobs all over the place, and if I know you at all Jack, you just can't settle. Your father had dreams, and he was always looking over the fence too," Lillian stated.

"Maybe he should have jumped over," I suggested, as I always did.

"Maybe. But he was a troubled man."

"Aren't all men?" Lake added.

"So true, honey. Jack, this woman's a gem, you know that?" Lillian said with a stare in my direction, as she daintily wiped her mouth with a cloth napkin.

"Yes, mom, I know how lucky I am, believe me." I had heard this many times from my mother. My mother had never given my two ex-wives much praise. She might have known all along those marriages were destined to fail.

"I went through the depression as a girl, and it looks like things are headed that direction again. People's greed will always be our downfall." Lillian took another bite of pizza and reached for her glass of milk.

'Politicians," Lake stated.

"Don't trust those republicans, not one of 'em. They are devious and don't play fair. It's the party of fear, if you ask me." Lillian was a democrat forever. Her father had been a state legislator, but lost his second run when he voted against prohibition.

"Couldn't agree with you more Lillian, but the democrats are suspect too," Lake added.

"Many are. Pass the peppers will you sweetheart?"

We stayed another couple of hours, and my mother showed us her new project, a photo album that went back a hundred years. I was glad we had stopped by. I hoped my mother would never learn our secret; it might put her over the edge.

At the station, the broadcast was minutes from airing. Anne was getting powdered at the news desk. This station was unique. It was tied to the journalism school at the university, and thousands of students had used it as a stage, to see if they had what it took to be in the biz. Some big names had gotten their start here, and gone on to become well-known news anchors. This was Anne's dream, and she wasn't going to let anything stand in her way. She had the goods and was at ease in front of the camera, but did she have the passion?

"Hi folks, I'm Anne Brewster. Welcome to the evening news. Tonight we have a channel-eight exclusive interview with Mr. Green Jeans. For those of you not familiar, yesterday at St Louis's annual VP fair, Minty Crow acknowledge Green Jeans by reading their Green Declaration of Dependence, or as the followers call it, The Creed. You can read the Declaration on our web site. Now I'm going to share with you parts of our exclusive audio interview with them just hours ago.

Lake and I caught the ten o'clock newscast on our couch with Barney, Smokey Joe and Pearl lapped over us. It was a family moment. As we watched, we became deathly concerned as our real voices could be clearly heard. No modification had been made to distort them. One and a half minutes later, the piece concluded, and the weather teaser began.

"Crap!" Lake exclaimed, in a loud whisper as if someone already knew.

"That's not cool," I said, clearly upset. "Look, I really doubt too many people could identify our voices, you know."

"Todd and Barb..."

"My mother," I quickly added.

"Yeah, your mother is a definite possibility. Maybe Kim, my principal?"

"Maybe some of my students? How could Anne be so thoughtless?" I said.

"Honey, I don't know, maybe she was in a hurry. I mean we could have changed our voices when we did the interview"

"True, but I imagine it's just a click of a button to disguise a voice, I don't like her anymore." I walked to fridge to find a snack.

"Yeah, that's just wrong," Lake announced.

The phone started ringing. I looked at Lake. "Let's just see who it is. It's ten-thirty!" The machine picked up. We still used our landline and didn't pay for caller ID. Lake's cell was in her purse and off most of the time.

"Jack, can you please give me a call, son. I'd like to talk to you. If you..." Her voice sounded like the game was up. She also never used the word 'son' unless she had something unpleasant to say. I picked up the phone.

"Hi Mom, what's up? It's late."

"You two never answer the phone."

"I know we're bad. So...." I was interrupted.

"Please tell me I'm wrong Jack, but I just watched the news, and I swear I heard your voice, and then it was confirmed when I heard Lake's. Now, tell me that wasn't you." Lillian waited. There was a pause on the line.

"What are you talking about Mom?" I had waited too long to reply.

"Honey, I'm eighty-seven years old, and my ticker is only going to tick so much longer. Just tell me it wasn't you." Another pause.

"It wasn't us Mom. We're watching the news, too. I guess you're referring to Mr. Green Jeans? You I know like that stuff, but Mom it wasn't us, okay?" I replied.

"Okay, honey. I just wanted to check. Now, if you two aren't doing anything Saturday, come by, and we'll order a pizza this time. Bye son." She hung up the phone. She knew. She knew my passion about the environment was deep. For years now, she had warned me I was turning into a troubled man, just like my father.

She decided a small glass of scotch was appropriate, and that she wasn't going to bring it up again. Pouring a few ounces of scotch over three ice cubes in a thick tumbler she opened up the photo album on the kitchen table. A loose picture of Jim, her late husband, my dad, was the first thing she saw. He was in his underwear kneeling by the tub, washing their first dog; a cocker spaniel named Mo. Jim had a big smile on his face as he looked up at the camera. It was a message, Lillian was sure of it. She took a sip of the scotch and silently thanked Jim for still being here.

Chapter Twenty-Four

TWO WEEKS PASSED. No funny stuff attempted. We stayed busy in the garden. We were both worried about continuing the Green Jeans journey. I had made one call to Anne to let her know how upset we were about hearing our own voices. She apologized and, of course, asked when we were planning our next outing. I said I'd let her know. Things had come to a point where we could stop and be glad we had at least done something. School wasn't that far off now. We both realized if we were to continue, it would have to get bigger, more demonstrative. We'd have to kick some butt and move it up another level. In today's world, nothing had much of a shelf life. Here one day, and gone the next. Mr. Green Jeans was on his way out if some more appearances were not scheduled. Then, it happened.

It was an early morning. Lake was out weeding a flowerbed, and I was running some string supports for beans in the garden. An old four-wheel-drive pickup drove up to the house. It looked familiar. It parked next to my old pickup and a man wearing a tattered cowboy hat, a pair of jeans, and a T-shirt that said 'Life is All right' got out and looked to the porch. Seeing no one, he turned to look around the yard. It was Gus. Oh no.

"Hey amigo," Gus said walking up to me in the garden.

"Can I help you?" I was on my feet pretending that I didn't know who he was.

"Just a friend of the earth, brother."

"What?"

"I ain't the enemy. In fact, I can help."

"How did you find us?" I said realizing there was no point in my ruse anymore.

"Wasn't too hard. Summers off, educated, it was either the university or the public schools. Took me a bucket of hours, but a married couple, while not rare at the public schools, narrowed my search. No kids I figured, and here I am." Gus held out his hand.

"Anne knows, too?" I asked, setting down the roll of twine on a weathered wood table in our garden.

"Are you kidding? That kid may have the looks and a good dose of short-term determination, but upstairs she mise well be fifteen. She has the stuff, but I don't know about the heart," Gus said looking over the vegetable garden. Lake was crouched down, weeding a flowerbed by our dilapidated shed a good distance off, and still hadn't noticed we had company.

"Lake!...Lake! Look who's here!" I shouted. She looked up with a handful of weeds in her hand. The recognition on her face couldn't have been clearer if she were two feet away. Dropping the weeds she hurried over, worried if this was the end to our life as we knew it.

Inside the house, Lake made a pot of coffee, and the three of us sat down to the rich patina of the harvest table in the dining room. The animals were all vying for Gus's attention, and he tried his best to give out equal amounts to everyone. Smokey Joe won out, as he jumped into Gus's lap.

"So, I believe in you guys. I know it must be keeping you awake at nights wondering what the hell you have gotten yourselves into. I've had the pleasure to meet a number of Earth First members and some freewheeling cowboys, too. The cowboys are the ones that don't answer to anyone. They monkey wrench a few bulldozers, an earthmover, bunch of trucks way out on some mining site, and then take back into canyons living primitive for a month or so, then come back out and do it again. Wild people, you hear me? Monkey wrenching or bust. That was all in the sixties and early seventies, pre- and post-Vietnam. A new generation is out there now, spiking the trees, monkey wrenching the equipment, letting the animals go free, but they missed the boat in my opinion," Gus said, petting Smokey Joe whose purr was audible.

"What do you mean, missed the boat?" Lake asked.

"When you destroy something, you have enemies. Sure, there will be some that applaud you, but very few who will join you. The way I see it, what you guys have been doing is civil disobedience for the planet. Non-violent measures to get your point across. Thoreau wrote about it, Gandhi and Martin Luther played it out. It worked. Two of them got shot, but it worked." Gus finished and looked at us.

"Gus, are you just here to encourage us?" I joked.

Gus laughed and sipped his coffee. "You won't get shot, I don't think. No, look, I am here to encourage you. Can't lie. Something has to be done. If we don't change direction, we are likely to end up exactly where we are headed. Unknown Chinese philosopher said that, and you two painted it on a banner. I knew I liked you then. But I'm also here to help you get networked if you want to continue. I know news folks from LA to New York and all parts between."

"You mean, do this without Anne?" Lake asked.

"That would be my advice. She only sees the value from her end, and I doubt that will change until she grows up and sees that she is part of the world. Doubtful though. Without that understanding, nothing great happens. You two have a lot of momentum right now. People are calling the station day and night asking for more news on Mr. Green Jeans. I even saw some college kid wearing a T-Shirt downtown with Mr. Green Jeans printed on the front. It wasn't one of yours from St. Louis either, he had made it himself. That won't last that long, and it's a bitch to start from scratch." Gus sipped his coffee again and looked at us.

"Wow. Well, we haven't decided what we're going to do…." I started.

Lake finished my thought. "We're really scared right now, if you want to know the truth."

"I don't blame you. Look, mums the word from me. Nobody's gonna discover who you are by asking me," Gus reassured.

"Gus, what suggestions would you have if we were to continue down this road?" I asked a bit reluctantly.

"How much time do we have?"

"We have all day," Lake said, filling up his cup.

The sun was setting when Gus left. We walked him to his car, and we all hugged. As he was pulling away, he rolled down his window. "You know, you guys have it good out here. I think the question you have to ask yourselves is, is it worth losing it all for what you might get in return? Passion's a tough road. I suppose we all get there in some lifetime. You guys might have arrived." Gus laughed. "Anyway, it was great getting to know you guys. You're true heroes in my book. You got my number," Gus said, rolled up his window, and made his way down our driveway to the gravel road.

I reached for Lake's hand. We stood there and watched Gus make the rise then disappear from sight. We waited silently for another few moments, watching the sunset.

"We're going to need more room than the Subaru. Shall we go find a new ride tomorrow?" I asked, still looking at the setting sun.

"As long as it's family friendly."

"Absolutely," I answered.

We squeezed each other's hand. Tight.

Chapter Twenty-Five

IT'S INTERESTING HOW when people are in-between commitments, everything else is also in between. They don't eat right, don't sleep right and don't love right. Last night, there was a peacefulness that overtook us. A decision had been made. It was settled. We were going for it. We were jumping the fence once again. This was different though. This was the crazy fence, the one that disappeared behind you.

"We're not getting any younger," I said, as I sipped the coffee from my stainless steel travel mug. We were driving down business loop I-70 in my pickup. All the car dealerships in Manchester were here. Lake and I were planning on doing some wheelin' and dealin' today. We wouldn't get out of the truck until we had picked the lots where we saw something of interest. Car salesmen displayed a sense of desperation we didn't want to experience until we saw something of interest. After a few hours of driving lots, we were ready to get out and take a look at a few vehicles that had caught our eye. First stop was Steven's New and Used.

"How long have you had this?" I asked, looking at a bright yellow, late-eighties, VW Vanagon, complete with the rack on top and one on the back hatch. It even had two hooks on the front grill to hang canvas water bags. This had the potential to be a desert vehicle, exactly what we wanted. Enough room for the family, and a small propane tank with two burners for cooking. One minus, as with all VW Vans, there was no undercarriage clearance. This would be a problem where we were going.

"Just got her in. Easy engine to work on, too. A bargain at this price," said Steven, a thin well-dressed older black man opening the hood. "Yep, she's got an easy-bake-oven engine, and that's a good thing these days. No computers." I didn't know engines. Lake didn't know engines. Didn't matter, because we weren't going to take any shop classes at this point. The price was in the budget.

"What would it cost to raise the chassis on this thing?" Lake asked. I gave her a how-the-hell-did-she-know-that-word look.

"More clearance? I can put you in contact with someone who could do that for you. I really don't know how much it would be. Ya'll taking it camping off-road, or what?" Steven asked, nodding and putting his hands in his well-pressed khakis.

"Maybe. Hey, thanks, we're going to look around," I said, hoping we could just quietly walk off the lot.

"Come on in and let me get your names. If you come back, we can probably work something out. I'll try to find out what the cost would be to raise the chassis. You two got a minute?" Steven said with a practiced coolness.

"Tell you what, you work on the numbers and the chassis cost, and we'll be back," I stated and took Lake's arm and headed us off to my truck. The truck was going to be our trade-in. The Kelly blue book trade-in value was about four hundred and twenty dollars. Every little bit helped, although I was going to be sad to say goodbye to my partner in crime for the last seventeen years.

"Okay. Hope to see you guys soon," Steven said, and waved.

Out of ear range. "He was pretty cool," I stated.

"We're buying a car, not a salesman, honey," Lake countered.

"Damn, first the chassis, and now some direct business logic. What has gotten into you?"

"I know, it's freaky. I'm just like streaming Wall Street and Auto World right now," Lake replied getting in the truck.

"Streaming? Did you just say 'streaming'?" I started the 95 Nissan, which turned over like a trooper, as it always did. Four hundred and twenty bucks, what a joke. It had another fifty thousand miles on it, if you didn't mind no air conditioning, no stereo, body in fairly good shape, and a lot of white spray paint covering up the rust that you couldn't see from a distance, no visors, no cigarette lighter, glove box held closed with a hook and wire, and the cab roof lining hung down and brushed against your head. But it passed inspection and ran like a champ. Somebody would appreciate it, I sure did.

We made three more stops to look at an F-150 with a camper shell, then a minivan with low mileage, and lastly a Volvo station wagon.

The decision was easy. "Sign here and it's yours," Steven said, probably anxious to call his wife and tell her the good news. It was hard for the small guy to compete anymore.

"Wow," I said, exhaling and passing the pen to Lake. She signed her name and smacked the pen down on the desk.

"Done! Congratulations folks! Here's the name of a good auto body shop. He said he'd have to take a look at it before he could give you an exact estimate. Sorry, I couldn't give you a solid number on the conversion." He handed us the keys.

"No problem. We love it," Lake said, taking the keys. I took a few moments to say goodbye to my truck. You get sentimental after seventeen years. I took a picture of her before I got into the VW.

"I love this thing!" Lake said pulling out of the lot.

"I do, too. I can't believe we just did this."

Then, we were on our way to grocery store. With bags of groceries filling the floorboard, I got up and moved to the back and sat at the yellow, Formica, fold-out table for the drive home. Opening a bag of sea-salt potato chips, I looked out the window, wondering what all the people we passed were thinking, knowing it was so very different from what Lake and I had bouncing around in our heads right now.

Back on the highway, we took the drive in silence. We were going back and forth between imagining the long stretches of road in the Southwest with great tunes blaring to the remorse of leaving our home in the country. As we passed the new 'BOX-MART' sign, now with lights and steel poles, I wondered how far down the rabbit hole we were going to travel. The biggest decisions most people make in life are a new job, a new home or a new partner. We'd both made all those decisions many times in our lives. This one was more than just a piece of cake. It felt like the whole cake.

"Baby, you think Brien might want to live in the house for a year? He just retired, he's single, doesn't know what he wants to do now."

"Other than write a sci-fi novel. But he's in Arizona, why would he want to come to Missouri?"

"We know he loves our place. He's visited us like four times since we've been here."

"I'll give him a call, but don't hold your breath."

"Okay." Lake turned into our driveway. I closed up the bag of chips. She turned to look at me.

"Let's take the babies for a ride and walk."

"Break in the VW, a little later, maybe?" I asked.

"You ain't seen nothin' yet."

Chapter Twenty-Six

IT WAS EIGHT O'CLOCK in the morning, and someone was knocking on the door. Lake was still asleep. She relished summer break and was now on summer schedule, not getting out of bed until nine o'clock. It helped that we weren't doing any more of our antics for a while. I had been up for hours. It was no problem getting up early when there was no school. I loved the mornings; it was when I was most productive.

"Oh my God," I said as I peered out the window. Next to Vanagon was my mother's car. She never stopped by without warning, and she would never come this early, either. I opened the door.

"Jack, I'm sorry for coming so early and without calling first, but we need to talk," Lillian stated, as she walked into the living room and sat down on one of ours chairs that had been all but destroyed by Smokey Joe's scratching.

"You want a cup of coffee, Mom?" I asked, already feeling what was to come.

"Is Lake still asleep?"

"Yes," I replied.

"Just as well. Sit down Jack," Mom was all business. At eighty-seven she had the right to say and do as she pleased. She had certainly earned it. I obediently sat down on the sofa across from her.

"I'm not sure how to say this. I know it's you, dear. I know that you are Mr. Green Jeans."

"Mom…." I started.

"No, don't interrupt me, son. I knew it was you when I heard your voice on the TV. I know you feel strongly about this. You've always felt strongly about the environment. I don't know if Lake has the same passion you do, or if she is doing this because you are. I want you to realize that you could lose everything if you continue. There are other ways to make a difference without risking so much. I am too old to visit you in prison. Now with that said, you will do as you please. You always have. What are your plans, sweetheart? And why, why would you do this?" My mother sat back and looked deeply into my eyes.

"Mom...I'm not sure what to say."

"You have a home in the country, a beautiful, delightful wife, a good job. I know you're both tired of teaching, but you are doing well. Tell me what you're planning on doing. I want to understand," she restated.

"We're going for it, Lillian." Lake stood in her bathrobe at the base of the stairs looking into the living room.

"Oh dear," she sighed, and looked up to the ceiling. I was dying inside. My mother was an incredible woman; a person couldn't hope to have a better mother. She didn't deserve to have to spend the rest her days worrying about me and her daughter-in-law being arrested and put in jail. This wasn't the kind of family she had.

"It's going to be all right, Lillian," Lake put her hand on my mother's arm. Mom rose, and the two gave each other a big hug. Lake always greeted my mother in this way, and I knew she appreciated it.

"Young lady, I do not want you doing this because of him, do you understand? He's got a screw loose," My mother had tears in her eyes. Lake had started to cry, too, and I sat there imaging how I could make this all better.

"Spend the day with us, and we'll talk. It's not as dangerous or criminal as you might think. Okay?" Lake asked.

"It's crazy, that's what it is. It's a nut without anything inside," my mother said, shaking her head and looking at both of us.

"Yeah, Mom, it is crazy. But we have to do this. We're going to be fine."

"That's the sixty-four-thousand-dollar question, isn't it?"

I was tearing up now, too. This was definitely one of those suck-ass moments in life, when a son has to tell his mother a deep dark secret. Problem with this secret was, there weren't any books titled *How to Deal with a Child Who's Told You He's a Radical Activist*. She was left with no books to read or support groups to join. She couldn't even talk to anyone about it.

The three of us sat around for most of the morning, Lake and I explaining our plans and my mother shaking her head and hoping she could get us to change our minds.

"It all comes down to living a life of quiet desperation, Mom. The influence the U.S. has on the world is immense, and the message we send out with our large corporations is, 'you too can live like us'. The problem is that living like us is killing the environment, and we need to change, show the world that living responsibly with the natural world is the only way our species can exist for centuries to come. We have to change our message. We have to change our ways. No, 'love it or leave it'. 'Love it and change it'. So, as ridiculous as it might sound, Mom, Lake and I are going to paste that message around the country in as many places as we can. Ten years ago, we couldn't have hoped to have the impact we can today. Today with the Internet and social media and a slowly burgeoning movement to be green, we just might have an effect."

"We just can't sit still, and we're grateful, Lillian, for our station in life to have the means to do this," Lake added. My Mom sat there without saying a word. She knew we were sincere, but she came from another era, and to grasp this was beyond her current repertoire.

As noon arrived, my mother had settled into a semi-peaceful resignation. She knew enough after over eight decades of living, that life was full of surprises, good and bad. This one just didn't seem to have an upside.

"I'm going to have a hard time making lemonade out of this, but I will try. If you two get caught, I am going to be very angry. I wish you could have waited until I was dead. That's not too far away, you know. Probably going to be much sooner now."

"Mom, can we take you to lunch?"

"No, I'll take you. You're spending all your money on paint and canvas, and whatever that thing is in your driveway. I sure hope you enjoy beans, because that's what you'll be living off of in a few months."

"Yeah, how about we drive, and you can check out the new wheels," I said.

"Your getaway car? That couldn't outrun a bicycle," my mother stated.

"We don't plan on being in any chase scenes," Lake said, grabbing her purse.

I helped her get up from the worn out chair. "I didn't plan on my kids being terrorists either."

"We're not terrorists, Mom. We don't hurt anyone, it's just the opposite, we're trying to get people to stop hurting the planet."

"You're hurting me, Jack. I'm sorry, I know this is not easy for you two. You probably wish you never had to tell me. Mr. Green Jeans? Whose idea was that?"

"Jack's," Lake replied.

"Honey, are you sure you wouldn't like a nice man that came home after work and fixed something in the house and doted on you? Had a good 401k, you knew you would retire in comfort, and you could do crafts and volunteer somewhere?"

"No Lillian, Jack is my hero. I love him to death, and you did a fabulous job raising him."

"I should have never let him play in the woods. I should have kept him in his room," my mother stated with a slight smile forming.

"Let's go, Mom. I love you." I was at the door.

"Let's go have your last supper. Don't drive too fast, Jack. But I suppose that won't be a problem since you only have a lawnmower engine in your getaway car."

"It's not a getaway car, Mom," I said, closing the front door. Lake helped her down the front porch steps.

"No, it's a look-at-me-I'm-driving-a-bright-yellow-bumblebee. You need to paint it a less conspicuous color," my mother said, as I opened the passenger door.

"Okay, we'll discuss that at lunch," I replied.

"What about the animals?" She said, climbing into the front seat with Lake's help.

"They're going with us," Lake replied, helping to get her seatbelt on.

"Oh my God! No, they are not," she said looking directly at Lake and then turning to me as I got in the driver's seat.

"Main Squeeze, Mom?" I said, ignoring my mother's ultimatum.

"You can go to the hippie restaurant on your own. I'm taking you to the bistro, and they serve fish and salads so you can have something to eat. Now, those animals are not going on your crusade to save to the planet, and that's final!"

I put the Vanagon in gear and slowly started down the gravel road.

Chapter Twenty-Seven

THAT EVENING, Lake and I were emotionally exhausted. I had just gotten off the phone with my mother, and she seemed to have calmed down a bit. It would be a roller coaster with highs and lows, and we promised to keep her in the loop. We wouldn't tell her everything, just enough to let her know we were all right.

We took the next two weeks to get things in order. We'd both been able take a year's leave of absence. Our explanation was to start a home-based business and travel. We were cashing out part of our retirement, which would give us enough to live on for a year or more, depending on how tight we kept the budget. We would get penalized for the early removal, but that was the only money we had. After a few calls with Brien, he said he'd love the opportunity to live in our house and split the mortgage for a year. He'd be here in ten days. He was planning on writing a book, and the old farmhouse was the perfect place to do that. Moms' request about the animals was taken to heart, and Brien had agreed to be their caretaker. He loved animals as much as we did and was bringing along his small mutt, Chance, to join the family. It was working out famously.

In bed that night, we fell asleep holding hands. It was a restless night. There would many more of these nights to come. There was really no end in this game plan. All we knew was that we would take off and display our banners in as many prominent places as we could get too. We'd called Gus, and he agreed to coordinate news stations to cover our ongoing messages. This was the plan, plain and simple. Anne Brewer was out of the loop from now on. We wondered if she'd figure out why. No worries, we only hoped Gus wouldn't be discovered as our accomplice.

The next day I drove to Phillips Auto Body, an old and trusted shop in Manchester. The estimate was thirty two hundred to raise the chassis six inches and do a full paint job, dark green. If we wanted to add four-wheel drive, it would be another two thousand. I bargained it down to forty nine hundred for everything and gave Lake a call to pick me up.

"You ready?" I said, as I got into Lake's Subaru.

"I guess so," Lake responded, pulling out of the Phillips Auto Body parking lot, leaving the VW for the makeover.

"I'm looking forward to it."

"I know you are," Lake replied with a knowing nod.

Lake waited in the car, as I walked into Boone High School. It was quiet. Summer school ended last week and just a few administrators and secretaries were left doing last minute preparations for the fall. I opened the office doors, and Jenny the head secretary saw me first.

"090, what are you doing here?" Jenny, a short, attractive, middle-aged woman said from behind her large desk stacked with files. She always addressed me by my room number, because I had told her I was really a special agent in charge of covert operations for a very secretive organization in Sweden.

"Isn't it cocktail hour somewhere?"

"It is. Is McCarthy around?" I had started calling our principal McCarthy last year. It seemed a good parallel – his way or the highway type of leadership.

"He's with the assistant super right now. What can I do for you 090?"

"Well, I'm here to sign my leave papers."

"What!?" Heather, another secretary exclaimed from her desk.

"No, really, what can I do for you?" Jenny asked.

"No, I'm serious. It's just for a year. Didn't someone tell you?"

"Jack, I'm always the last one to know anything around here. What did you do, win the lottery?" Jenny asked.

"I wish. No, I got an assignment to do some top-secret, highly classified, very sensitive work in Nova Scotia. That's all I can say."

"Sounds dangerous. But you're the man, No, really, what are you going to do?" Jenny asked.

I stayed for a few more minutes and told them about the fictitious home business and traveling that Lake and I had formulated as our story. We were supposedly going to network all the farmer markets across the country, and then set up a website that gave times and location for each market so anyone traveling could visit the local markets as they passed through on their vacations. Good idea, really. Jenny found the papers I needed to sign, and I said goodbye to both secretaries, promising to send pictures of our travels.

Next stop was Richmond Junior High, Lake's school. I waited in the car and waited and waited. Finally Lake appeared, walking out with her principal Kim Ashford.

"Hi Jack. We're sorry to lose you guys for a year. Sounds like the farmers market idea could really work though," Kim said, standing by the passenger window.

"Yeah, she told you, huh? We're trying to keep it quiet until we get started," I said with a look at Lake who was standing behind Kim and smiling through a few tears.

"I won't say a word," Kim turned. "We'll see you in a year Lake. Please keep me updated," Kim said, giving her a hug.

"Thanks. I will, Kim." One more hug, and Lake opened the car door.

A few more stops, hardware store for supplies, bookstore for maps, grocery store and then home to plan our great adventure into the unknown.

Chapter Twenty-Eight

THE LAST WEEK had been filled with preparations for our departure, and we could already tell that money was going to be tight. Our mortgage would be split with Brien, and we'd leave enough money to keep the animals on good food for a year. Our biggest expenses would be supplies for the banners and gas. Camping and cooking our meals was cheap. Any stays at hotels would be short. If there were no unexpected expenses, at least no grand unexpected expenses, we'd be fine. We had one more month of pay coming to us, and the plan was to live off that for our first two months on the road. The VW was paid for. When we returned home, we'd start back in on another teaching year. This was the plan, and we all know how best laid plans work out.

"Let's go, baby," I said, standing at the front door.

"Coming!" the toilet flushed upstairs.

Driving down the highway on our way to pick up our new-and-improved Vanagon, I laid my hand on Lake's leg and she covered it with hers.

"It's like a new life, huh?" I said.

"And then some," Lake added.

"Brien should be here tomorrow."

"When's Gus coming over?" Lake asked.

"About two or three today," I answered, looking out the window at all the billboards on their monolithic steel poles.

"Honey, you think your mom's going to be all right?"

"I hope so. I've promised we'd be good about calling her. It really bothers me that she's going to be constantly worried, but what are we supposed to do, right?"

"Yeah. We just can't get caught, period," Lake said, and looked over at me.

"We're not going to. Okay, here's our exit."

"The Green Jeans Machine!" Lake said, squeezing my leg.

"Oh yeah baby!"

It was a sight to see. The three seasoned mechanics that worked at Phillips all came out to take one last look and see our response.

"Far out! Right on, guys!" I exclaimed, staring at the now-forest-green VW. Its new clearance was obvious, and I imagined it going over some bumpy-rutted desert roads without a problem. My mother had thrown in the money for new tires; she was always concerned about me having good tires, something she had picked up from my father. They were all-season, double-walled, back-country-treaded, kick-butt tires.

"Well, it's not a Hum-Vee, but this thing will get you back in there without a problem," one of the mechanics stated standing next to me.

"It looks incredible," Lake said, with a big smile on her face.

"We had a problem in the beginning with the conversion of the van's chassis which involves the removal of the old two-wheel-drive components, and the installation of a front-drive axle, transfer case and other related parts, but we found the parts, and I'll put my reputation behind it." The lead mechanic said handing me the keys.

"Well, it looks fantastic. Thanks," I said, shaking his hand.

"Send us a picture from somewhere," said the youngest of the three mechanics.

"We will. Thanks guys," Lake said, closing the drivers' door on me as I strapped in.

'King of the road, baby," I said from my new perch.

"Just don't wreck it on the way home," Lake said, as she watched me pull away.

It was a beauty. The forest green paint job contrasted beautifully with the classic white bumpers and VW emblem on the grill. It was a piece of rolling cultural history. As I drove down the highway, I turned on the new stereo and ACDC 'Back in Black' immediately blared from the speakers. One of the mechanics must have forgotten to take out his CD. It was a perfect song though, and I turned it up even higher. I began to imagine rolls of canvas and gallons of paint filling up the back of the van, a desert vista in the foreground, and the thrill of hitting another site before making camp for the night.

The Southwest was our old haunt and a place we cared for deeply. This is where we planned to spend much of our time in the coming months. The fragile environment of the desert had a hard time restoring itself when it was damaged and damaged like it was. John Muir and Edward Abbey were a few of the folks that had spent their lives fighting for its preservation, and they along with others had done much to bring focus to this land. Now new blood was needed to carry on the fight. Mr. and Mrs. Green Jeans to the rescue!

After taking some back roads to see how the VW handled, I pulled up our driveway, and Pearl and Barney sat in the yard, wondering who had just entered their territory. Lake was holding Smokey Joe and came off the porch steps with tears in her eyes.

"What's wrong baby?" I said, hopping out of our new ride.

"I'm going to miss them, Jack," Lake said, kissing Smokey on the head.

"I know. I am too. They're going to love Brien," I stated, with hopeful assurance.

"Want to take a test drive!? It's a stellar machine here."

"You betcha. Come on guys. Pile in!" Lake said, and took the keys from me.

When we returned from a short drive along the Missouri River with the family, Gus was sitting on our front porch.

"Hey comrades! That's a nice set of wheels!" He said coming off the porch.

"Thanks! How are ya, Gus?" Lake said, giving him a big hug as the dogs jumped up trying to get some attention as well.

"Doing good. We've got a lot to talk about," Gus said, trying to give equal attention to both dogs.

"Let's get started, I'll make us a plate of nachos," I said opening the front door.

We sat on the back deck for hours discussing plans, pouring over maps and hashing out logistics. As the sun went down, we moved inside and spread out the maps on the harvest table. Gus gave us a long list of news media contacts that he knew personally. They would be eager to cover our latest clandestine missions.

"You know, you folks already have a following on the web," Gus said firing up his notebook.

"What?" I said, truly surprised.

"I didn't think you knew. I uploaded a bunch of your endeavors months ago and made it easy for anyone to copy the pics. I've been updating ever since. I didn't know if it would go anywhere or not. Turns out, there are a number of blogs out there and even a site devoted to you two. They've been requesting your response for a few months now."

"What!?" Lake responded.

"T-shirts for sale. They have your Green Declaration of Dependence on the back and made up caricatures of you two on the front. The explosion really began with Minty Crow and then your audio interview made you more real, and everyone is just waiting for you to get back in action."

"Wow, you gotta be kidding?!" Lake said, looking at Gus's notebook.

"This is freaking crazy, Gus," I said, with my mouth opened as Lake navigated through the site.

"That's the way the world is right now. Someone can sit down at a computer and make up a site and boom, instant communication with the world. It's not that hard. I think I can probably earn you guys some revenue."

"Really?" Lake said, looking up from the screen.

"Yeah, I have some ideas."

"Why didn't you let us know before now?" I asked.

"I didn't want you guys getting cold feet. Selfish, I know. Now, I think it would be good to keep these sites informed. This is going to be very helpful, and at the same time, there's really no fear of identity exposure. You take the pics, send them to me, and I'll do the rest. We can even do audio interviews from the road. The goal is to reach a critical mass, so the big boys take notice."

"Yep, the big boys need to listen up," Lake agreed, pulling up the picture of the columns.

"Oh they will, especially if you call them out by name on your banners. They're not going to be happy, either," Gus said, getting up to stretch.

"That's the goal. First scare 'em, and then keep it up until they have to change," I said, looking at the computer as Lake scrolled through more pictures.

"What's new with Anne?" Lake asked.

"She mentions you guys every once and awhile, but she's found a boyfriend, a rich boyfriend. I think her hard news days are over. She's trying to get him to fund a local talk show featuring her as the hostess with the mostess. The new Oprah she calls it. Basically, she's an ego-driven, spoiled girl that wants a halogen light overhead twenty-four hours a day. She'll probably get it until her boobies start to sag."

"That will take her down. You got time to go over the map one more time?" I asked Gus, who was bending down trying to touch his toes.

"That's what I'm here for."

After Gus left that evening, Lake and I made love. We were on another high.

"Maybe this is what it feels like to be a rock star?" Lake said, lying in bed with the sheet pulled up.

"I think it is," I replied, kissing her on the lips and turning over on my side, wondering if either one of us would get any sleep tonight. Tomorrow Brien would arrive. The next day we were scheduled to depart.

Chapter Twenty-Nine

NOT BEING FAZED by a restless night, we were ready to rock and roll the next morning. The excitement of taking off on the road tomorrow, put us in overdrive and most of the morning we spent packing up for the adventure. Todd and Barb were coming over for breakfast in a few minutes to say farewell. We hadn't seen or talked much to them after the VP Fair in St Louis. Something had changed. Lake was fairly certain that they were being cautious now, and we couldn't blame them. It wasn't like they were associating with hardened criminals, but since Lake and I had dived into this and currently had made national news, they were reluctant to associate with us as freely as they once had, which didn't surprise us. This particular road had very few travelers. It was completely against the wisdom of the logical mind. Our attempt to help the planet wouldn't reap us a new career path and certainly no paycheck, but if we didn't get caught, all would be good. That is, if the road allowed us to return.

"Hey guys! Jack, they're here!" Lake said, opening the front door and calling up the stairs to me.

Sitting on the back deck, eating the cinnamon buns Todd had made that morning and sipping on freshly ground, Costa Rican, fair-trade coffee, the conversation was strained. We shared no details of our venture, and just told them we needed to take a year off from teaching. They were suspect, of course, but asked no questions they didn't want an answer to.

"Okay you two, we need to get going. We want you guys to be careful out there. If Brien needs anything, tell him to let us know. We'll stop by and meet him sometime this week," Barb said getting up from the table.

"Thanks, we'll let him know," Lake replied, tapping her foot on the floor, something that had just started this morning. She wasn't a foot tapper.

"I bet you guys have a lot of packing to do, so we'll let you get to it. Be careful, okay?" Todd said, opening his arms to give Lake a hug and then me.

"Yeah, you guys have a good year; we'll send you a postcard," I said, moving to give Barb a hug.

"No, don't do that. We'll find out from Brien how you're doing," Todd said, obviously uncomfortable with the idea of a mail trail to their house.

"Oh, okay," I responded.

Barb and Lake had a good long hug and whispers. Barb knew what we were doing. Todd knew, too. I just couldn't talk to him about it.

The morning visit lasted all of thirty minutes. As we waved at our neighbors who were walking back down their drive to their cozy home in woods, I turned to Lake.

"We freak them out, don't we?"

"I know we freak Todd out. Barb not so much. Things might change in the future, who knows? We're doing some strange stuff, Clyde. Can't blame them for being cautious," Lake said, slapping my butt. She hardly ever did that. It was sign that she was building up her commitment to our departure.

"Well, shall we get the Green Mobile packed and ready?"

"Yeah," I answered, slapping her on the butt to let her know I was there, too.

I was in charge of attaching the plastic roof cargo case. I wasn't that mechanical, but I was inventive, and two hours later, it was done. I attached it on runners so we could pull it on and off fairly easily and make use of the van's pop-top. I crammed the cargo case with ten rolls of canvas already painted with words for the 'Mother'. The canvases ranged in size from four to five feet in width and thirty to a hundred feet in length. Two cases of bright color paint and various brushes and sponges were stuffed anyplace there was room. This was enough material for three jobs. Canvas wasn't cheap. Every sign had to have an impact.

Lake was busy making the inside of the VW comfy and cozy. Without the animals going along for the adventures, and undoubtedly misadventures, the van needed to have some semblance of home. Lake could take a space and make you want to spend time in it. The windows had thin white curtains, a few small paintings of mine were hanging from the little wall space we had. Both were abstract heavy impasto acrylics, one was a heart, and the other was a peace sign. We were hippies, yippies, whatever ippes and proud of it. The animals not going was a relief to both of us. The idea of a litter box where we ate and slept and did just about everything else was extremely unappealing, but doable. Some good video could have come out of that. We had decided to do a video log, and not worry about having our exploits recorded. If a documentary could come out of this, and we could hide our identities when we shot the footage, it might be worth it. It might be something that could further the cause. We were totally thinking outside the box, and we felt like kids again. That is a very fine thing to feel. Indeed. Indeed.

"There, that's done," I stated closing the cover to the car carrier. It didn't close without a fight.

"Where did you put those new plastic tubs?" Lake asked, sticking her head out the back of the Van.

"Up in the bedroom, where you wanted them," I replied.

"Yeah, two of them are up there, where's the third?" Lake asked.

"Oh, filled with books and notepads, laptops in there too," I replied, knowing I was about to unpack it.

"No, one's for your clothes, one's for my clothes, and the other is for our rain and cold weather gear. I told you that when we bought them," Lake answered, familiar with this conversation.

"I suppose I wasn't listening that closely. I usually hang on your every word."

"Yeah, that's funny. So aahhhhh…," Lake replied, not having to finish.

"Un-pack it. Got it," I said, walking to the house.

It was dark when we felt everything was done. Twenty-degree-North face bags, two couch-thickness, Therma-rest pads, very comfy, solar lantern, folding chairs, dishes, pots, pans, silverware, food for a few weeks, two five-gallon containers of water, video equipment, computer, and a few board games was the short list. A lightweight, sixteen-foot extension ladder was attached on the driver's side, under the now curtain-lined windows.

Brien called and said he had to stop or he was going to drive off the road, he was so tired. He had tried to do the non-stop, nine-hundred fifty-mile drive from Albuquerque. One hundred twenty miles short of making it here, he stopped in Kansas City and would be here early tomorrow morning.

That evening sitting on the floor in the living room eating a double-cheese, black-olive pizza, Lake cheating on her vegan diet again, we watched a black-and-white episode of the Andy Griffith Show. It hit us like a bulldozer slamming against a concrete wall. Lake was holding Smokey Joe, he was nursing her neck still at seven years of age, and Pearl lay across her legs getting her head scratched. I had Barney lying by me, staring me down for any crumb of pizza I might share. I obliged as always with my crust. On the screen, Andy and Aunt Bee and Opie were sitting down for dinner, and Opie was about to say grace. And it hit. We looked at each other, found each other's hand, and Lake dropped a few water bullets. I followed, rata tat tat. This was the last family night at home. Mayberry would not be ours for some time to come. Not that Mayberry ever really existed, but as far as our lives went, we were as close as we'd both ever been. We knew that at our age, fifty-and-counting, we could be blowing it all. Boom. This was really happening.

"Amen," said Opie.

Chapter Thirty

"ALL RIGHT, we're not leaving today," Lake said, standing by Brien's truck, and taking two large, black trash bags of clothes out of the back of his U-Haul trailer, which was packed to the brim. It was 11:00 a.m. and too late to leave, knowing we needed to give Brien a quick orientation to the area, house and our kids.

"I agree, we've got to give you a tour of town and do a good hang out this evening," I replied, grabbing two more trash bags.

"Sorry, I was a day late. A little over-ambitious with the long-haul driving. Used to be able to drive for twelve hundred miles without stopping," Brien said, pulling out an antique floor lamp from the trailer.

"Those were the days," I replied.

Brien had lived in an apartment in Phoenix for the last twenty years, and everything he owned was crammed into his extended cab pickup, and the small rental trailer he'd pulled across the country.

After getting him somewhat settled in the house, introduced to Pearl, Barney and Smokey Joe and allowing Chance, his cute small mutt, to do the 'meet and greet' with everyone, we climbed in the VW and drove him around Manchester. We pointed out the university, the library, our favorite grocery store, Main Squeeze, of course, and generally gave him a quick orientation to the town he'd visit often over the next year. When we returned home, we walked the property. It was a beautiful August day, not too hot, which was unusual, but weather was these days. Sitting outside under the Walnut grove in backyard, conversation turned to the demise of the Southwest, a subject as heartfelt to Brien as it was to us. He'd spent the last thirty years in Arizona, teaching in the back country of the Navajo Reservation to the inner city of Phoenix. He'd loved teaching. He taught social studies to middle schoolers, a tough crowd. He was sad to leave the profession, but he knew he was burnt out and needed some time off to figure out what to do with the rest of his life. Writing a science fiction book had been a dream of his for years. He had his retirement. He had run the course with steadfast determination. For the rest of his life, he would receive a well-deserved check each month that would at least keep his head above water.

Brien knew Arizona's public lands better than we did. He'd backpacked, car-camped and canoed for weeks at a time all over the state. We drilled him on places where we could camp for a week or more at a time, and not expect see anyone. We might never go to these places, but having a list of safe retreats was comforting. He gladly went over topo maps with us, as we highlighted the places we didn't already know about.

After a dinner of veggie-burgers and a salad from the garden, I let the beans spill and Lake filled in the details. We could trust Brien. He'd seen a snippet of the report from St Louis on a local station in Phoenix, and heard about our national coverage. Sitting on the couch with Smokey Joe draped across on his lap and Chance by his side, Brien looked at us with a blank expression. "You're doing what?! You've got to be kidding! Of all the people I know, you two would be the ones to do it, but I can't believe it!" Brien exclaimed.

"I shouldn't have said anything." I took a deep breath.

"We thought we should tell you in case something happens to us, and we can't take care of our part of the mortgage," Lake blurted.

"Sure, that makes sense. I mean, I don't know what to say." Brien was looking at us like we'd just told him the earth really was flat.

"We're crazy, that's all," Lake stated, sitting on the wood floor across from him.

"Well fudge cake city!! Mum's the word. I mean you don't ever have to worry about me. I mean, I didn't even hear what you said, right?"

"Are you cool with staying here, we might be caught," I yelled from the kitchen, putting our dinner plates in the sink.

"Yeah, you didn't tell me anything. All I know is you are taking the year off!"

He had finally escaped Phoenix, was about to live a nature-filled existence at our house, and now we tell him we're Mr. Green Jeans, about to leave on a year tour.

"You know this is all on the down-low," I said coming back into the parlor, still worried that maybe we shouldn't have said anything.

"I can only imagine what you guys are feeling, how long it took to get to this point, and I still can't believe you're doing it. How you two are going to communicate in this day and age is a crap shoot. I'll tell you, the only way to know you can't be heard by someone is to purchase a forty thousand dollar satellite phone from someone who hadn't sold the encryption technology to NASA or NSA. In short, you have to know someone who is deep underground. This obviously is not going to be an option for all sorts of reasons. In truth, it's probably ridiculous to be thinking about it and getting paranoid. You're only hanging banners, not blowing up things. Right?" Brien asked looking back and forth at the two of us.

"Right. No boom, boom," I replied.

"No boom, boom," Lake agreed.

"Good, then your disposable cells, un-hooked when not in use, is a good way to go. It's what all the criminals use, I think." Brien yawned, as did we.

"Great, we're acting like criminals," Lake said and laughed.

"Dude, are you sure you're cool with this? 'Cause, we're off in the morning and not looking back," I asked, as Chance came over to re-introduce himself.

"Very cool. I'm already living vicariously. I gotta hit the hay, okay? I am not what I used to be."

"Nor are we," I agreed, and the three of us climbed the stairs to the bedrooms, followed now, by four furry friends.

The next morning with two full mugs of coffee and hugs and kisses for the animals, we got into the VW. All our kids were there with Brien. I grabbed Lake's hand and turned the key. We both looked at the house, the animals, and I slowly backed up to head down the driveway.

"Call, if you need anything. Don't hesitate to take anybody to the vet. We'll send you a check."

"It's going to be all right. You guys take care of yourself and be very careful. You call me anytime. I'll get a disposable just for you guys," Brien said, holding Barney who wanted to go with us.

"Okay. Thanks, man," I said, looking Brien in the eyes.

"I love you, babies!!! Thank you Brien!" Lake shouted, out the passenger window.

"Get out of here, everything is going to be fine!" Brien said, holding Barney at bay, as Pearl and Chance inspected a spot in the lawn a few yards off.

Putting the VW in first gear, we slowly drove the driveway and headed down the gravel road to I-70 West.

The first hour was the toughest. Not too many words and a few tears. The second hour going through Kansas City was just as bad. By the time we reached Wichita, five hours into the first day's drive, we were starting to feel a bit more resolute. Our children would be fine as long they got love and foodies. Brien would give them that and more. Besides, we were going to be back. Dodge City, our first target was five hours northwest. We'd case out the town and then find a place to camp.

Chapter Thirty-One

DODGE CITY WAS A CATTLE TOWN. Its history was filled with the lore of the Old West. Wild Bill Hickok, Wyatt Earp, Bat Masterson, just about all the ole gunslingers had passed through here, and many even made a home here for a spell. It sat on top of the world's largest underground water system, the Ogallala Aquifer. Presently, Dodge City was like any other town in America, the geography of the franchises and, of course, our favorite, the Super-Sized Box-Mart, made it look like you hadn't left home. Downtown was still alive, thanks to the old gunslingers. On Front Street you could visit the Wild West museum, eat frozen yogurt in the same spot where many of the infamous outlaws had once eaten steak and grits. You could take your picture beside a cut-out of Wyatt Earp, or wander around Boot Hill and look at the gravestones of the fallen men who now served to draw tourist money. Otherwise, it was a town that had seen its heyday pass. That is, unless your business was cattle. And the cattle business is why we had stopped in Dodge.

"Ready to find a spot for the night?" Lake asked as we drove past literally miles of stockyards on the outskirts of town.

"Up wind of this," I said, looking over at the square miles of feeding stations and tens of thousands of cattle bunched together, getting fat by way of hormones, antibiotics and cheap corn. Two years was the average life of a pasture cow in America. These cows lived less than half of that. Many of them spent their entire existence in stockyards, with the smell of the slaughter house drifting across their mild consciousness every day. It was truly a disgusting sight, and our hearts physically ached as we drove by. This one was for the COWS!

"I saw a small campground as we came into town," I said, turning around in the middle of the two-lane blacktop.

"Sounds good. We need to get an early start to beat the people around here."

"Yep. Can you get out the list Gus gave us?" I said, straightening out the VW on the two-lane blacktop.

Lake opened up the glove box and pulled out a small tablet. She had organized the list of reporters geographically.

"Dodge City, Vincent Gunter. Sounds like an old guy," Lake said.

"Old hippie probably. He is Gus's friend. What's the number?"

I dialed the number on our new cell phone with a pay-as-you-go plan.

"Hi, is this Vincent?...Yes... uh...I'm a friend of Gus Hobart He said I could call when we were in town and give you a heads up on some Green Jeans...."

"Haaa-ha.... he said, he had a few dedicated folks going on the road. What time and where?" answered Vincent, and I paused. "Your secret's safe, I swear on the green goddess," Vincent added.

"Tomorrow morning about four-thirty at the Cattleman's Association. Five o'clock at the stockyards east of town, just drive down the blacktop, and you'll see it."

"Two sites?" Vincent asked. It turned out he had been waiting for our call for three days. He went on sipping a greyhound on the porch of his cabin, which sat on ten flat acres, the sunset was killer.

"Yeah," I answered, wanting to be done, but also liking the contact with someone else who was seemingly on our side.

"Hey, I know your current reality leans toward caution, but you guys are welcome to stay here for the night. It's all cool."

"Hold on." I looked over at Lake. "He said we can stay at his place tonight. He sounds nice."

"What do you think?" Lake said, caught off guard.

"I think...yes, I guess?" I said, holding the cell phone against my chest. Lake nodded.

"Okay. How do we get there?" I answered with trepidation. We were in yin yang time now. Lots of decisions would be based on guts.

Vincent's place was a few miles outside of Dodge City proper. Dodge City was a watershed for a few rivers. At the turn of century, back in the days of the large cattle drives before deep-well drilling solved the water problem, this watershed, along with the train, made Dodge City a prosperous town.

Driving to the dead end of a gravel road and then continuing on a rutted dirt track four hundred yards, we reached Vincent's cabin. Vincent, greyhound in hand, was there to greet us. This place was isolated. Nothing but prairie as far you could see. We liked it.

"Hi, cowboys! Welcome!" Vincent said, holding his glass tumbler trying not to spill any of its contents as he made his way to our vehicle. He was a small man, about sixty-five years' old, mature, grey beard, red suspenders and thick glasses. He seemed kind from the moment we laid eyes on him.

After getting the VW set up for its virgin sleeping, we joined Vincent on the back porch of his cabin. When he had bought the property, there was only a turn-of-the-century, hand-sewn, one-room cabin and a working well. Over the last ten years, he had restored the cabin and added three more rooms and a huge porch on the backside over-looking a seemingly endless field of prairie grass. The entire house was sided with cedar. He'd done most of the work himself, and his calloused hands were evidence of the hard labor. Coming out of the kitchen, through an antique screen door he had restored, he held a heaping platter of fried potatoes and beans, showered with a spicy red sauce. He was vegetarian himself, an oddity in Dodge City. You could hear the moos' in the distance, even at his place. Lots of cows in Dodge County. Eerie freaking place for an animal lover.

"You have to be true to the road," Vincent stated, already having eaten dinner and sitting back his rocker, lightening up a three dollar cigar.

"Our road is unknown, Vincent," Lake said, with a forkful of potatoes dripping with red sauce.

'Unknown, untested and unreal. Been there, done that," Vincent said, with a smile.

"Old activist?" I asked, stuffing my mouth with another bite. I was a sauce guy, and this was excellent sauce.

"Long story, but yes. You two are the sweet scent of old memories. I used to believe we were going to change things. Live with land and not just on it. For a while back in the sixties, it seemed to be catching on. Of course, I was surrounded by people of like mind, and that has a way of putting blinders on ya. Now, some of the people I used to know that were on the 'sustainability love train', have switched rides and hopped on the 'money express' and never looked back. The baby boomers have a lot responsibility for the ways things have changed. You hit 'em hard. If you don't mind answering, why are you stopping in Dodge City?" Vincent asked, taking a draw on his cigar.

"The cows," Lake answered.

"Oh, those poor sentient beings. Every time, I pass those stockyards, I throw out blessings. Rips my heart out."

"Why are you here, Vincent?" I asked, finishing my last bite.

"Oh, that's for another time," Vincent replied, with a long laugh.

The windup alarm clock had been ringing for a good twenty seconds before Vincent slapped it off. It was 4:00 a.m. He struggled to get out of bed. Looking out the window, he saw that we had left. By 4:15 he was on the road to the Cattleman's Association, a large monolithic structure with columns supporting a grand facade like the Taj Mahal's, in honor of the cow's gold. Attached to the columns across a thirty-foot expanse and up twelve feet was a brown, painted banner with green text. The letters were four feet tall. It was quite noticeable.

WOULD YOU CONSIDER CLOSING OUR PRISON? MAYBE LETTING US HAVE OUR TWO YEARS IN A

FIELD? IT SEEMS LIKE THE LEAST WE CAN ASK? A COW'S PLEA.
COMPLIMENTS OF MR. GREEN JEANS

The sun would be up in thirty minutes and the natural light would reveal our newest words to all who passed. The building faced east, toward Mecca, the cattlemen wouldn't want that fact pointed out.

Vincent pulled into to the 24-hour minimart to grab a coffee. He'd wait for the dawn, snap some pictures and then head out to the stockyards. As he sat on the hood of his car he reflected on the story he was going to write today. His job was tied to the town and running this wouldn't garner him any friends. He just hoped he would still have a job at the Dodge City Globe. He just hoped he had the balls to remember who he was or had been.

Five miles down the road from the Cattlemen's kill office, Lake and I laid down a set of banners on the grass just off the blacktop and walked up to a three-wire, barbed fence. The enormous head of an Angus heifer came up to the fence and stuck out her head, carefully resting its neck on the barbed wire. The huge dark eyes looked at us, and Lake melted.

"Hi sweetheart, I wish we could take you with us. We're on your side, babies," Lake said to the helpless heifer, and the sea of her family that stretched to the horizon in the early morning dawn. Lake withdrew her hand, kissed it, and then placed it back on the short rough brown and white hair of the young girl's soft forehead.

"Baby, hurry!" I shouted, having run the first banner down the fence line. With a sigh and another blessing of hope, Lake picked up her end of the banner, began running hemp string through the holes we'd made across the top of the banner, and tied it to the fence. Finishing the last knot on my end, we hurried to our next banner. Done with that one, we ran to the VW parked behind a pair of cottonwoods, just a few hundred feet down the road.

"Baby!" I shouted, grabbing Lake's hand and pulling her across the road. A super-duty pickup truck was coming straight toward us. The headlights hadn't reached us yet, as we jumped in a ditch on the opposite side of the road and laid flat on the dewed grass. The truck slowed as it passed our banner. We could hear country music coming from the cab. Good chance he worked the early shift at the stockyard. We lay motionless in the ditch as the truck slowly drove the three hundred feet of fence line, now draped with Mr. Green Jeans' latest message. He gunned his engine at the end of the canvas, and the truck flew off over a small rise. We got up and ran as fast as we could to the van. Inside, I reached behind the seat and handed the video camera to Lake in the passenger seat.

"Okay, one pass, make sure the camera's night light is on," I said now backing out onto the blacktop. Lake held the video camera out the window. The morning light was arriving. I drove in second gear down the length of our latest message to the world and then turned at the next junction on highway WW heading west out of Dodge.

When Vincent arrived at the Stockyards, there were already several trucks parked on the side of the road. He realized he had to get the shot quickly. These were cattlemen and that sign would be down in a few minutes. He pulled off the road and climbed on top of his Geo Metro. He was using a wide-angle lens and was able to get the entire message in three shots, which he could then piece together on the computer. As he carefully climbed off his car, he was greeted by Jim Solomon, a Dodge City native, who ran cattle south of town, and also paid for a large herd to be grown in this stockyard.

"Vincent, how did you hear about this?" Jim, a tall, lean man wearing Lee jeans and worn work boots approached Vincent, an over-sized silver belt buckle of a steer's head, emblem of his fraternity, leading the way.

"Quick Mart. Saw an ole boy there who just passed this way." Vincent was quick on the draw. He'd lived here for way too long. He spoke their language when needed. A reporter needs to be able to do that.

"Up early, aren't ya?" Jim said, looking him straight in the eye.

"Always am on a Sunday," Vincent answered, reaching through the open window to set his camera in the driver's seat.

"You plannin' on putting this in the paper?"

"Have to see how the pictures come out, Jim. Talk to ya later," Vincent answered, as he got in the Metro, put it in gear and cantered off. Last thing he needed right now was politics. Avoid, avoid and avoid, and it would usually go away.

Vincent did a U-turn in on the blacktop and headed back into Dodge. He snapped off a few more pictures of the ranchers taking down the signs as he passed. It was quite a sight. Short-lived, but quite a sight. Three hundred feet by four feet. Green letters on a manure brown background.

WE ARE VEGETARIANS. WE THANK OUR HUMAN VEGETARIANS FOR THEIR COMPASSION—WE KNOW WE WILL BE EATEN SOON, BUT IT WOULD BE NICE TO LIVE OUT OUR LIFE ON A FIELD OF GRASS WITH OUR FAMILY—WE GET TO SPEND SO LITTLE TIME WITH OUR CHILDREN BEFORE WE ARE KILLED AND EATEN, AND THEY ARE LEFT WONDERING WHERE WE WENT—WE CRY OUT FOR A LIFE.

PLEASE GIVE US A LIFE!

MR. GREEN JEANS

"I'll be damned. That was beautiful," Vincent said, out loud and knew he had to put this to print as he drove back into Dodge. He'd landed here ten years ago after finally getting fired in Seattle, for being drunk on the job. Here in Dodge, he could be drunk everyday if he wanted. But he wasn't. The open space out here gave his spirit a place to roam. He only drank on weekends now and not that much.

To the west, we cruised across the plains on our way to New Mexico.

"That one was for the cows!" I shouted, out the window as we rolled over the empty blacktop, the early morning dawn awakening before us. Shrub bush and yucca were beginning to dot the landscape. The desert wasn't far away. This was the flora that marked the perimeter to the place we called our true home. The transition from the Midwest to the Southwest crept up on you, and then before you knew it, the green was gone, replaced with brown and a smattering of cacti.

"God Bless the cows, God Bless all the creatures that have no voice, and God Bless the Southwest," Lake shouted, out the window.

"Beautiful baby. That was one for the record books. I sure hope Vincent has the balls the get that in the paper."

"Woooooooooo! I'm sending the pics to Gus, and I bet he can get them out there!" Lake was still yelling out the window. I slid in our Xavier Rudd's 'Food for the Belly' CD.

We were on our way back to the place we felt most at home in. The Great Southwest! She needed us and many more stewards to come to her rescue.

Chapter Thirty-Two

WE STOPPED IN ALBUQUERQUE and purchased more canvas, giving us three thousand feet to work with. That night, after sixteen hours of hard driving between the two of us, we made it to Malpais National Monument, Spanish for the Bad Lands.

The Malpais was between the Acoma and Zuni Indian reservations, eighty miles southwest of Albuquerque. The Malpais National Monument was a huge lava field, one hundred and fourteen thousand acres set aside in 1987. With extreme care, I drove with the high beams on twenty-three miles down a dirt road that ran the edge of the lava field. Tires here were the victim for the arrogant visitor. Lava is a metamorphic rock, meaning it underwent great heat and dried quickly. It can be as sharp as a knife in places and pieces are always breaking off, birthing new blades for the unsuspecting traveler. This was one of my old playgrounds when I taught elementary school on the Zuni Reservation. It was a great place to get lost. There were lava tubes that went into the ground for miles, cinder cones to climb, a bitch to get up; but a blast to run down, and there was the field. The oldest lava was estimated to be well over one hundred thousand years old; the youngest and topmost layer was just a few thousand. All the volcanoes were extinct now. This grand blanket of lava, pinions in the relentless struggle for sustenance, and many varieties of cacti dotting the landscape, made for an eerie landscape. This is where we would spend the next week making the banners for Phoenix.

Phoenix was going to be our build-up to our grand crescendo. We hoped it would surpass St Louis. It would cost us fifteen percent of our cash. Fifteen percent in only three weeks. It was a calculated risk. The evolution of the Mr. Green

Jeans would hopefully take a leap if all happened as planned. It was a simple supply-and-demand-economics model of activism. To keep our audience, we had to keep the show going.

Camped out just off the main dirt track that ran around the perimeter of the lava field, Lake and I got busy. We were well hidden, and very few people ever visited the harsh landscape of the Malpais, especially not as far back as we had come. It was open to the public year round, but most people who did make the drive from the interstate went to the monument's tourist center and walked the half-mile trail that started and ended at the nature center's back door. It gave them a taste of this unearthly world. Some purchased a souvenir from the gift shop that went to protecting the monument. They left contented, having visited a place few even knew existed.

It was three digits hot here, and the paint on the canvases dried quickly, allowing us to roll up the each banner after a few hours and start on another. Five days later, we'd completed the thirty banners. Stored on the floor of the Vanagon, each one was marked on the back with its message written in pen. The banners were getting more and more artistic, colors were bold, and the text contrasted nicely on top of swirls of colors. Our green background idea had metamorphosed just like the landscape before us. We were proud of these pieces. We took pictures of each one and when we were in a Wi-Fi zone, we'd send them off to Gus to put up on his site after they were hung in Phoenix. One of Gus's ideas about making some money had been to use the banners for T-shirts and posters. Maybe it would work, couldn't hurt.

That night, during our fifth dinner of rice and beans, we went over our targets. Phoenix was a sprawling city, still growing by the hour, a true conundrum of civilization. Our focus was the Sonoran Desert or what was left of it. It is arguably the most beautiful desert in the world. It stretches from Arizona into Mexico and is the only place on earth where the Saguaro cactus lives. Many of these obelisks of the desert are over two hundred years old. They are home to the Cactus Wren and Desert Owl and many other desert creatures, and mark the boundary of the Sonoran Desert. They can reach heights upwards of forty feet. It is unlawful to destroy or maim a saguaro in Arizona. Over a decade ago a few ole boys with shot guns blasted one to pieces during the consumption of a twenty-four pack of Natural Light in the desert outside of Phoenix. They were caught and did a few months in Florence prison because they couldn't pay the five-thousand-dollar fine. There are a lot of unconnected rednecks in this country. There were septic-tanks-full of them in Arizona, and they were the least of the desert's problems. The desert doesn't have much resilience. When she gets hit, she feels it, and recovery is a painstakingly slow process. The Valley of the Sun, Phoenix or the 'Blob' as Edward Abbey called it, was now home to hundreds of golf courses, thousands of pools and millions of people. It's truly unbelievable what is being done to this ecosystem. That's what happens when there's money, sun, water piped in from its rightful home up north, and masses of people who could care less. The Saguaro shadowed the foreground of this picture with an example of the truth.

The next morning, leaving the Malpais, Lake carefully drove the tire slashing lava track back to the blacktop and onto state highway 53. We were both ripe and in need of a hotel stay. Taking a left and heading west, we gained elevation and passed through a sparsely wooded landscape. Pinions and ponderosas were the largest flora, and elk and mule deer the counterpart fauna. Sparsely populated for the next ninety miles, Ramah was originally a Mormon settlement that was now interspersed with Native Americans who'd left the reservation, Anglos who either taught on the reservations or worked in the medical field, and a few artists in the outlying hills and canyons living off of nature's beauty. Twenty miles from Ramah was the Zuni reservation, and the place I had lived for three years in a trailer leased from the tribe. Teaching their children at Ashiwi Elementary School had been a good experience, but sad and lonely was the reservation. Sad and lonely was a common theme on any reservation in America.

"Turn left here," I said, as we sat at the only stop sign in Zuni.

"Are you sure?" Lake asked.

"I'm sure. Frankie will appreciate this. The whole Zuni population will appreciate this. Plus, there's a chance we can get some more support, and I'd love to see Frankie. He's going to like you."

"Okay, but I say we keep going. You better be right about this." Lake eyes were looking forward at the long stretch of blacktop that took us out of Zuni.

"Trust me on this."

"Okay," Lake responded, making the left.

"Baby, it's cool, I promise." She wasn't buying it right now, and who could blame her? We were on an Indian Pueblo, and I was telling her I wanted to let an old friend know what we were doing, thus opening ourselves up to another possibility for mistrust. This hadn't been planned, but what really had?

Pulling up to an ancient adobe house in the middle of the Zuni pueblo, I got out of the VW and went to the door. The pueblo was a tangle of dirt roads that spidered through rows of adobe homes, most built off of one another and sharing a common wall. In the center of the pueblo was the five-hundred-year-old Spanish Mission, which still held services every Sunday. It was living history. The Spanish under Cortez, looking for the seven cities of gold, had tried to conquer the Zunis in the 1500's. The Zuni were the only tribe that held fast and defeated them, sending them on their way. It was a proud heritage. Now, times were bleak. Dogs roamed the streets in packs, and the unemployment was near fifty percent. Animal fetishes and jewelry craftsmen were the mainstays of their economy. Their workmanship was unequaled. China had stolen their designs and created a town named Zuni, so they could label their products 'made in Zuni'. China duplicated hundreds of products, even BMW's. I knocked on the weathered, wooden door.

Frankie, a forty-five-year-old fetish craftsman, who also ran the local radio station from his home, opened the door. "Jack, *Keshi!*" He gave me a big bear hug.

"*Keshi*, Frankie, this is my wife, Lake," I said, putting my hand on Lake's back.

"Very glad to meet you. What a prize, Jack," Frankie said, opening his arms for a hug.

"Thank you, it's nice to meet you." Lake blushed, as she hugged Frankie.

"What brings you here, Jack? It's been years, brother," Frankie asked, standing outside the door on the red dirt. Frankie was a respected member of the tribe and still held to tradition. He was often frustrated with the youth, and there was a time when he almost completely succumbed to the tragedy of his people and joined many of the lost souls drinking for days on end in Gallup. Gallup, was a town of twenty thousand on interstate 40 thirty miles north that served as the convergence point for many Indian nations, Navajo being by far the largest. Alcohol was not sold on reservations. So Gallup was where you went to buy alcohol, drink alcohol and shop at Box-Mart. Gallup was an ugly town, a town of desperation and last rights. Today it was in much better shape than it had been, but it still served as the last stop for many a Native American.

"You have a few hours?" I said.

"Jack, you stop by after all these years, I'm not letting you leave until tomorrow, so I have more than a few hours. Looks like you two could use a shower, too," Frankie replied with a deep laugh and pinched his nose shut.

"Yeah, we've been camping at the Malpais."

"Not much water there," Frankie said with another deep laugh. Frankie was a large man and displayed a robust belly. Outside his house was a clay oven, and these ovens dotted the landscape of Zuni. It was in these ovens that the people made their famous Zuni bread. Zuni oven bread, mutton stew and an assortment of fried food was the mainstay of their diet, not recipes found in healthy living cookbooks. Frankie had a ponytail that ran the length of his back, wore jewelry like Liberace, and his smile could warm the heart of any crying child.

"Jack, let's take a walk before you guys get cleaned up, that okay?" Frankie said closing the door behind him.

"Sure," I replied.

"Jack was well-liked here, Lake. We don't keep the good ones too long, though. You can never really feel at home here if you're an Anglo, it's a temporary place for them. The ones that do stay are the misfits, the ones who have trouble fitting in with their own people."

"I think that might be us now," Lake said, grabbing my hand.

"Oh, why would that be?" Frankie said, with an expression of curiosity.

"Can we go in the mission today?" I asked, changing the subject.

"We can. I have the key." Frankie paused, looking at me for an answer and then led us off toward the mission that sat across from his house. He walked swiftly crossing the red dirt road running just a few feet from his doorstep.

"We'll tell you in there," I said, as Lake and I followed Frankie to the mission.

"Hmmm…this sounds good. After you, Lake," Frankie said, opening the gate to a small graveyard that sat in front of the mission. He turned and gave me a wink and a thumbs up. Frankie was a good judge of character.

Chapter Thirty-Three

THAT EVENING sitting in Frankie's house, a simple three-room, one-bath, adobe-walled home that was probably over four hundred years old, Frankie listened to Lake and me tell another story about our adventures so far.

"You two are crazy. Indian crazy. I love it!" Frankie said, laughing so loud he shook the tea out of his cup.

"Now, before you ask, the answer is, Yes!" Frankie said, setting down his cup of Earl Grey.

"You don't know what we…" Lake was interrupted.

"It doesn't matter. I have more to offer than what Jack thinks. Come with me," Frankie said, getting up and walking toward a closed door off the main room. He opened the door and turned on the light. Inside a fifteen-by-fifteen adobe room was a state-of-the-art radio station and recording studio. It was small but with today's technology you didn't need to have a lot of space to do what once took a whole building.

"I have been busy Jack," Frankie said, with an enormous smile.

"This is a major step up from what you used to have, brother!" Frankie and I gave each other a high five.

"It is the communication center for the pueblo. I'm working on my Wolf-Man voice. I have about forty thousand regular listeners, White, Navajo, Zuni, Mexican, Jemez, Acoma, almost all the pueblos listen. We even have a website with streaming video. Satellite feed for a little TV station might be up in a few months," Frankie explained, with a great deal of pride.

"To have a voice is a beautiful thing," I said, putting my hand on Frankie's shoulder.

"Mr. Green Jeans will be shouting from here my friends; you can be sure of that. The journey of the Takers must soon end or we will all be at each other's throat."

"Well said, Frankie," Lake replied, laying her hand on Frankie's other shoulder.

"Frankie, look we don't want you getting into any trouble over…"

"Can you shut him up, Lake?" Frankie looked to Lake, and she shook her head.

"How 'bout some green chili, no meat, before we turn in?" Frankie offered and laughed.

"The famous New Mexico green chili is never turned down," I said still looking in the room, amazed at what Frankie had put together and realizing that he was a brother from another mother.

The next morning after sleeping on our Therma rest pads in Frankie's living room, we awoke to Frankie broadcasting his morning show.

"This is All Tribes Lone Wolf Frankie Z saying good morning New Mexico! There's a slight chill in the air this excellent dawn, a perfect beginning to a new day. *Keshi*, my brothers and sisters. On this day August twenty-ninth, we kick off our support to Mr. Green Jeans. An organization that has made headlines in the Midwest and nationally. If you don't know Mr. Green Jeans yet, we'll keep you up to date on this ground-level, coming out of the Kiva earth steward. We here at the All Tribes growing network offer our unwavering support. Maybe we'll even get an interview someday?" Frankie looked at us on the verge of laughing. "Now, here's a tune that puts this new partnership in perspective."

"What do think!" yelled Frankie from the studio.

"Outstanding!" I shouted.

"Lake?" Frankie said, coming out into the living room.

"Thank you, so so much!" Lake replied, sitting up with a blanket across her legs.

"I think I've passed the audition," Frankie said, letting out a big gut laugh.

The Beatles 'Come Together' filled Frankie's small house.

"Okay, I made you guys a little care package: some Zuni bread, Jiffy Peanut butter and a bag of hot fries. You know the mainstays. I don't eat this way anymore, not too often. Ha-ha. Here's a list of some of our people that will be happy to help you. You tell them Frankie sent you." Frankie handed me a paper bag and a sheet of paper with five names written on it.

"Thank you Frankie." Lake gave him a big hug.

"My sincere pleasure. I always knew Jack was special. I didn't know he had the courage of a bear, but it seems he does, and you must, too. I have a feeling we will see each other again someday soon. Now, I have to get back to the broadcasting. I do a question-and-answer hour called 'One is not Enough'. Mostly I listen to my people's problems, but sometimes I can help. Oh, you made the Dodge City newspaper, whoever wrote that story probably needs to get out of town. I put a print out in the food bag. *So'a:ne*, my brother and new sister," Frankie said and gave me a huge hug. He placed a turquoise, spirit bear fetish in my hand.

"*So'a:ne*. brother," I repeated 'goodbye' in Zuni to him.

Frankie disappeared into his studio and shut the door. I packed up our blankets and sleeping pads and Lake took another shower. Fifteen minutes later, we were on the road. The turquoise bear sat on the dashboard as we drove the dirt roads through the pueblo waving at the children playing in our path. Corporate America was making offers daily to bring their brand of culture onto the reservation. This was truly a place lost in time, and if the Zuni nation could hold out and keep to tradition, they might have a chance to regain their honor. As I turned onto the highway that ran through Zuni and headed west to Arizona, I saw a few teenagers walking along the road wearing colors. There had been a gang problem here for years. It was a natural transition for these kids to join a gang. Every Zuni was already part of a tribe and a clan with passage rites and traditions. Zuni was also part of the drug traffickers' highway that ran from Mexico to Canada. With few opportunities for the youth, a short-lived place of power and identity was attractive. Gangs flourished on reservations, just like they do in the impoverished areas across America. Without strong people like Frankie in the tribe, things could go from bad to worse very quickly.

As we came to a rise in the road, I looked in the rear-view mirror at Zuni. It was a beautiful and tragic place at the same time. I took Lake's hand, stepped on the gas, and we headed off the reservation and back into the world that was causing all the problems.

Chapter Thirty-Four

AN HOUR LATER, driving on Interstate 40 heading west to Flagstaff, we passed through Holbrook. Another thirty miles and we hit Winslow. Lake began singing 'Take it Easy' by the Eagles. Downtown Winslow has a statue erected commemorating the line in the song, "sitting on a corner in Winslow, Arizona." For us, its crowning attraction was La Posada, an old train station that had been restored to its glory days as an upscale hotel. Bogart and Gable were a few of the stars that used to take sanctuary here when filming the old westerns. The Petrified Forest and the Painted Desert National Parks were a short drive. Otherwise Winslow was a town in need of a face-lift. Given its location, Winslow could easily go off the grid with a solar power plant. The big boys didn't want that to happen though. The fossil grip was still strong, even in places where the transition could happen in a matter of years.

We didn't stop; it was only sixty miles to Flagstaff and our favorite coffee shop, Macy's. Mount Humphrey loomed in the distance, the tallest peak in Arizona at 12,633 feet. When we had completed our work in Phoenix, we hoped to return to Winslow and stay a few nights at La Posada. They made a corn chowder that was out of this world. We both knew that probably wouldn't happen, but it was fun to dream.

An hour later, we rolled into Flagstaff, home to Northern Arizona University, NASA Research Center, Snowbowl Ski Resort, rock climbing, hiking and mountain biking. It was two and half hours north of Phoenix, thirty minutes north of Sedona and one hundred miles south of the Grand Canyon. To the Northeast was the Navajo Reservation, which I knew well. It was through the Dinah land that we would make the final trek to our last target before taking some time off to re-group, unless we were behind bars.

Parallel parking in Front of Macy's Coffee Shop in downtown Flagstaff, Lake got goose bumps. This was her town for many years before we met and took our vows. Flagstaff had one of the most liberal populations in Arizona, and true to form, there were two other VW buses parked across the street.

Inside Macy's, you felt you might have returned to the sixties. Neil Young softly played from two box speakers, and you couldn't tell the patrons from the staff if they hadn't been separated by a counter. It was an organic crowd, a happy crowd, a crowd of people we missed since moving to the Midwest. Macy's scent was the earth, patchouli, sandalwood, coffee and fresh-baked bread. Lake went to order coffee, and I grabbed a table with a street view and turned on the laptop. Moments later, she returned, placing two steaming mocha lattes and freshly baked croissants on the table.

"I'm going to do it baby," I said.

"Go for it, it can't hurt. We need the help, if we plan to get all those banners up. I'm going to call Brien and check on our babies," Lake said, settling in her chair.

We spent the next hour at Macy's. I emailed Gus to fill him in and sent some excellent pics from Dodge City, gave Frankie a shout and thanked him for his help in Zuni and then sent an email to the people at MrGreenJeans.net. Gus told us that it looked like their IP originated from somewhere in Arizona. I hoped for a quick response. It took only ten minutes before I had a message back from them. I opened it with hesitation. We hadn't wanted to involve too many people in our activities, but we couldn't do what we had planned for Phoenix alone. We needed help, and after all, it was our intention to get a movement started. We just wanted to remain as anonymous as possible. But maybe our anonymity was coming to an end. I opened the email.

"They said absolutely yes!" I exclaimed, looking at Lake who was talking to Brien on the phone. She gave the thumbs up with her mouth wide open.

I emailed back that I would be in contact with them tomorrow. I quickly emailed Gus to see if he could find out who was behind MrGreenJeans.net, and if they could be trusted. We were now weeks into our activist trip. In the next month, Phoenix and then our crown-jewel target would be hit. We planned to lay low after that for a few months and see what kind of publicity we generated. We'd hang out camping in the desert, moving every few weeks.

"Okay, Pearl has been sleeping by the door every day since we left, Brien says she seems happy but it's obvious she misses us. Barney sleeps with him, he never slept with us. And Smokey Joe is, of course, just fine. Oh, there was leak under the sink, but he fixed it. Okay, tell me what you found out!?" Lake asked with some anxiety.

"I think we are about to meet some loyal followers," I said.

"Seriously?" Lake said, putting down her mocha.

"Let's get some disguises."

"Why don't I dress as a man, I can bandaged boobies and you can dress up like a woman?" Lake responded.

"I'm going to be a pirate this time."

"A swashbuckler with a hook?" Lake said, sipping her Mocha again.

"You got it! Desert Viking, baby."

Lake laughed. "I think you'd make a great Marilyn Monroe."

"Don't kill my dreams."

"You can be a pirate, babe."

"Thanks. We should get going," I said, closing the laptop.

Lake wanted to stay in Flagstaff longer and visit some old friends, but we both knew that was too risky. We had to get to Phoenix and set up shop. After Phoenix, maybe we could pass through, depending on what our 'state of affairs' was after what we hoped would be our largest crash thus far. Thirty minutes later, we were driving south on I-17.

I-17 runs from Flagstaff to the Phoenix valley. It starts at 8700 feet and drops in 120 miles to 300 feet on the desert floor. Lake drove while I did more emailing and made contact with Gus on the phone. He said he was looking into the dot net site. He gave me contact numbers for three reporters and said he would make the initial calls to warm them up. He also told us his wife was getting a little heady about all of this, so he had to be discreet. Gus wanted me to only contact him by emails from now on, and he would call us back. Any more and it was almost impossible to not leave a trail. Because, we had pledged to never vandalize again and be only peaceful in our efforts, we hoped anything we might be charged with, if ever caught, would be only minor offenses. How wrong we might soon be.

Dropping abruptly over the Mogollon Rim, which cuts Arizona in half we began on our descent into the desert. We passed through the town of Camp Verde and crossed the Verde Valley, gateway to Sedona, Cottonwood, Jerome and Clarkdale, then gained elevation again crossing atop a large mesa with yuccas and prickly pear cacti. Just past Sunset Point rest stop, we made the final drop into the Sonoran Desert. Here the saguaro is king and stands majestically against the harsh landscape. Seeing the first saguaro caused a moment of pause for us. It was one of the reasons we had chosen Phoenix. Somewhere deep inside our beings this amazing life force spoke to us. It was a sad voice that spoke of death and fear but still held out hope for a return to harmony. The saguaro had become a symbol for Arizona, and they were decorated like Christmas trees in December. Plaster, plastic, wood and metal saguaros were mass produced from a few inches to over twenty feet in height. The saguaro was good business. A few golf courses left some real ones in prominent places for effect. Whenever a development went in, and that was with the frequency of the tides hitting the shore, the saguaros were dug up and placed in makeshift wooden planters because they were protected by the law. They were then either replanted elsewhere or sold to homeowners. But many never saw the ground again and slowly died in the huge wooden boxes. Oversight, once again, was a joke.

Hitting Anthem, a planned community of fifty thousand on the outskirts of Phoenix, we had arrived in the valley. Anthem was an example of everything that was wrong with Phoenix. It had been built in just a few years. Gated neighborhoods, schools, shopping centers, and a world onto itself. It filled quickly with people either moving to the valley or escaping the crime and traffic of the metro area, and it wasn't cheap. Before we moved to Missouri this is where I had seen rows and rows of saguaros standing on the edge of the development with earthmovers in the background raking the land of any life to prepare for building. I knew many of these hundred to two-hundred-year-old glories had reached the end of their life in one fell swoop. The few saguaros left served only as a reminder of what once was.

Any doubts we might have had about going through with this immediately vanished as we passed Anthem and drove into the heart of the valley, a dull cloud of smog hung in the skyline before us.

"Look at that layer of smog!" I sighed.

"It will be worse in a few months when all the snowbirds return, and the temperature drops," Lake added.

"Wish we could have waited until then," I replied.

"Yeah, but it's our pictures and coverage that count the most. You think we're making a difference, babe?" Lake asked, looking out the window as we drove seventy miles an hour down I-17 into the heart of the Blob.

"Absolutely. This is going to be a big one, baby. We might just elevate our name here. You scared?" I asked.

"Yep," Lake responded.

"Me too." I took the Camelback Road exit and headed west.

Marriott Suites at the corner of Camelback and 24th Street was a good central location in Phoenix. We could get to any of our banner hangings within forty-five minutes from here. We were going to spend a lot of money on this one. Parking the VW and getting out our necessary bags, we walked to the office.

"I'm looking forward to getting this done," Lake said. She took the lead across the parking lot.

"Believe me, I can't wait." I hurried to get the door for Lake. Chivalry was still alive.

Now, it was time to check into the Marriott and blend in with the rest of the folks.

Chapter Thirty-Five

A TWO-ROOM SUITE, cable, mini bar, nice big shower with all the amenities, even a phone next to the John. We wouldn't see this for a while, unless we stopped at La Posada when we headed north again. It was looking more likely that La Posada, our favorite hotel on earth, would have to wait. Money always goes quicker than one thinks it will.

"Okay, tomorrow we scout?" I asked.

"Tonight we party!" Lake stated.

"Baby, we have some planning to do."

"Our banners are done, we've got the numbers for the reporters Gus gave us, as well as his buddy at the Scottsdale Airpark. We're set," Lake said, ready to head out for some real Mexican food. The kind we hadn't had in the decade we'd been living in Missouri.

"Well, what about the MrGreenJeans.net people, for one?" I responded.

"So, take the laptop with us."

"I'm waiting for Gus to call and give me the okay," I said.

"We'll turn on the phone. It will be okay." Lake was putting on chapstick, a sure sign she was almost out the door.

"You know, you're right. There's nothing more for me to do tonight. I'm still an infant. I'm a baby. I need to suckle, honey," I responded moving in for a kiss.

"Goo, Goo, Gah, Gah, let's go. Suckling can happen later." Lake grabbed the keycard.

Taking a left onto a dirt track off of Camelback Road we wandered through towering palms for two hundred yards before we arrived at the Monastery, a very unique bar and restaurant. It was stuck back in a grove of palms in the middle of prime Paradise Valley real estate. Paradise Valley is one of the oldest and richest burros of Phoenix metro, and it encircled Camelback Mountain. It was amazing the Monastery had resisted the temptation to sell, with prices for land at an all-time high just a few years ago. It was a hidden jewel. Word was that it was owned by an old Arizona native, who purchased it in the 50's. It was paid for, the revenue from the business was enough to pay the exorbitant taxes, and the owner was fine with that. Who knows if that was true? But it was still here. Kudos to the owner for not selling out. Now, it was time to devour some real Mexican food.

The waiters wore monk attire, a long brown hooded gown. This was no meat market bar; it was a sanctuary, a getaway from the noise of the city. We couldn't believe the place had survived, surrounded by multimillion-dollar homes in every direction. But you wouldn't know it if you were here. It was an oasis. We found a table on the outside patio, which had an eclectic assortment of chairs, tables, church pews, and was completely surrounded by enormous, bottomless planters containing ocotillos, saguaros, prickly pear and many other varieties of cacti. You could barely hear the hum of traffic from the city just a hundred yards off through the palms.

After an hour and three baskets of chips with fresh guacamole, a half dozen veggie tacos, and a margarita, I turned on the laptop. Message alert. Gus wrote, "All cool with MrGreenJeans.net. Seems its bunch of desert rats haven't caused too much commotion, but you never know. It only takes one, Jack. Good luck, my *compadres*. God Speed, and be careful. Big brother is surely sneaking around somewhere!" The next email was from MrGreenJeans.net. They wanted to meet tonight. I zipped back an email confirming the meeting.

"Baby, we need to go right now," I said as I closed the laptop.

"What? What's going on?" Lake asked, dipping a chip in the last of the guacamole.

"I'll tell you in the car."

Thirty minutes later, I pulled into Piestewa Peak Desert Preserve in the heart of Phoenix. Formally named Squaw Peak, but changed to be more politically correct. It was now named after a Tuba City, Arizona Native American soldier who lost her life in Desert Storm. Driving with the lights off, we crept along the two-lane blacktop through the desert preserve until we reached the locked gate to the parking lot. I turned the VW around and parked on the other side of the road a few yards down from the gate. I hoped we wouldn't be long. I was sure a regular patrol passed throughout the night. This was the most popular hiking spot in Phoenix. If you wanted a good view of the madness that is Phoenix, an hour-and-a-half hike to the top of Piestewa Peak offered a spectacular view in every direction.

"Jack, I don't like this," Lake said, trying to focus while she waited for her night vision to kick in. I turned on my headlamp and scanned the desert as we made our way around the gate and onto the large parking area that would be completely full by six a.m. tomorrow morning.

"I don't either. But Gus said he couldn't find anything to give him a warning flag about these people, and we can't do this job by ourselves," I said, looking into the desert watching for anything that moved.

"I think he gave us an educated guess, Jack. We're supposed to be meeting a guy that calls himself Groundhog. I really don't like this. Let's just leave, scale down and do this ourselves. What was that?!" Lake said, grabbing my hand. We both saw something moving in the arroyo to the right of us.

"Hello," I whispered into the darkness. It was a quarter moon tonight and hard to see more than a few feet ahead. I turned my headlamp toward the arroyo. There was more movement and then a pair of eyes.

"You see it?" Lake grabbed my arm. She wasn't scared of animals. Lake was a veteran desert camper. People are what scared her. Me too.

"A coyote. They're all over the place. I know people who used to see them downtown in the morning waiting for the street light to turn green before crossing."

"Turn off the light," a voice whispered from behind us.

We turned to see a huge figure standing next to a Palo Verde. He must have been six five.

"Groundhog?" I asked as my headlamp illuminated him against the tree. He looked like he could have crawled out of a hole. He was filthy, long beard, worn-out hiking boots, and overalls. He wore a big silver watch and one of those embroidered skullcaps you get from Southeast Asia. He was somewhere between forty and sixty years old. It was hard to tell.

"Turn off the light," he said again with more emphasis this time.

I turned off my headlamp and he started toward us. Lake held tight to my arm. I straightened up and used the Blowfish tactic of making myself look bigger by pushing out my chest. It probably didn't work so well.

"I'm Groundhog. Behind you is Jumping Mouse and off in the desert is Cactus Wren."

I turned to see a smaller figure appear from the arroyo.

"Hi," Jumping Mouse whispered, half out of the arroyo.

"Hi, nice to have the desert fauna here to greet us. I'm Prickly Pear and this is Little Cholla," replying impromptu and continuing to puff out my chest.

"Funny." But Groundhog wasn't laughing, and he walked within three feet of us and stopped. He was burly, and the spider web of creases on his face could only come from living under desert sun. He smelled like a mesquite campfire. "We really like what you're doing. We're here to help." Groundhog held out his hand.

I returned his gesture and shook. His hands were like one big callous. We paused, I look around to see if Jumping Mouse was still there. And who the hell was Cactus Wren, and where was he or she? This was definitely something my mother wouldn't hear about.

"Great. So, you're the ones who put up MrGreenJeans.net?" Lake asked, still holding my arm.

"My lady did that. She's of the digital era. She'll be helping with the banner hanging too. So, did you bring a list?" Groundhog asked.

"Yeah. Look, we want to remain as anonymous as possible. We really don't want to meet with anyone but you," I said relaxing my chest.

"You bet. We don't want any unnecessary attention either. Just make the drop at Papago Park, tomorrow at 2:00, and we'll do the rest," Groundhog replied, and I handed him a folded piece of paper from my back pocket.

"It's a partial list. I'll bring the full list when we deliver the banners," I said as Groundhog stuffed the paper into his pocket.

"That'll do. The Mother thanks you. Mr. and Mrs. Green Jeans, it's been an honor," Groundhog said, and he began walking off into the desert.

We turned to the arroyo. Jumping Mouse had disappeared.

"Hey," Groundhog said from the darkness, "after we're done putting up the signs, we're doing a round-up out north of here. Take the highway through Fountain Hills to Payson, go to Sugarloaf Mountain, just after mile marker 131—you'll see a dirt track—take a left, park at the end of the road and walk a mile due northeast." The song of a cactus wren, which I knew well, sung a short verse, followed by a coyote yipping. Both were fakes. This was weird, after spending the last decade in Missouri, I'd forgotten how far-out people can be, and I missed it.

"Okay," I answered, but there was no reply.

"Prickly Pear? Little Cholla?" Lake said, grabbing my hand and leading us back to our VW.

"Pretty good, huh?"

"Not bad."

Back at the hotel, we both tossed and turned all night. Waking up a little past seven, we showered and ate with the other guests at the free breakfast in the lobby. All the stale bagels, tasteless fruit and instant oatmeal we wanted. Spreading cream cheese with a plastic knife onto a multigrain bagel, I checked my emails.

"Hey, Groundhog wrote," I said, as Lake stirred her instant cinnamon-and-raisin oatmeal. She was still trying to go vegan. Pretty tough to do on the road.

"Let's hear it."

"Switch the drop point to the end of Fortieth Street. Back side of the peak. Same day. Same time. Sorry for the change. Security. G.H."

"What do you think that's about?" Lake asked.

"Don't know. Have to trust now," I replied.

"Trust? Love many, trust few, was what my father used to say. I don't know, baby."

"Sometimes you have to do the opposite, I guess. I've been scared since we got to Phoenix," I said putting my hand on Lake's face and giving her a kiss across the small glass top table.

"I guess some of that's just being here. The energy in this city is intense. I remember living here and many times feeling nervous for no discernable reason," I added.

"Bad *juju* in this valley," Lake agreed.

"What do you expect from a place that takes and doesn't give?" I said and finished the last bite of my bagel.

"I expect it's time is ticking away," Lake said getting up to throw away her Styrofoam bowl and plastic spoon, which gave her pause.

"Tick-tock, let's go Prickly!" She said ready to start our first day of reconnaissance.

"I'll give you some prickly."

"No Cholla till we leave Phoenix"

"Love you, baby."

"I love you, too. Let's go"

"Right behind you, Mrs. Green Jeans."

"Sshhh! That was stupid."

"I just got excited when you said Cholla."

"You are such a guy."

"Yep."

Chapter Thirty-Six

FIRST STOP WAS SCOTTSDALE'S AIRPARK. Gus had a friend here from his days in Vietnam. He flew charter for the rich. We were news now, and even though he was Gus' friend our nerves were on high alert. Groundhog's menagerie was unsettling enough.

"I'm looking for Ham?" I said to dark-tanned teen sitting behind the small terminal's reception counter. He was texting two girlfriends at one time, trying not to get busted.

"What?" said the dark-tanned kid with a pimple the size of an acorn on his chin.

"Looking for Ham?" I repeated.

The kid got on a Motorola walkie-talkie.

"Ham, you out there?" the kid said into the Motorola and gave us a once over while he waited for a reply.

"What's up, pimple chin?" replied Ham through the walkie-talkie.

"Funny. Somebody here to see you."

"Be there in a minute. Pop that thing before I get there." A laugh could be heard coming from the talkie.

"You hear?" the kid said, getting back to his texting.

"He was hard on you, dude," I said, looking over at Lake with a smile.

"He's a freak, pulls down a load of cash, did pull down a load of cash. Times have changed, they tell me. Anyway, he's a freak. Good pilot, though." A few minutes passed, the kid furiously texted, and I thought better before I poured a cup of stale coffee from a pot that obviously hadn't been updated since early that morning.

The back door behind the counter opened, and in walked a guy who was definitely a friend of Gus's. Ham was five-foot-eight, stocky, had a well-groomed goatee and a ruby earring. All Gus's far-out characters looked like they had flown under the radar for years. We were beginning to realize we had entered another world. Almost everyone that was any help to us was odd in some way. Maybe I'd have to get a tattoo to fit in better.

"Hey folks, what can I do you for?" Ham said offering his hand.

"Gus said to look you up," I responded, and Ham's customer smile turned into a wide grin and the beginnings of a laugh.

"Follow me folks. Let's take a look at the birds. Peter, you'll pass that puss soon. Don't worry, we all went through it. Right this way guys," Ham said, holding open the back door that led to one of many hangers.

"Up yours Ham," Peter responded.

Walking through the open-door hanger, we followed Ham past a few single props. Ham turned and faced us.

"Mr. Green Jeans?" Ham asked.

"Mr. and Mrs.," Lake corrected.

"Right on. Gus is impressed with you two."

"We really appreciate all he's done for us," I replied.

"He never sold out, not really. Not as much as I have. I've been chartering these rich bastards for too many years. I think the hole in my heart is just about complete."

"You gotta do what you gotta do," Lake said, knowing it was just something people said, but didn't necessarily believe.

"No, you don't. Let's go check out the aviary," Ham replied walking out of the hangar and onto the tarmac.

There were six helicopters, and a wide assortment of two-winged birds, single and double props and a long row of lyre jets. This was the parking lot of the wealthy. It was a gorgeous day, about 85 with blue, smoggish skies.

"Let's talk price first," Lake said.

"This one's on me. Weird thing is, I need this as much as you need me. This town is a black hole. If I had brass balls, I'd be blowing up the dams to the north. Take away the life stream of this place. A typical human in this valley uses more water brushing his teeth in a year than the average yearly rainfall. You feeling me?"

"We feel you. And we thank you. We want to drop a bunch of flyers, trail some banners and have some skywriting. We're happy to pay for all of this, really."

"I'm telling you, it's on me," Ham said while he walked to a bank of dual props.

"You're going to get in trouble for this," Lake said

"I've got that covered. Look, Gus is the man. I flew the bird, he had his Nikon, and we kept each other sane over there. So, when's the explosion?" Ham asked.

"Day after tomorrow, during morning rush hour," I answered.

"Can't drop anything over the freeway. I don't want to cause any accidents," Ham said with some concern.

"No, no highways," I qualified.

"Okay, Look, I'm quitting here anyway. So this is balls out!" Ham said.

"What?" Lake asked.

"I got a bankroll honey; this valley has been burning my belly for years, so bad I'll turn into a worse cantankerous old ass than I already am if I don't get out. You guys were just the medicine I needed. They might come after me, and right now I could do with a little chasing. See, sometimes you need someone to chase you before you get your act in gear and do something," Ham said, walking toward a 3500 Corvalis Cessna, single-engine prop, a beauty.

"But we don't want you getting into any trouble," Lake responded.

"What do you think is going to happen if someone does what you want done? Homeland security ain't no joke here," Ham countered again.

"Nothing happened to the pilots in Missouri. It was all for hire," I said.

"That's because it was Missouri and not Phoenix. It was also because no one knew who you were then. That's all changed now. You two are a show, and people want to know the names of the actors. Look, I'll take care of the details. Tomorrow, what do you say you follow me to this place in the desert where we can cook dinner and spend some time in the glorious Sonaron before all our lives change?"

"Yeah, okay," I answered looking at Lake.

"Actually, that would be nice," Lake added. She was already getting worn out being in the city after just a day.

"Okay then, Mr. and Mrs. Green Jeans, it has been my pleasure. Be here at 5:00."

"Can we bring anything?" Lake asked.

"A bag of ice and plan on staying. You need some time on the desert floor under the stars before game day," Ham said and continued toward the terminal and Chin Zit.

"Thanks Ham," I said, and Ham waved his hand up over his head but didn't turn. We walked to the van.

"You feel good about going out there?" I asked Lake.

"Yeah. He seems committed," Lake replied, nearing the van. We were off to scout the Valley of the Sun. We had thirty banners to hang. That is a lot of places to locate.

The rest of the day we spent driving from one target to the next making sure we could get in and out easily. Lake had purchased five dozen Amazing Putty tubes, advertised to hold almost anything to any surface. We tried it out in the Malpais, sticking a hundred foot banner from the lip of a lava tube. Winds at thirty MPH, it held steady. Amazing Putty would soon be worth its weight in gold. We also purchased medium-gauge wire for the banners above overpasses.

"Let's hope the Desert Gods are full of benevolence two days from now," Lake said as we pulled into the Marriott parking lot about seven o'clock that evening, having completed our search for targets. Tomorrow we'd run the route again and double check driving times between targets. The opening game of the Eco World Series was about to begin.

Chapter Thirty-Seven

IT WAS THE EVE of the Phoenix hanging. Before meeting Ham, we needed to make the drop to Groundhog. Pulling into a dirt parking lot at the back side of the Piestewa Peak, a number of cars were scattered about, their owners out walking, running or biking. We drove to the back of the parking area and parked behind two large Ocotillos. A few minutes later an '83, blue, four-wheel-drive Ford pickup slid in beside us. It was Groundhog and a gentle-looking, dark-haired woman, who was sitting in the passenger seat. I rolled down the window.

"Hey," I said looking around the parking area for anything suspicious.

"We set?"

"Yep. I've got the final list. You think you can handle 16 banners?"

"We sure can," The woman next to Groundhog spoke up.

"This is Cactus Wren," Groundhog said with an adoring glance.

"Nice to meet you," Lake replied.

"Let's do it," I said, getting out of the VW.

Opening up the back of the van we began pulling out the rolled-up banners and handing them to Groundhog and Cactus Wren. We placed them in the bed of the pickup, and Groundhog covered them with a black tarp.

"Here's some adhesive. It works really well. And two rolls of wire for the banners above any car traffic. Holes are already cut in those banners for quick installation," Lake said, handing Cactus Wren a small box of Amazing Putty and two rolls of wire.

"Excellent. We going to see you guys at the round-up?" Groundhog asked securing the tarp.

"We're going to try and make it." I closed the VW hatch.

"I hope so; you two have a lot of fans," Cactus Wren said adjusting the tarp.

"I wrote the times next to each banner. It's really important that they're up at those times because we have reporters we're going to be contacting throughout the morning. If we don't get the coverage, all this is in vain. You comfortable with that?"

"We'll have them up."

"Thanks." I handed Groundhog the list and shook his calloused hand.

"Yeah, thank you so much!" Lake held out her hand too, and we all shook and got back into our vehicles and drove off.

"That was a weird experience," Lake said as we drove to meet Ham.

"What hasn't been lately?"

Two hours later, we picked up three veggie subs at an independent sub shop I used to patronize regularly when living here. Then, we met Ham at the airport and followed him through Carefree, a small town west of Phoenix, and out into the desert. We drove down a dirt path through a maze of Saguaros that stood like watchdogs. We stopped in a small clearing and set up camp.

"I think you folks were a bit impetuous when you started. I understand this quality well. I signed up for Vietnam because I was impetuous. From what I understand about your exploits to date, you two are taking a peaceful track, and that is key. What you put out is what you get back," Ham said, sitting down against the giant saguaro.

"Yeah, we hope so." I responded, noticing Ham had just sat down and leaned his back against a saguaro.

"If you are starting fires all over the place, chances are you're going to get burned too. Granted, what you're doing is not killing or destroying, but in a way it's more powerful. Do it with respect and you will get respect. Respect will get you numbers, and there are people out there that don't want those kinds of numbers rearing up on them. Follow?" Ham gave us each a deep stare.

"Doesn't that hurt?" I asked, sitting next to Lake in our aluminum foldout chairs.

"Let me show you something." Ham took off his shirt and sat back down against the cactus.

"See I just feel the lady and become part of her. Give it shot," Ham said, offering the bait.

Taking off my T-shirt, I got up and carefully sat down at the base of a thirty-foot, two-inched needled, spring-green, trunk of beauty and long lost stories. Slowly feeling the groove of the needles, I cautiously laid back vertebra by vertebra until I was supported.

"Bonnie, your cactus awaits," I said.

"Cactus awaits! I love it!" Ham said quickly getting up and taking a jug out of his cooler and, without any hesitation, sitting back down against the Saguaro.

Lake walked over to one five feet from me and with shocking brevity found her backrest. A smile appeared on every face. The connection had been made. The truth of what we were doing came down to this in so many ways, sitting up against the giants of the desert. Making the connection.

"See a man, a person, can't expect to live out their life in peace if something is dogging 'em day in and day out, and they don't do something about it. It's a crying shame to look back on your life and realize all you've done is put out fires. But that's what we do, most of us. That's all we do most of the time. Deal with the dogs, deal with the dogs! Deal with the dogs. I ain't talking about Nam. Let's get that clear. See, the breath slowly gets taken out of a person as life passes, in the worst cases, that's all a person does anymore, breathe. I'd say we're breathing mighty fine right now, wouldn't you say? Little celebration, huh? Cause we have a cause, and we're doing something about it, not just yakking away! Here, take a drink of this." Ham tossed the jug to me.

"What is it?" I asked, barely catching the plastic jug as I tried to keep my back motionless against the cactus.

"Green tea with honey. I brewed it yesterday. Since I stopped drinking, that's my go-to beverage."

"Nice." I took a swig and tossed it to Lake, who caught it with no problem.

"Now, mise well tell ya. Tomorrow is my last day in the good ole USA."

"What?" Lake said after taking another drink of the tea.

"Well, since I stopped drinking 295 days ago, my head cleared up, and I realized there's better places for me to be."

"Where are you going?" Lake and I both asked in unison. We did that often.

"Guatemala!" He filled us in on his plans to leave the country and become an Expat. He was done and this would take him out in style.

After finishing our veggie sub sandwiches, we filled Ham in on what we wanted written in the sky. We gave him the banners to trail and told him where to drop the flyers. It was ten o'clock. The stars were in full bloom, and the full moon cast its glow across the Sonoran gatekeepers. The three of us made our respective nests.

The silhouette of the saguaros and a thousand sparkles sucked Lake and me back into memories of years past before moving to Missouri. Snuggled in our zipped-together bags, alarm clock set, we were feeling the sensuality. Ham lay just thirty feet away, atop a sleeping pad covered with an old Pendleton wool blanket. A gentle-but-constant snore filled the air. Lake and I made silent love and then drifted off for three hours of sleep. Tomorrow was going to be one of the best days of our lives, or the worst.

Chapter Thirty-Eight

"HAM, WE'RE LEAVING." I gently shook his shoulder. Slowly his eyes opened, and he smiled up at me.

"Jack, it is Farewell Day." This was going to be Ham's last day as a charter pilot. Last day as a resident of the U.S.A. He'd told us that Guatemala had always been one of his favorite places. The tropical weather and cheap living, it was a great place to get lost. It seemed perfect for Hamlin.

"Yeah, big day." I stared into Ham's eyes. Lake was sitting in the VW checking for any phone messages.

"About time. It is about time. Don't think I could take another day of seeing this sacred land being raped. It's literally been giving me hives for years now." Ham was up and threw his bedding in the back of his suburban.

"We should be through by six, and then it's all you."

"I want to say, you two have balls, big earth balls, and whatever happens, this is one of those I'd do it again moments before we've even done it. Follow me?"

"Shazam!" I replied.

"Shazam! Good way to sum it up."

"Jack! Gus left a message and said MrGreenJeans.net let the cat out of the bag. He said they posted an alert to watch for the Phoenix banners. Oh my God!" Lake was out of the van and pacing.

"I don't think it was Groundhog. He was already worried about something, that's why he changed the drop-off location."

"So?" Lake was sitting.

"So? We go for it, it's not like it's on the morning news. Right? We can't turn back now."

"Jack's right. But after today, that would be a big ole caution flag, follow?" Ham said as he put some fair trade, Guatemalan beans with his manually -operated coffee grinder.

"Let's go, okay." Lake was all business right now and quickly went to say goodbye to Ham.

"Ohhhh, that's a good hug, sweetheart," Ham said as Lake gave him one of her famous deep warm hugs. You two stop by Guatemala and ask for Ham. It ain't that big a place." Ham smiled and put a peace sign to his lips, took it down to his heart and then blew it to us.

Lake climbed into the driver's seat, and we were off down the dirt track through the Sonoran Desert, headlights leading the way, on the lookout for Jack rabbits, Gila Monsters, and diamondbacks. It was one a.m., and the desert was alive. We were very cautious not to run anything over.

Back on the blacktop, I sorted through the banners. We had fourteen to put up and Groundhog had taken the other sixteen for his people. I got on the phone and rang the first of Gus's reporter contacts. It was on, but if there was ever a time to turn back, it was now.

"This guy said he was going to be there," I said after making the first of many calls today.

"Okay," Lake replied, keeping her eyes on the road.

"If we get caught today, I want you to blame everything on me."

"Shut-up. We're not getting caught. Don't say that again," Lake said, turning around and popping me on the head as I went through the banners.

The Fountain Hills upscale residential development took off in '80's. It was north of Phoenix and bordered Scottsdale. We turned into the main entrance, a cannon of water intermittently shot up fifty feet from the center of a small, man-made pond a few yards to our right. There was nothing aesthetic about it; it was a pipe sticking up in the middle of a mundane pond of water that was supposed to let everyone know they had arrived at the beautiful Fountain Hills. It was an unnecessary waste of our most precious resource. Good symbolism and target one.

As with almost all communities in the Valley, a prominent entrance was an important feature, often times with water. Fountain Hills had a fourteen-foot arch that went over the main entrance. I took the extension ladder off the van. It was dark, my headlamp lit the way. Lake held the bottom steady as I climbed up with the banner over my shoulder and a tube of 'Amazing Putty' in my back pocket. My right foot still touching the top rung, I swung my left leg over the top of the foot wide arch until I was sitting upright.

"There's a tingle between my legs, baby."

"I know there is, be careful."

"Whoa, this is intense," I said, trying not to look down. I hated heights.

"Just hold on. If you have to come down, we'll scrap it," Lake said in a loud whisper as we weren't far off from a house in this upscale community of consumption.

"I got it." I slid my way across the arch, adhering the banner as I went. Topping the apex, I swear I felt a drop might pee exit.

Reaching the opposite end of the arch, I applied the last glob of putty. Something caught Lake's attention as she was moving the ladder to the other end of the arch.

"Jack, someone's coming" Lake whispered. I hurried to position myself on the ladder.

"Hold the ladder," I said.

I scrambled to get my footing on the ladder, almost slipping halfway down and then jumping off four rungs up from the ground.

Sure enough, an early a.m. walker was headed our way. I pulled down the ladder and quickly attached it on the rack with a few bungees. Lake already had the VW humming as I jumped in the passenger side and slammed the door.

'Whoa, Danny boy!" I exhaled with heavy breathing.

"Nice start to the day!" Lake snapped a picture and then was pedal to the metal.

The early morning walker, an older man wearing a baseball cap passed under the arch looked up. He got out his cell phone and took a picture.

Draped across the top of the pink arch covering the Fountain Hills bronze letters, hung our first words of the day.

EXCESS LEADS TO DEATH—STOP STEALING THE WATER THAT BELONGS SOMEWHERE ELSE! TURN OFF THAT RIDICULOUS FOUNTAIN!
MR. GREEN JEANS

We hoped the reporter I called would arrive before the Fountain Hills maintenance was able to remove the banner. I made calls to three more reporters about the next targets. Groundhog had better have his people following the correct order of display. It was all about timing. Get the banner up, and the reporter would arrive as the hangers left, hopefully before it was taken down. Next stop, Scottsdale.

Scrump Ranch Country Club was our next hit. Good size money around these parts. A golf course is a beautiful sight, and here in the valley, there were over a hundred and fifty eighteen-hole courses and many more nine-hole, three-par courses attached to apartment complexes and even trailer parks. However, if you knew what went into making and maintaining these oases in the desert, the beauty disappeared.

It was now 2:30 a.m. Parking the VW on a side street off Scrump Parkway, lined with half million- to ten-million-dollar homes, I pulled out the correct banner and slung it over my shoulder. We ran down the side street, then up Scrump Parkway to the entrance of the country club. We had picked a line of palms that fronted the entrance to the two-hundred-and-fifty-dollar, green-fee course. Amazing putty on all four corners and up it went, much quicker than the first one. Then we ran. This one would get some good face time. It couldn't be missed if you were driving down the Parkway.

TWENTY TONS OF HERBICIDE, FORTY TONS OF PESTICIDE, 90 MILLION GALLONS OF WATER

EVERY YEAR. DOES ANY OF THIS MAKE ANY SENSE IN THE DESERT?
FOUR!!!!!!!!!!!
MR. GREEN JEANS

Lake took a few pictures as we drove by. After we were done with all fourteen, we'd upload them to Gus and Frankie in Zuni. It was all about the publicity. Most people would never see more than one or two banners at best, but they would live on digitally forever.

We successfully did another golf course just a few miles away with the same words and now headed to the freeway overpasses. These were going to be tricky, but there was no doubt the viewership was guaranteed.

Unknown to us, Groundhog and his crew had already put up ten banners without a glitch. Eight over freeway passes in Chandler, Gilbert, Mesa, Phoenix proper, and another two at the entrances to the South Mountain Preserve, one of the largest desert preserves in the city. This was definitely one of our favorites, but logistics didn't allow us to be the hangers.

ENJOY YOUR WALK—WHEN YOU LEAVE DON'T FORGET ME—I AM PART OF YOU—WE ARE BOTH FRAGILE—WHEN I AM HURT I OFTEN DON'T RECOVER HAVE YOU EVER FELT THIS TYPE OF PAIN?
THE DESERT'S VOICE
MR. GREEN JEANS

Marnie Tyden, one of Gus's oldest friends, a veteran environmentalist, had promised her twenty-two-year-old videographer a two-night stay in a Sedona B and B with his girlfriend, if he would get up early and tromp around the valley with her. He was glad he did. He realized this was something he'd probably never see again. This was one of the reasons he had chosen to do this work in the first place.

"This is wild," The young videographer stated panning across the banner.

"Like the old times, little marshmallow," Marnie stated, as she directed her young videographer.

Ham arrived at the airport about 4:00 a.m. The sun would start to rise in an hour. He needed the time to set the banners in the runners and have an easy take off before anyone important arrived at the airfield. He also had to get the sky-writing device filled and mounted on his biplane. Ham wouldn't begin until he got the call from me, and that was hours away. His involvement was the riskiest because word would be out that Mr. Green Jeans was in Phoenix. Ham expected a prompt response to his participation. He would probably only receive a fine or two if his record had been clean. It wasn't clean. He had a few FAA violations for flying too low. Now his dream of banana trees and warm salty water was simply common sense.

At the Lincoln Boulevard overpass on the Piestewa Peak Freeway, Lake and I ran along a narrow sidewalk and began to lay out a banner. All the banners that were placed above the freeways had holes that we would string wire through and then secure around the railings next to the sidewalk. We did not want any of these banners falling into traffic.

We were beginning to drape it over the rail when a car stopped in the opposing lane of the overpass. The window rolled down.

"Hey, what are you guys doing?" a young guy wearing a Paradise Valley Mall security uniform spoke with all the authority he could muster.

"Promotions for the Macy Sale at Metro Mall." We had practiced this shtick just in case.

"So you got permission to hang on public property?" he lighted a Marlboro light and waited for an answer.

"We went through a training class yesterday on safety and were given our locations. We have to come back and take them down tonight." I hoped he wouldn't get out of his car and see what the banner said.

"What a job. Pay well?" the guy was always looking for an easy way to make a buck.

"Two hundred each for the day," Lake stated, holding the canvas so he couldn't read it.

"That's some change. I'll have to give Macy's a call. Watch for traffic now. Crazy people out this time day." The mall cop was off and taking the ramp onto the freeway that would give him a rear-view shot of the banner. We quickly wired it to the railing. From the overpass, we watched his car merged onto the freeway. His brake lights flashed, and then he pulled over to the shoulder. He got out of his car, cigarette dangling and looked up at the banner. He read it, took a picture with his cell phone, got back in his car and took off. We ran to our VW double parked a few yards away and peeled off to our last target.

"Oh my God, was it this crazy in Kansas City, babe?"

"No, I wasn't dealing with freeway overpasses. These things suck," I said, looking in the rear-view mirror.

"Want to skip the last one?"

"Absolutely not." Nobody was following us, as I kept checking the rear-view mirror.

"Alrighty, let's go Clyde." Lake replied. She must be feeling the same rush I was. We were super-heroes right now. I eased on the gas, and we peacefully rolled down Lincoln Blvd. On the Piestewa Freeway, early-morning commuters and late-night bar hoppers streamed past our words.

WHEN THE EARTH BLEEDS—WE BLEED—
SO WHAT ARE YOU GOING TO DO?
MR. GREEN JEANS

Most of the signs were painted with our brown earth background and bright green letters. Soil and growth meet. A few though, had wild-colored backgrounds with white letters. If Groundhog's crew was sailing, all thirty signs would be displayed soon. Maybe this wouldn't change a thing, but we had hooked ourselves in now, more so than we knew. The wireless world was humming our message as we breathed. There were concerned parties taking notice since we had made national news, and unknown to us, our Phoenix outing was going to call them into action. We were overstepping our role as consumers, and for some companies this was a threat. Ham was just a few hours away from taking off. When the cake was done, he would provide the icing.

Chapter Thirty-Nine

CAMELBACK MOUNTAIN springs from the desert floor with its double-humped, monolithic, sandstone outcroppings in the heart of Paradise Valley. It was the target of our last four banners. Backing the VW into a space at the trailhead parking lot, we were surprised to see so many cars already here. It was four thirty in the morning. It took about an hour to reach the top and catch the sunrise over the Phoenix valley, so I guess it made sense. It just seemed awful early for city folks, but many in the city didn't come from the city, and getting up early to hike and watch the sunrise was essential to their well-being.

It was obvious we were up to something carrying two banners apiece slung over our shoulders, but this was our final installment, and we figured anyone we passed was either concentrating on getting up or looking forward to getting down. We were right. A dozen or more people passed us on the way up, but no one said a word, they were focused on their destination, no time to question the strange couple carrying large rolls of canvas.

An hour later, we stopped a hundred yards before the trail ended at the top. Here we separated and went off trail, both heading to opposite sides of the rock-rimmed peak.

"Get it done and get down, okay baby?"

"You got the hard side. Be careful Clyde."

"Love you."

"Love you, too." I was off with my two banners draped across my back.

Maneuvering through the strewn-about, sandstone boulders, we both hurried to get our last job done and reunite. Out of sight, successful hikers sat above us waiting to take in the sunrise. The sun's rays would envelope the valley floor, up over the skyscrapers downtown and spread west up and over Camelback. It was a painting that happened every day. Lake laid her first canvas on the ground and continued walking with the second around more boulders. She was careful to stay hidden from any onlookers peering over the edge.

As she reached what she calculated to be the starting point for the first of her two canvases, she pulled a new tube of putty from her pocket and climbed up a rounded, sandstone boulder with the banner draped over her shoulder. She scaled the 20-degree course, grit curve of sandstone, like a spider keeping her center of gravity close to the rock. Putty applied to the first two ends, she pressed the canvas to the rock and then jumped to the next boulder with the remaining sixty feet in hand, allowing enough slack so the banner wouldn't pull off from the rock where she had just applied the putty. She used more putty, and with another jump, the far end of her first sign was secured. One more to go. She slid down the sandstone and picked up the second banner. Then she heard footsteps behind her.

"Can I help you?" A woman about Lake's age, platinum-blond, wearing top-of-the-line boots, scientifically designed synthetic shorts, a shirt for best wick and comfort in the climate, and a chartreuse bandanna around her neck stood looking at Lake.

"What!?" Lake slung the second canvas over her shoulder.

"I'm Brenda and I'd like to help you. I saw you on the way up here and wondered about that long roll of canvas you were carrying. See, we passed a sign on I-17 on our way here.

WHAT YOU HAVE COMES FROM ME—I'M NOT INFINITE—THERE'S ONLY SO MUCH OF ME LEFT—TREAD GENTLY
MR. GREEN JEANS

I just think what you're doing is lovely and I really want to help," Brenda stated, standing at attention and attempting her best Botox smile.

Lake was speechless.

"Please," Brenda, a frustrated homemaker, degree from Williams and Mary never put to use, stood in awe staring at Lake.

"You're serious?" Lake asked as she took out another tube of putty from her pocket.

"Dead serious. You're one of the Mr. Green Jeans people, aren't you?"

"Yeah," Lake admitted, knowing it was of no use to lie at this point, and even proud of her newly developed persona.

"Yes! I knew it!!" Brenda said, adjusting her bandanna.

"Okay, take this end and stretch it out as soon as I get into place up here."

Lake scaled the boulder, applied some adhesive to her end of the canvas, pressed it down and Brenda carefully navigated the uneven ground as she unrolled the canvas along the way. Standing tippy toe and sticking down the lower right corner to the rock. Lake made her way across three boulders separating herself from Brenda, adhering the top of the banner as she went until she reached the end. Stepping back Brenda gazed at the virgin slogan.

> THE EARTH HAS A DIS-EASE—IT IS US!—
> EITHER WE CHANGE OUR WAYS NOW
> OR
> THE EARTH WILL CHANGE THAT FOR US
> MR. GREEN JEANS

"I love it! I really love it!" Brenda exclaimed.

"Thanks. I gotta get out of here." Lake jumped down from the boulder, grabbed her camera and took the best picture she could of the banners and then began walking away.

"Hey, you really believe we are in the last days?" Brenda asked.

"If we don't change, our memories of the past will only be pictures we can look at." Giving the peace sign, Lake vanished around the corner of a large boulder. Brenda took the first civilian picture of the banner and zipped it off to her entire address book. This was how it was happening. The exponential expansion is just what Mr. Green Jeans needed. Within a few hours, Mr. Green Jeans would reach critical mass and within a few days, the headlines across the country and various Western nations would be splashed with our messages.

Reaching the main trail, Lake didn't see me. She checked her watch, she was right on time. She waited five minutes as planned and then headed for the parking lot, a thirty-minute descent. If I was not there she would drive around the other side of Camelback Mountain and hope I had made my way down through a maze of million dollar homes to stand on the corner of Tatum and 47th Street. Plan B. Something had obviously happened. Lake never wanted to split up, but with time running against us, it was the only way to get the job done before sunrise. I was nowhere to be seen at the parking lot, which was now filled to capacity with hikers on their way up the trail. She noticed people pointing up from the parking lot at the newly hung banners

"Kids, Mr. Green Jeans wrote that," said a young man to his two sons as they prepared for the hike.

"Is that who wrote that stuff about the cows?" asked the youngest son.

"Yep."

"Cool, I like him."

Lake looked up at the top of Camelback Mountain. Her placement was grand. It was a clear, sunny morning, and the message could be seen from a long way off. Getting in the VW, she hoped I would be easy to find, hadn't fallen off the mountain, wasn't in need of helicopter rescue.

Driving out of the parking lot and taking a left onto Tatum, she spied two cruisers coming from the opposite direction and slowing to turn into the trailhead parking lot. She hoped she hadn't left too soon, and that I wasn't on the trail, encircled by a group of vigilantes making a citizen's arrest.

"Jack!" Lake said out loud scanning the side of the road.

Coming to the intersection of the 47th and Tatum, there I was, sitting on the curb in front of Hardees eating an egg-and-cheese breakfast burrito and looking up at my handiwork.

"What the hell happened!?" Lake said, pulling into the Hardees parking lot and yelling out the window.

"I got caught. People up there were taking pictures of me and a few told me to stop. I resisted the middle finger. Then a few others were telling those people to leave me alone, that I was part of the Mr. Green Jeans, and that I was doing a good thing. I felt like a rock star."

"Well, you're not. Get in! Because two police cars just went into the parking lot as I pulled out," Lake screamed opening the passenger door.

"Jeez, calm down. I called Ham. He said to tell you *adios.*" I got into the VW still eating my burrito.

"Calm down? You had pictures taken of you, and a woman saw me plain and clear up there. We can be identified, Jack!" She was borderline frantic right now.

"Someone saw you, too!?"

"I'll tell you all about it later. Let's get out of here." Lake pulled out of the parking lot and headed down 47th Street toward Scottsdale.

"We're done, now. We just have to wait for Ham to do his magic in the air. It's going to be all right." I tried to assure her as Hardee's special sauce dripped from my chin.

"We're completely certifiable now." Lake was looking in the rear-view mirror every two seconds.

"Let's just get to Papago Park and watch the finale." I took my final bite of the burrito.

"And why are you eating fast food?!" Lake replied.

"I know, this was wrong."

"It is, but you should have gotten me a cinnamon roll or something."

"Sorry."

Lake's knuckles were turning white as she gripped the wheel, and her eyes didn't leave the rear-view mirror for more than a few seconds at a time.

"Is someone following us?" I asked, realizing I shouldn't feel as calm as I did.

"No. No. Not yet. Do you even realize what we just did today, did since we left our home? Crap, Jack!" Lake exclaimed hitting the steering wheel.

"I don't have the words right now."

"Then howl or something! You're killing me."

"Oooowwwwwwwww!" I shouted out the window.

"That's better."

We sat for a few minutes in silence as Lake concentrated on driving and calming her mind. I was having this conqueror euphoria that I knew wouldn't last, but I wanted to ride it out before some kind of paranoia crash would inevitably arise.

"I want to call home tonight, see how Brien is doing and see if our house is staked out. And we need to call your mother," Lake added, taking a deep breath and still scanning the rear-view.

"Baby, we're fine."

"They took your picture, dammit!" Lake responded, switching emotions and slamming the steering wheel again.

"Right. Well, maybe it didn't show me. I was wearing a hat and sunglasses. Come on, we're fine," I said, looking out the side window.

"Once we finish the big target up north, we're going home." Lake was gripping the wheel, her knuckles still white.

"We'll see," I replied, wishing I hadn't.

"No, we're going home!" Lake made a sharp turn onto the entrance to Papago Park, and I put on my seatbelt.

After a short hike, we sat atop a large, sandstone boulder in Papago Park, a desert reserve that borders the Phoenix Zoo. I called Gus even though he'd ask us not to. Lake was beside herself and hadn't said a word to me since she had declared we were going home soon.

"What's up, *amigo!?*" Gus said from Missouri.

"You tell me," I said, looking over at Lake who wouldn't exchange a glance.

"I'm watching the net right now, and you just made Yahoo's front page. There's a picture of a banner on an overpass in Phoenix. Son, you two are becoming the real deal. How you two doing?"

"No freaking way!?" I turned to Lake. "We're on Yahoo's home page!" Lake turned to look at me. She couldn't help it. A smile and a tear emerged. I took her hand.

"Gus, the fireworks are not over. Your buddy is about to fly over the valley."

"I know. He called me this morning to say goodbye. Jack, we can't talk anymore on the phone. You have a voice, a powerful voice. You want to keep going, or are you done?" Gus didn't mince words; there was no time for that now.

"One more for sure, then I don't know."

"We're not stopping!" Lake exclaimed just as suddenly as she had when she called it quits minutes ago. I loved her, but would she just make up her mind?

"I heard that. I'll get in touch with you today by email. I'm proud to know you guys." Gus hung up.

At the Scottsdale airpark, Ham took off in his Sky-writer and reached midtown Phoenix in five minutes, releasing a continuous green plume of smoke. He turned, banked, looped, straightened, and looped again, writing words in the sky. He wore a big smile. What a stellar way to exit the USA. Straightening out for the fly off, the message stood proud.

THE TIME IS RIGHT NOW!
G. J.

"Wow," I said looking up at Ham's handiwork and still holding Lake's hand.

"Sorry, babe." Lake squeezed my hand.

"No apologies. We're past that, I think. So?"

"Let's go to that round-up."

"Maybe make love in the parking lot first?"

"No."

"Okay."

We sat on the boulder, arms around one another and waited for the last message.

Ham returned to the airpark, knowing his time was limited. His personal plane was ready to go. Guatemala would be his at day's end. Pimple-face ran onto the tarmac as Ham exited the sky-writer.

"Ham, there's two officers here wanting to see you."

"Tell 'em, I'll be right in."

"Are you in trouble?"

"Kid, I want you to remember the only piece of advice I ever give out anymore."

"Okay."

If you can't be yourself, then who are you supposed to be?" Ham tossed the keys to his Suburban at the kid.

"It's yours, titles in the glove box already signed over. See ya, kid. "

With that, Ham turned and walked to his Cessna already filled with all the things he could carry to start his new life south of the border. The banner lay on the ground, hooked up and ready to stream. The kid just watched, not really understanding what was happening, and at the same time he knew his brief acquaintance with Ham was something he was going to remember. He turned to walk back in the office and saw the two blues already running across the tarmac towards Ham.

Ham climbed aboard and started up the twin prop. It was already hot out and no time was needed to warm the engines. He began to taxi down the runway and saw the young blues running after him. Ham knew it might turn out this way, Gus had warned him that Jack and Lake might be trouble, but it was the kind of trouble he missed so dearly.

Thrusting to full-throttle, the wheels left the tarmac. Flying back over the airpark Ham tilted his wings to say 'Hi' to Phoenix's finest below and then sailed off trailing the last banner of the Phoenix mission.

HELP ME—PLEASE—I AM IN SO MUCH PAIN
MOTHER EARTH

Ham made four passes over the metro area from Scottsdale to Tempe to Chandler, and from downtown Phoenix to Paradise Valley. While he did this, he dropped ten thousand notecards with 'The Green Declaration of Dependence' printed in bright green ink on 100% recyclable paper. He threw out a few hundred at a time. He was feeling groovy.

He had been ignoring the blinking red light on his radio indicating a transmission had been coming in minutes after takeoff. A big FAA violation. Off to the West, he saw a helicopter approaching and knew it was time to 'exit stage right' this scene. Banking south, he straightened the plane and headed toward the border, a seven hour flight with just enough fuel to make it. Last year, he had added extra tanks just so he'd be ready when the time finally arrived for him to go. He always had the feeling he would have to leave the US. He was just too out-of-place to make it here anymore. He had just hoped he wouldn't die first. With the helicopter on his tail, he blessed Lake and me, picked up speed, and left the helicopter behind. The copter would have no chance of catching up to him. He only hoped that the Luke Air Force Base wouldn't be called to assist. Homeland security was now loaded with money, and just making it across the border might be the challenge of his life. Outside of the city expansion, he dropped off the radar, flying below observable levels across the desert floor. He knew from other pilots that to cross the border undetected was tricky at best, so he rubbed his first wife's garter belt hanging from the control panel and prayed to God. His first wife was nuts, just like him, and he had loved like no other. He was just too young to know what he had, and divorced her after returning from Nam. Thirty-eight minutes, and he'd reach Mexico. He released the banner from its hook by pulling a lever on the plane's floorboard. He watched it drift slowly towards the desert floor. He'd send the coordinates to Gus when he landed. Gus had told him the banners were prized and he didn't want to drop it and cause an accident over a road way. He picked up more speed and headed due south. He'd make Guatemala today, and tomorrow, he'd vow to do his part to live with the earth and not just on it.

Chapter Forty

WE DROVE BACK through Phoenix, Paradise Valley and Scottsdale and were now headed north passing through Fountain Hills. Passing our first sign, we saw that its demise was seconds away. Two maintenance workers, one holding the ladder and the other ripping our banner from the Fountain Hills arched entrance, made a quick end of our protest.

"Uhh, we did that!" Lake pointed and shouted from the passenger seat.

"Yes, we did, baby!" I said, feeling about as well as I could ever remember feeling. We were done with Phoenix, and it was time to escape. "This outlaw thing is…"

"Making you feel like you're really doing something with your life?" Lake interrupted.

"When you put it that way, yeah. It just feels extremely good, ya know? Yahoo front page, what is that!? I mean, in two hours, tens of millions of people saw our banners!"

"Rags to riches, my dear. And don't say outlaw. We're fighting for nature's law. You got that?"

"Nature cops?" I asked.

'Stewards, baby. We don't want to be cops. We're Mother Loving Stewards."

"Mother Loving Stewards! Yeah, that's what we are! I love you so much."

"If it weren't for you, we wouldn't even be here. I loved you before, and now you're irresistible," Lake said.

"So, let's pull over?"

"Men just have a constant sex stream going on, don't they?"

"Baby, some do. I'm talking about love here."

She put her hand on my crotch. "We'll get to it, lover,"

Taking highway 87 north toward Payson, CD player blasting some Midnight Oil, we drove through the far corner of Sonoran desert where the round-up was planned. We were ready to lay low for a few days. The VW had been doing great. Its four-wheel-drive, raised chassis had cleared all impediments and easily taken us up some pretty hairy terrain so far.

Twenty miles past Fountain Hills after snaking through the boulder-strewn, scenic hills of the higher desert, we turned off just past mile marker 131 onto a dirt road marked with a single drooping, green balloon tied to a grandmother saguaro. Slowly driving for a mile on the rutted dirt track that was lined with fourteen-foot ocotillo soon-to-be-in-bloom, we parked at the road's end. Thirty to forty vehicles of all makes and conditions were parked off the road in the desert. Donning our packs, we hiked a mile following a crystal-clear stream with saguaros, mesquite, Palo Verde, jumping cholla, prickly pear and barrels lining our path. Arriving at a clearing, a hundred people were milling about, setting up tents, a cook site, even a bathroom. After we all left, it was to look like we had never been here.

We were going bare, no disguises, just us. Groundhog saw us, approached, and put his huge long arms around both of us at once. He didn't smell anymore.

"Hoooooooooooo, here they are, my good loves!!!!!!" Groundhog stepped onto a granite boulder and addressed the gathering that looked like a throwback to a Woodstock crowd.

"This, my fellow desperados, is Mr. and Mrs. Green Jeans, part and parcel. They are a celebration walking. Their voice is ours, and ours is theirs. Raise your containers and give a cosmic toast to the best thing to hit this desert since us!" It was just shy of noon, and the party had started.

"Now remember, there are no pictures to be taken. If you haven't turned off your cell phone and given them to Reggie to hold for you, do that now. Anybody takes a picture loses their device. Period. Now, a few words from our sponsor, Mr. and Mrs. Green Jeans!" I took Groundhog's position on the granite boulder.

"Thank you. There's no way we could have ever done this without you guys. This has been a family effort, and we are family." My hands in prayer I bowed to the crowd.

The collection of twenty- to eighty-year-olds erupted. Everyone was beside themselves for the coup attained today. It was a win for the people against the machine. We were truly humbled. These were our people. A collection of misfits who truly cared about the earth. Lake stepped up.

"Well, hello and thank you for making it happen. We are the Stewards!" Lake shouted. A loud howl came from the crowd. Lake had definitely recovered from her previous state. But that's how she was. She wasn't one to let fear take hold for very long.

"Okay, you earth lovers, celebrate and pat each other on the back. Good job today!"

Groundhog shouted over the jeers. Tents and gear were scattered across the ground. Some people were setting up their camps, others soaking in the creek and some were starting a cook station for a big victory meal. Lake joined in at the cook station, and Groundhog and I took a walk.

"How did it go for you guys?" I asked Groundhog as we strolled away from the gathering following the shallow desert stream. We were three-thousand feet above the desert floor and the weather was like spring in the Midwest.

"Well."

"Any photos taken of you guys?"

"Not that I'm aware of. You?"

"Yeah, I think someone got a shot of me on Camelback. I had a hat and glasses, but I don't know."

"I suppose we'll find out soon enough. Look, I know you're worried. This business is fraught with worry. You guys are as high up on the eco-action scale as anyone I've ever known. You're really making a difference and opening up some dialog. We have a few safe places where you can lay low for as long as you need to. There's a good chance you'll need them."

"Thanks. Why your website was compromised?"

"We have a good idea who that was. I confronted him, he denied it, but I know it was him. He's just a lost kid who's been staying with us for the past month or so. He has no family to speak of except our wayward crowd. He didn't know what he was doing. The password's been changed, so it's just me and the Cactus Wren who have access." Groundhog sat down on a boulder a few yards away.

"It's a wild collection of people out here."

"What did you expect? Grassroots, man. You've changed things. We got some donors out there, and if you're in the game, they're ready to help."

"Donors?" I sat down on the ground.

"There's people out there with big money looking for people like us, believe it or not."

"Our finances are good for another six months. We have one more target before we're going to hang low for a while," I said, holding off, not wanting to get any deeper than we were already.

"Can you tell me what the target is?"

"This is our life, you know?" I rearranged myself on the desert floor.

"I know all too well."

"All right. This is meant to shake, rattle and roll 'em for a while." I stood and began to pace.

"I'm all ears."

"Frackzon Corp. and their proposed gondola into the canyon at the confluence of the Little Colorado and Colorado rivers, among other things. It's on native land, but they're putting on the pressure. Some are caving for the promised money. They also have large mining claims adjacent to Native land," I answered, knowing we needed all the help we could get for this one.

"Whoa. I know about them. Frackzon is an international corporation with tentacles in mining and energy across the globe and now they're sprouting out to build casinos and this gondola ride to the confluence in the canyon. They're bad, man," Groundhog said, taking a seat next to me.

"We're going to need big numbers on this one."

We sat alongside the stream, and I filled Groundhog in with the details. We hiked some more spending some silent time together meandering across the top of a mesa. As the sun began to set, Groundhog looked at the huge watch on his wrist.

"We need to head back. I have a surprise," Groundhog said getting up.

"Oh yeah?"

"Oh yeah." He gave me a hand up, we slapped and walked back to the gathering.

As we approached the camp a loud eruption of hoots, whistles and lots of animated shouting exploded. I gave Groundhog a curious look.

"I think they got the satellite working," He said, giving me a pat on my back.

A twenty-eight-year-old, discouraged environmental engineer, who dropped out and was now just living in the desert and pulling survey markers, among other things, pulled a white sheet off a 52-inch flat LED screen hanging from a Palo Verde tree. Three car batteries were attached and a satellite dish on a tripod was adjusted to get a feed.

"Gather round, *mi amigos!*" Groundhog yelled at his people.

The TV came to life after a few adjustments.

"It seems they're not done yet. The infamous Mr. Green Jeans, which began its banner campaign in the Missouri, and garnered the support of Minty Crow at a large concert in St Louis, is still going strong. This campaign has stretched over five months, crossed from Missouri into Kansas, and today into the Valley of the Sun, Phoenix, Arizona. We take you live now to our affiliate, KLPH in Phoenix. Stuart, what's going on out there?" Matt Roker asked from his evening news desk in New York.

"Well, Matt, we've been hit."

The desert gathering erupted in screams for two seconds, then came back to a dead silence as the correspondent continued.

"Mr. Green Jeans, under the cover of darkness, has hung thirty or more banners in the valley today. 'Earth Messages' as people are calling them here in Phoenix. We have some footage to show you from earlier today. Most of the banners have been taken down."

"Stuart, before you go to the footage, can you tell us if anything is known about the identities of Mr. Green Jeans?"

"Authorities say they won't comment at this point, but tell us they received some very useful information just hours ago as to their identities."

"It seems there may be quite a few, considering the scale of their conquest today?" Matt surmised.

"He said Conquest!" Groundhog operatic voice sung out with his fist in the air like Braveheart. The gathering erupted again for another two-second explosion.

"Yes, it was a well-planned event that took a number of bodies to complete. There was even a plane involved today. Here's the footage. Enjoy."

The energy was palpable, now. The hundred or so gathered out in the desert were hugging and even kissing each other in congratulations on a job well done, with the quintessence of their life blood leading the way. Rare indeed. I weaved my way through the crowd and found Lake hugging a very cute flower child. Lake saw me and our eyes locked. It was the kind of moment that comes only a few times in one's life. It was a moment where we sank deeply into all that had transpired since we had begun our life together ten years ago, and now our life as eco-stewards. We would have never predicted we'd be here at this moment in time. Currently, our love for each other and ourselves had an extraordinary patina to it.

The footage had been shot from a helicopter. It showed thirteen of the eighteen freeway overpasses and many spots in between. Groundhog and his gang had put up six on a two-mile stretch of I-17 in the heart of Phoenix. In order they read: PHOENIX DOESN'T NEED COAL OR NUCLEAR, next overpass, IT HAS THE SUN, next overpass, TELL YOUR UTILITIES TO CHANGE NOW, next overpass, CLEAN ENERGY ONLY, next overpass, I'M VERY SICK, last overpass, BUT IT WILL BE YOU THAT DIES IF THERE IS NO CHANGE. The footage finished with Ham's banner streaming behind his plane HELP ME—PLEASE—I AM IN SO MUCH PAIN—MOTHER EARTH

"So there you have it Matt. We'll keep you posted here on any new developments. One other thing: Frackzon Corp., the biggest utility provider in the Southwest, has offered a twenty-five thousand dollar reward for the identities of Mr. Green Jeans." Stuart waited for a response.

"Why an energy company, Stuart?"

"No one knows for sure. Speculation is that many of the messages inferred that energy is a great source of concern for these people. Arizona, like most states rely on coal for their power, and coal is believed to be one of the major contributors to climate change. So take what you will from that, maybe Frackzon sees them as a possible threat."

"Interesting. America, it seems Mr. Green Jeans is exercising his right to the Declaration's freedom of speech. That's all for the nightly news folks. Goodnight." Applause erupted again, this time for much more than two seconds.

That night we feasted. No one seemed to care about a wanted poster. The collection of characters in the round up ranged in age as much as they did in education. There were organic, off-the-grid farmers with a high-school education, young, new age hippies, professors, white-collar this and that, and a bunch of folks who made it their business to do this work time and time again as discreetly as possible. There was a shared pride in the air. In this peaceful attack, we had all been victorious today. Partying, kissing, hugging, dancing, and most of all smiling the night away, we were glad we had decided to come to the round up. We needed this boost. It had been hard living in a vacuum.

Just before I couldn't keep my eyes open anymore, I rolled over on our Therma-rest pads to kiss Lake goodnight. We were both thinking about the twenty-five grand price tag on our heads, and also about our final target.

"We're good." I whispered.

"We're good." Lake found my hand and held it tight.

Chapter Forty-One

FOR MOST OF THE PEOPLE at last night's celebration, the next morning was mix of hangovers, leftover elation, and depressing thoughts of going back to reality. For Lake and me, it meant heading out and getting our last job done. Groundhog said he would arrive with troops. When I had asked last night about why he had changed the pickup spot in Phoenix, he informed me that it was the same kid who compromised the website that was his concern. He had a bad feeling about this kid bragging and talking. Groundhog pointed out the kid last night to us, and over the course of the evening we noticed him watching us on more than one occasion. We did our best to avoid him. It was already dangerous enough to have shown our faces to all these people, but we needed some camaraderie. Everything has its price. Now, with twenty-five thousand in reach, this kid could be very dangerous.

"You guys all ready to go?" Groundhog came up to us as we were adjusting our packs.

"Think so. Hey, thanks. No way could we have accomplished this without your help." I took Groundhogs' hand.

"Groundhog, thank you!" Lake ran over and threw her arms around this grizzly of a man, and Groundhog was forced to reciprocate.

"You're very welcome. Now, we'll see you soon," he said with a laugh.

"Safe travels," I replied.

"Happy trails, guys." Groundhog walked off to help clean up the camp. Pack it in, and pack it out.

Starting down the trail to the parking area, I noticed the kid in question was strapping on his pack.

"We might have company." I motioned with my head for Lake to look at the kid.

"Well, let's get move on!" Lake tightened her waist buckle and marched ahead.

As we reached the primitive parking area on the BLM land, the kid, who wasn't more than twenty, was just a few yards behind us and closing in. We threw our packs in the back of the VW and as I closed the hatch he was there. He took out his cell phone to take a picture and told us how honored he was to have met us. We weren't fooled, Groundhog's concerns were playing out. Photographs were one thing that Groundhog had addressed last night. The kid knew better.

"Hey, no pictures." I unlocked the passenger door for Lake.

"Put the phone away, please," Lake added, about to get in the VW.

The kid ignored us and snapped a photo of the back of the van with his cell, license plate and all.

"What did I just say?" I repeated walking toward the kid who was six feet, maybe 175, and in good shape. I had an inch and 30 pounds, but any semblance of catlike instincts I used to have had long since vanished.

"Give me the phone," I said within a few feet of the kid now.

"Man, I don't know what you're talking about. This is free country."

"Give me your phone, and let me delete the pictures."

"In your dreams." He began walking off. I followed him and when I was just behind him, he turned and shoved me, almost knocking me to the ground.

"What is wrong with you?"

"Hey Jeremy, you know you're not supposed to take pictures!" Rachel, a young girl Lake had spent a lot of time with last night had just emerged from the trail and was quickly making her way to us. Jeremy turned to look at her, and as he did, I grabbed the phone out of his hand. He turned back and was about to take a swing at me when I took both my hands, phone in one, and shoved him in the chest as hard as I could.

He lost his balance and fell to ground right on top of large jumping cholla.

"Owwwww! Damn!" covered across his back with possibly a hundred or more cactus needles, he was having a hard time getting up. I ran to the van and quickly got in and started the engine. As soon as Lake shut her door, I roared off spraying gravel and dirt. The kid was up and hurling rocks at us as we sped up the bumpy track to the highway. Lake turned to see a rock hit the back window, cracking it, but not breaking it.

"Oh my God! This is nuts!" Lake said still looking back at the kid. Rachel stood next to him now, obviously giving him a piece of her mind. It was going to be a few very painful hours before all those needles could be removed.

"Here, check his phone for pics." I handed her the phone. Adrenaline was coursing through us. The VW banged over the ruts, until we hit the blacktop and headed north on highway 87 toward Payson. We were both still trying to catch our breath.

"Okay, that sucked," Lake said, turning on the phone.

"I didn't want to push him."

"I know. You did what you had to do. He could have ruined everything."

"We gotta be more careful. No more roundups."

"Definitely, no more roundups. Oh no, he took some pictures last night of us too!" Lake was searching the phone

"Let's just hope he didn't send any of those pictures to anyone."

Obviously, he hadn't given Reggie his phone last night. Now, we had about a hundred people who could give a description of us with a healthy monetary incentive from a multinational energy company. We just hoped he was the only bad apple in the bunch. The sun began to peek over the high desert hills as we wound our way north, headed towards our last target. If our plan went smoothly, this would be our grandest event to date, hands-down. I leaned over and gave Lake a peck on cheek.

"We're hiding out after this one," Lake stated still going through the kid's phone.

"Yeah, for a long time." I replied.
"Your words to spirits ears."

Chapter Forty-Two

BY NOON, we were driving through Payson, a more conservative Arizona town on edge of the Mongolian rim. We were both on the lookout for cops. Many people around here didn't follow the word we were trying to spread. Climbing up the rim through the Tonto National Forest, enormous pines dotted the landscape amongst the crags of granite jutting out on the rim's crest. This conifer forest had been hit from the right, left and all points in between these last few decades. Excessive logging, thoughtless campers, man-made forest fires, dry conditions bringing out the dormant bark beetle, and climate change, which was the major reason this piece of heaven was battling for survival.

An hour later, we reached I-40 and crossed the interstate heading into Hopi Land. I knew a few people to hole up with for the time we needed. Having spent a few years teaching high school English in Tuba City on the Navajo reservation, my students had been both Hopi and Navajo. After a number of sweat lodges with my Navajo friends and a dozen or so ceremonial invitations with Hopi families, I had made a few close friends. One in particular was where we were headed now.

These two tribes had been neighbors for several generations since the reservations had been established. The Hopi were a pueblo people, the Navajo a more nomadic tribe; and both were breaking at the seams to keep their way of life. Unemployment, alcoholism, poverty and loss of culture were sited when describing the Native Americans, regardless of the tribe. And it was true. It was true throughout the world with hundreds of other cultures too. The Native American people still faced extreme discrimination, and assimilation into the mainstream culture of the America happened only rarely. Lake and I had been dis-assimilating from the mainstream for years. We wanted to reconnect to the real steam, Mother Earth. In the end, our most ardent foe is our-self. And that foe appears with greater frequency the further we separate ourselves from her.

An hour into Hopi land, I pulled off the two-lane blacktop onto a dry, red-dirt track that seemed to lead to nowhere. Ascending the dirt road, I crested a ridge and saw Elroy's stone house. It was built near the edge of a cliff at the road's end. It had been his great uncle's, a shaman of legend. Elroy, who possessed the same gift as his uncle, was thirty-five. He had lost his way more than once, taking monthly trips into Flagstaff, drinking till in four days, he had spent all his monthly disability from the army, he'd thumb it back home to live off beans and food from his family for the rest of the month. This went on for three years, until one sunny afternoon in August, he had accepted the wrong hitch home. Two redneck boys from some rural town bordering the reservation had picked him up on 1-40 and beat the living crap out of him before dumping him in the median. Near death, he walked across the reservation for three days with no food or water. He stayed clear of houses; he wanted no help. He wanted to die. It had been a well-needed wake-up call and the closest thing he had ever had to a vision quest. A young Hopi girl out walking with her blue-eyed cattle dog found him face down on the high desert floor.

Ten years later, still sober, he'd become a private guide for the rich and famous doing backpacking trips to sacred sites across the reservation with the sanction of the tribe. The trips were extremely expensive, and he and the tribe split the profits. He'd made what he needed for a month in a week. It was all very private, and only advertised with a few exclusive travel agents on both coasts.

I pulled between two stands of sage twenty feet from the cliff and parked.

"Wow, this place is great. Let's just stay and never leave, okay?" Lake exclaimed as she got out of the VW. Before us was a red, sandstone house, and as far you could see in any direction there was nothing but nature. Ten feet from the house, two solar panels absorbed the sun's light.

"That would be nice," I answered, thinking the exact same thought.

She walked up to the precipice and looked over the vast Little Colorado gorge. It was like looking into a mini Grand Canyon. Not far from here, the little Colorado converged with mighty Colorado River in the place where we hoped to stop Frackzon Corp.'s plans to forever change her landscape. I walked around in back of the house. No sign of Elroy. He had no phone number I knew of, so I had no choice but to just show up. I hadn't seen or spoken to Elroy for many years.

"Is it all right to be here, honey?" Lake asked, turning and admiring the twenty-by-twenty adobe house with a wind-weathered, wood door, maybe as old as the house itself. The smell of fresh sage and a welcome isolation gave us both a bit of needed peace.

"Yeah, it's cool. Elroy likes his privacy. But he won't mind us stopping by"

The door flew open, and Elroy appeared talking on a cell phone. His grin bust out. Instead of saying hi or giving me a hug, he handed me the phone and then approached Lake with his arms opened.

"Hello?" I took the cell phone.

"Jack, you are the warrior!" Frankie said in Zuni, with a big laugh from the other end of the cell wave.

"Frankie!? What's going on!?"

"Jack, you two are the smoke across the reservation right now. Elroy and I have been friends for years. He's my Hopi brother and I'm his Zuni brother. He said you might be stopping by."

"How would he know that? Oh…. forget I said that." Elroy was a sensitive and trusted his feelings. He saw many things before they happened.

"Yeah. I'm proud of you, Jack. Give that sweet lady a Frankie hug, and have Elroy go online for you. Surprise, surprise. See you my brother"

"What are you talking about?! ... Frankie...?"

Frankie had hung up.

I stood there holding the cell phone in the middle of the Hopi reservation looking at Elroy and Lake, who were staring at me and laughing.

"What is going on?!" I exclaimed, looking at Elroy.

"It's all over the Res., Jack. Frankie's been waiting for something like this forever. How you doing my brother?" Elroy and I gave each other a good wrap.

"Good. It's so nice to see you again."

"Let's take a hike."

"What's up with the cell?" I asked.

"My cousin a few miles north of here is getting the big bucks for a cell tower by his house, so he bought me a phone. Don't always like it, but it came in handy just now." Elroy laughed and picked up a small pack lying on an old cedar bench by the door.

"How long has it been?"

"A hundred moons," he laughed. "Looks like you've done well." He pointed to Lake.

"Lucky bro."

We walked along the ridge of the cliff, until we reached a break in the sandstone, and took a steep path down to the desert floor and the Little Colorado River. Hiking another thirty minutes, we began to follow the murky, shallow Little Colorado with three-hundred-foot, red sandstone walls on either side. We looked up and saw an ancient Anastasia ruin. The base of the cliff where we stood was littered with pottery shards and small corncobs of days gone by. The ruin itself was situated halfway up the cliff face, under the lip of a natural shelf. A precarious climb was the only way to get there, well serving the need for protection. The former inhabitants of these dwellings were called the Ancient Ones. Why they took to the cliffs across the Southwest and then disappeared fifty years later is still a mystery. That was eight hundred years ago.

They must have been worried about attack and withdrew into the safest refuge they could find. Mesa Verde in Colorado is the most accessible of these ruins to the public, but by no means as real as what we were looking at.

"Long ago, my ancestors retreated from a devil. From 1200-1250 they were said to have been here in the cliff dwellings, and then, they disappeared. Archeologists have no real answers to their disappearance. My people only have stories that the earth was in transition. A drought caused havoc, and many warred, taking others' stock and crops in the desperation that ensued. These places held the best water, as the rain drained through the rocks and emptied into the narrow valleys where the crops could be grown. Today, we face the same, but much worse times. The earth is screaming now, and she will change course soon, as she needs to rid herself of this rash. Our species will need to find its way, or the end will arrive with short notice. This is what my people say."

"This is what we are trying to avoid." Lake sat, looked up the cliff dwelling, and imagined the life that once went on here.

"The ancients bless your efforts." Elroy lit a sage smudge stick and let the smoke go where it wanted.

"Until you start, you head nowhere, right?" I replied.

"Just remember there is no ending. There is just the now that we create. Let's go eat." Elroy started back down the trail holding the burning sage in the air.

Returning to Elroy's home, we feasted on green chili, fry bread and roasted corn. Late that night, I stayed up searching the Internet. Frankie's site had exploded with comments, almost all favorable. I double-checked all I knew at this point about the Frackzon Corp. and its invasion plan. We couldn't do this one alone. We needed a movement to show up. Get in. Get Out. And Get Lost. That was the plan. Hopefully, this blast would make a real difference.

Chapter Forty-Three

THE NEXT MORNING, our cell phone had three messages. Lake and I sat outside on the cedar bench against the red stone of Elroy's home, as the sun crested the ridge and began to warm all in its path. We listened to the messages together. The first was from Frankie.

"Hey, Jack, I have had people from Acoma, Jemez, and Taos pueblos, and of course, the Dinah, since it's on their land. I also have people from the Cherokee and Sioux nations all telling me they're coming. It could get big. Don't worry my friends, we are good at keeping secrets."

The second message was from Gus.

"Hey Stewards! My wife and are going to be there! She's actually excited. Been great for the sex life. TMI, right? Also LA to New York media will be represented. No need to call back…. Blend in, my heroes. See you soon."

"Oh my God!!! LA and New York!" Lake was jumping up and down on the red dirt.

"He's having sex," I spoke like a true male.

Message Three: Lillian.

"Jack, what are doing? Stop it, okay and come back home. What am I saying? You're not coming back, Jack, honey, Lake dear, has he got you hostage? You're smarter than this. Please, honey, Jack… call me, oh, I haven't said a word. I don't think they know who you are. Lake, dear, please don't…. Goodbye, I love you both."

"We have to call her," Lake stated without pause.

"Yeah. I think she was drinking bourbon."

"So would I, if you were my kid." Lake hit me in the arm. The phone rang.

"Hello."

"Prickly Pear, its Groundhog."

"What's going on?"

"I got a growing caravan ready to take off when you give the word."

"What!?"

"Yeppers, dude, they're lining up."

"Okay, man, that's great. I'll let you know."

"I'll be waiting.'

I hung up. I was speechless, breathless and blown away.

"What's wrong?" Lake asked.

"Groundhog has a caravan coming up." I looked up at the sky.

"Wow, this is really happening."

"Yeah, it is."

We both sat and breathed the sage in. A light rain had fallen last night and there was hardly a scent better than the desert after a rain. Elroy appeared climbing out of the little Colorado canyon just a few feet from us, from what looked to be an impossible access point.

"Did you just climb up that?!" Lake's eyes were wide open.

"There's a rope just over the edge here. I shouldn't have told you." He let out a long laugh.

"Okay, are we ready to paint!?" Elroy asked.

"It's on!" I yelled.

"Are you guys open to a suggestion?" Elroy asked, looking at both of us.

"Sure," Lake answered.

"If I take this soil under our feet and mix it with water from the Little Colorado it will make a nice soup you can use to easily cover these canvases with. It will also be of the place you are going." Elroy was letting a handful of dirt sift out through his fingers.

"That's beautiful, Elroy," Lake said, bending down to get a handful, too.

"Beauty is in the details, and that's a beautiful detail!" I added, joining in and grabbing a handful myself.

We worked for the rest of the morning mixing, stirring and spreading the Colorado plateau soup over the canvas. These banners weren't destined to be hung and taken down. People would be carrying them.

After another hike, we returned to find the banners dried. It was time for the messages. The red clay paint had adhered well. By dusk, we had finished. This time some of our messages were more directly aimed. Frackzon Corp. had put a price our heads. We might as well earn it.

The next morning, we woke early and rolled up the banners. They completely filled the van. We had to squeeze in the front two seats, but we were used to that by now.

"Elroy, thanks brother, for everything!"

"It is my pleasure, Brother Jack, you two are one of us, and we are part of all, and that's how it is, and will always be. We'll see you in a few days." Elroy gave Lake a squeeze and a kiss, and patted the side the VW.

It had been good to see my old friend, and I felt like I was getting back into what it meant to be alive. There was some vague remembrance of feeling this alive. Seemed like I'd felt this alive before in my life, for a few moments at least. It had been a long time ago, but you don't forget those feelings. You just bury them, and I was in the process—we both were—of digging up that treasure. Rolling up the ridge and away from the stone house, we saw Elroy light another smudge stick and watch us drive away.

Chapter Forty-Four

VISTA CANDY. That's what Lake and I called the Southwest. The Colorado Plateau was by far one of the sweetest pieces in the bag, and she was in serious trouble. Frackzon was doing everything it could to convince the tribe to let the gondola project move forward and 'share' in the immense promised profits.

The confluence of the Little Colorado and the Colorado was a sacred spot to many Native Americans. It was believed that these two rivers were male and female, and that where they met life begins. It was also believed to be the spot the spirit returns to after death. This was where the gondola ride would end, and restaurants and gift shops would cater to the riders three hundred and sixty five days a year. It would be a goldmine for the Frackzon Corp. It would be one more slice of death for the canyon and the native people.

Lake drove fifteen miles an hour over the bumpy dirt track paralleling the blacktop nine miles away. I had out the computer and was downloading stills and video from our digital camera. Short video pieces of putting up our banners, painting them and even some great rolling landscape shorts. These and a slew of still shots, I sent off to Gus. The only images of us were either our hands or our feet. With a twenty-five-thousand-dollar reward on our heads, we realized what had once started as just a simple 'rage against the machine', had already changed our lives forever. Five months ago, we were classroom teachers. Now we were wanted agitators.

The level of attention wasn't going to be ignored by Homeland security, either. It needed as much good press as it could muster, and if some yahoos were painting the town and escaping time and time again, it didn't bode well for the relevancy of the agency. Our minds wandered over all the possible outcomes, bad to good, and then often back to bad. If we were caught, would we be judged as 'enemies to the state', homeland terrorists? We had garnered more national and now international press than we could have ever imagined. If we were caught, that same attention would explode. The news would eat it up, and any lore Mr. Green Jeans was beginning to create would end on that note: captured, imprisoned and awaiting trial; or captured, imprisoned and awaiting charges. You don't need to be necessarily charged to be imprisoned, even in this day and age. If we didn't get caught, then who knows what we'd do after this. But we would have hope, and hope goes a long way, especially in our current line of work.

"Jack, I'm starting to worry again," Lake pronounced, eating a granola bar and navigating the dirt track that was rising steadily to a crest.

"Makes sense," I replied turning off the computer.

"That's all you have to say?" she looked at me with the beginnings of a melt-down expression on her face.

"What do you want me to say? We have a price on us. I think that picture of me from Camelback is currently being analyzed by the authorities somewhere, and soon will be the front page on newspapers across the Southwest and beyond. Going home after this may not be an option. What? What is there to say? I'm freaking out, too, right now." I sat looking out the window at the untouched desert of the Navajo reservation.

"It's not just you here, buddy," Lake countered.

"I know that. Where's that coming from?"

"I don't know." Lake brought the VW to an abrupt stop at the crest of the ridge.

"There's doesn't seem to be any end game here, babe. Whether we get caught or not, if our identities have been compromised our lives are changed forever."

Lake turned off the engine, leaned her elbow on the steering wheel and cupped her hand across her forehead. I got out of the van. I quit smoking almost three months ago, but I wanted one right now. Lake did a long exhale, got out the van and joined me. We stood side-by-side, resting against the front grill, not saying a word to each other. The only sound was that of the wind and a raven cawing from his perch on twisted, desert pine behind us. The last conquest lay a short distance from here, and we were scared to death. Not scared of what we were planning to do. Scared with the realization of what we might have given up to do all this. Everything has a price. The piper always gets paid.

Chapter Forty-Five

WE SAT ON THE LIP of the Little Colorado gorge, miles downstream of Elroy's home and less than three miles from the confluence, where the Frackzon Corp. was planning to install its absurd gondola ride to the canyon's floor. The postcard view changed each minute, as the sun set across bluffs and buttes in the distance. I had our little backpacking stove going, cooking up some boxed organic mac and cheese.

The Grand Canyon held a special meaning for both of us. Lake had backpacked the canyon a half dozen times from the north rim to the south. She had also explored many of the lesser trails, spending a week or more at a time living on the canyon floor. She knew this place. We both did. It was in our DNA.

"They can't do this!" Lake said, looking across the vast expanse in front of us.

"They do it all the time," I said stirring the noodles.

"I always heard the rumors of someone wanting to do this, but I thought there was no way that would be allowed," Lake stated, transfixed on the ever-changing picture in front of us.

"I heard the rumors, too, when we used to live out here. I thought the same thing. That will never happen."

"Bless you Canyon!" her arms outstretched, she shouted her words over the vastness.

"Bless you, Mother!" I followed in suit.

After we finished our mac and cheese and split a chocolate bar, we lay side by side on our Therma-rest pads and went over what we were doing the next day.

"Okay, we'll stop at the confluence tomorrow morning, take a few moments there and then check in at the El Tovar to decompress for a day. The next day we meet with Elroy and Frankie outside Tuba City. That's it, I think."

"I love you," Lake said, touching my hand.

"I love you too, baby," I replied, gently squeezing her hand.

We hadn't set up the tent, preferring the ceiling of the southwest sky. Our nerves didn't allow for much sleep, and before dawn began its spread across the Colorado Plateau, we rose and packed and headed down the dirt road to the confluence. We passed some Hogan's, still inhabited, and few other stick-built homes, also with occupants. These people had lived here for generations. If the project went through, this road would be paved and thousands of tourists would travel it daily. It was quiet now, and outside of the few dwellings scattered about, it was mostly wild here. The flora and fauna were safe and lived free. It was the way it was supposed to be.

Arriving at the rim of the Little Colorado, we stood on the edge, where we could see its meeting with the Colorado. Two life forces coming together. It is an awesome sight.

"I think I'm going to throw up, Jack."

Lake turned her back to me and emptied her stomach. Lake's emotions ran a direct current to her physical well-being. The idea of Frackzon's potential destruction literally made her sick.

"Oh, baby," I said, getting out a few Kleenexes from the VW and handing them to her.

"I love this place. I love all the animals and plants, the river, the clouds, everything," she said, getting back into the van. Her face was pale, and beads of sweat covered her forehead.

"Let's get to the hotel, shower, and take a nap?" I said, starting the VW.

"That sounds good," she answered, and climbed into the passenger seat, leaning her head against the window.

This was it. Our grand finale. We just needed to make it through this and take a break.

Chapter Forty-Six

CHECKING INTO THE EL TOVAR LODGE on the canyon's south rim, we stepped back in time. This lodge was built in the early 1900's when the railroad from Williams, Arizona to the canyon was completed. At the time, it was said to be the finest hotel west of the Mississippi. Old plank floors and huge structural timbers made the bones for this amazing lodge, and it fit comfortably into the natural scenery, unlike the many chain hotels lining the road outside the park in Tusayan, a small community that exists outside any major national park in America catering to tourists.

"Oh baby, I could stay here for a while," Lake said, opening the door to our room and rushing to the window to pull back the curtains.

"There she is," Lake whispered, staring out the window.

I tossed a Duluth pack on the bed and joined her at the window.

"Wow," I said using the most frequent word heard at the Grand Canyon.

"We both have so many memories here," Lake said, putting her arm around my waist.

"Yes we do, and now we're going to try and give her something back," I said wrapping my arm around her waist.

"Yes, we are!" she added in full agreement. "I'm sorry for freaking out, sweetheart." She turned and faced me.

"Baby, I've been a mess, too. I think most people would have stopped a long time ago. We're just borderline nuts." I grabbed her with both arms.

"Most people wouldn't have even started. Now, let's go downstairs and get those biscuits and eggs we talked about last night," Lake said, giving me a nice kiss on the lips.

"How about a shower first? I could wash your back?" Her kiss took me away from our troubles and on to brighter things.

"Ahh, I suppose my back could use a little washing."

After a delicious shower fit for a high-quality, steamy movie, we sat in the El Tovar's restaurant awaiting a hot breakfast. We wore the same getups we had on when we checked in. Lake sported her long blond wig and wore a baseball cap with a peace symbol embroidered on the front. I displayed oversized black plastic reading glasses and a Raiders-of-the-Lost-Arc jungle hat. Not much of a disguise, but this would be our last protest for a while, and we felt that our identities were still safe. If word got out that the Frackzons newest destructive project was going to be the next Green Jeans landing, then the reporters and bounty hunters would appear quickly.

"So, we got today and tomorrow's the party," Lake stated looking around the dining room for anyone suspicious.

"Yep."

"You okay?" Lake said and reached her hand across the table.

"I think so. And you?" I grabbed her hand.

"Dandy, thank you, Clyde."

"Bonnie, look to your right, please." I spied the waitress across the dining room coming towards us with a tray of food.

"Is that our food?!" Lake responded following my hopeful line of sight to the tray the waitress held at head level, its contents just out of view. We hadn't had too many table meals since we left Missouri. Each one was like winning the lottery.

After a scrumptious breakfast and a three-hour nap, we left the Lodge and took a walk along the rim trail that started just feet away from the El Tovar's large front porch. Five million visitors a year roamed this sidewalk, taking pictures and standing in awe of something that has no words for description. The canyon was eighteen miles across at its largest span and a mile deep on average. Many visitors would hike a few miles down and return to a good meal somewhere. There were many other people who were perfectly satisfied with walking her rim and getting lost in her majesty, a soul trip to be certain. And some would hike her entire length from north to south, if they had planned ahead and got on the waiting list. The cross-canyon hiking permits were filled years in advance, and that was a good thing. We have to keep places sacred, and that means limiting the number of us in them. We counted ourselves very fortunate to have spent so much time in this incredible place.

With Frackzon Corp.'s asinine gondola ride at the confluence, the canyon would lose more of her skin, and too much had already been taken. She was damned, with Lake Powell above, and damned with Lake Mead below. Only a trickle of her life's blood, the Colorado River, made it to the delta in the Sea of Cortez. Only a trickle.

"Screw them!" Lake said, looking out across the canyon with her arms raised.

A few Japanese tourists turned to look at her and then snapped a picture. "Angry American at Canyon."

"I mean what are they thinking!? Screw them!"

Snap. Snap.

"Baby, let's go," I said, turning to walk back to the lodge. Lake took the cue and followed.

Chapter Forty-Seven

"I MEAN she contains five of the seven life zones! You got to travel from Mexico to Canada to experience that! Frackzon's going down!" Lake exhaled, still on fire, as we drove through the strip of motels, campgrounds, restaurants, an IMax and the convenience stores that made up Tusayan, the small community just out the park. Only five hundred people lived here year round. During the height of tourist season, that number was in the thousands. The majority of the service employment was seasonal and maintained simple quarters during the season or drove here daily from Flagstaff, Williams or the Reservation.

At the south edge of Tusayan, I turned onto a newly-built gravel road that the Frackzon Corp. had built to access their property. A sign said private road, no trespassing.

"Keep an eye out for anyone," I said, as I took the VW down the clear-cut road. Dead ponderosas lay off to side, and we could see bulldozers in the clearings through the trees. Survey stakes filled the property, mapping out where water, sewer and utilities would go.

"I didn't know they'd already started," Lake said as she looked through the trees to see large wafts of land already stripped of any vegetation.

"I know. I thought it might be surveyed, but that's all," I replied, surprised to see how quickly a natural place can change with a few earth movers.

"Looks like we're going to do some real monkey-wrenching," Lake said, eyeing the machines that created a change with no thought and in no time.

"What?" I responded, hoping she hadn't lost it.

"They're here. They've started it. The war is on," Lake said, looking at me with enough seriousness to make me worry.

"We can't do any monkey-wrenching. We destroy their equipment, and we lose the war. You know that."

"I know, I know. I just want to blow the machines up!"

"I do too."

"I'm definitely pulling those survey stakes!"

"No, Lake. We do that, and we lose the support we're hoping to get. You know that," I said, stopping the VW and looking at her.

"I know. I know. You're right, but do you really believe the stand here is going to stop this development?"

"We just have to hope. I know if we start going illegal, we definitely aren't going to change anything."

"Who comes up with the idea to make those machines?" Lake said looking at a large earthmover that had a seven-step, steel ladder incorporated to reach the cab.

"Those are small compared to the monoliths they use for mining," I stated, wondering the same thing. If the industrial revolution had been aligned with the natural world, our world today would look much different, and Mr. Green Jeans would never have been a thought.

After looping through the newly made road and back onto the blacktop, realizing we might be a little behind the eight ball, we headed back to the hotel. We had one more day before the march.

"Okay, I'm going to check the messages," I said, as Lake pulled up to the entrance gate, ready to show the ranger our park pass.

"Whoa! We have a bunch of messages," I said, showing Lake the phone.

"Let's hear 'em," Lake said, rolling down the window and showing the female ranger our pass. The ranger gave us both a few curious looks before she raised the gate to let us enter.

"What was that about?" I asked.

"I don't know. She was checking us out. Play the messages, baby."

As we drove through the park to the El Tovar Lodge. I put the phone on speaker, and we listened to the messages.

The first messages were from Frankie. Frankie was excited in the first one, and told us all the tribes who would represented at the march. It was the second one that stopped us in our tracks. Lake pulled the VW into a parking area overlooking the canyon.

"Play it again, Jack," Lake said, staring out the front window, hands clenched on the steering wheel.

"Hey guys, sorry about this bad news, but things have changed. Your pictures were on the evening national news. They know who you are. Wherever you are now, get to the camp immediately. Word is out that something's going to happen at the canyon. Seems someone leaked it to social media. Our plan is still in place, and it might even be to our advantage, because there's going to thousands more people coming now. Everyone wants to see a celebrity. Get to camp, we will see you soon. I'm serious guys. Good chance they know what you're driving too."

"What do we do!?" Lake shouted banging on the steering wheel.

"We can't go back to the hotel," I said looking at Lake.

"That's okay, we have all our gear in back."

"It's just clothes and crap at the hotel, right?" I asked.

"Where's the camera!?" Lake asked, mouth opened wide.

"I reached under the passenger seat and revealed it.

"Oh God. Good job, baby."

Lake did a one-eighty. We headed back down the road. The camping spot was the same place we'd been last night before coming up here. We exited the park out the Desert View entrance. We both had put on sunglasses and hats, but didn't have to stop leaving the park. That might change soon. Lake and I didn't speak for the entire forty-five-minute drive off the canyon and back onto desert floor to our camping spot. I played the other messages.

"Jack, Lake, I know there's no sense in scolding you two. I want you to know the police visited me yesterday, and I told them I had no idea what you were doing or where you are. I don't think I'll have any problems here. Your pictures were on the front page of the Manchester Tribune. The headline read 'Home of Mr. and Mrs. Green Jeans'. The article was favorable – I might be a celebrity back here. Now, I want you to come home, face the music and things will be all right. Please Jack, Lake you still have some sense. Come home, please."

The next was from Gus, "Be careful. Big brother is watching now, as I hope you already know. Be careful, my friends." Elroy was next, "I will see you tomorrow. Don't worry, Great Spirit is with you two." Groundhog followed: "We'll be at the canyon tomorrow, and it was probably the kid we've been trying to help that gave you guys up and posted on social media. Sorry." Brien was the last call. "I'm thinking of painting the house red?" that was our code for trouble.

Before making the turn down a dirt track to our camp, we passed hundreds of cars with their occupants milling about and making camp on the side of the road. Arriving at last night's camp, we both got out and walked to the rim of Little Colorado River Gorge. It was close to midnight, the skies were partially cloudy, and it smelled like it could rain. We stood there looking at the moon's reflection casting its glow through the high-floating clouds moving over the canyon. We stood there for minutes before either of us spoke.

"So much for keeping our identities hidden," I said, staring out into the vastness that is the Colorado Plateau.

"What are we going to do, Jack?"

"I really don't know, Lake."

Chapter Forty-Eight

EMOTIONALLY AND PHYSICALLY, we were spent. We'd been asleep for just a short time when I heard a vehicle coming down the dirt track to our camp. I nudged Lake, and we both sat up in our bags. We'd slept under the stars again. You can do that in Southwest. No mosquitoes, just rattlesnakes and scorpions, which have no interest in you. Headlights flooded across the ridge, and then an old pickup appeared coming directly toward us. We had nowhere to run to. As the pickup slowed to a stop ten feet from us, the lights went off. The driver's door opened, and out stepped Frankie.

"Keshi!"

"Mr. and Mrs. Green Jeans!" Elroy said, getting out of the other side.

"God, am I glad to see you two!" Lake said, getting out of her bag and rushing to give them each a hug.

"Yah tey hey," said a middle-aged Navajo woman with a long, gray, braid down her back, and a glow coming from her being, as she got out of the truck.

"This is Savannah. She has been fighting this development for half her life," Elroy announced, and both Lake and I shook her hands.

"You two are something else. Thank you for choosing this fight," she softly said with a gentle smile.

Elroy got a lantern and some folding chairs out of the pickup. I started the stove and made coffee. We sat in a circle and talked for hours under the stars.

"Our people are much divided on this development. Some see jobs, which we badly need. Others like me, see a sacred place and habitat destroyed, which we will never get back. Both are true. Only one is temporary. We use this earth as though she is a bucket that is filled each day for our infinite consumption. I have cried too many times in my life, and don't want to show my children and grandchildren only drawn pictures of what this place once was. When it is gone, it will be gone forever, and that is something I cannot live with." She sipped her coffee and looked across the lanterns glow, at Lake and me.

"Jack, you and Lake have much power in the Green Jeans name. True power only grows when it is shared. It is then that the power can be discovered to be real or something that only serves few," Savannah added, bowing her head and looking off in the distance.

"Green Jeans was never ours. Our hope was, it would bring together people to fight for the earth's health, our health," Lake said, smiling at Savannah, who returned her gaze.

"Well said," Savannah remarked, sitting between Frankie and Elroy and patting them each on the back.

"What does tomorrow look like?" I asked, looking at the three of them, knowing this was their show now.

"It will be big. I'm sure you saw all the cars parked off the highway before you came back here," Frankie began.

"Yeah, it was crazy seeing all those people out there." I replied.

"You saw only a little bit. Tuba City is flooded with people from all the country, and I'm sure more are coming each hour. It was a blessing that word got out this was happening, but I'm sure you are worried about your part, your safety."

"Just a little, Frankie," Lake said, trying to show courage.

"If you still want to march, I have your outfits in the truck, no peeking," Elroy said with a mischievous smile.

"I think we're game," Lake said looking at me.

"Definitely," I said, agreeing, also trying some semblance of bravery.

We talked for another hour. Savannah spoke of all her ideas about creating sustainable, earth-friendly jobs on the reservation. We spoke about our escape plans. Frankie and Elroy assured us we would have safe refuge with them if that's what was needed. We all gave coyote cries to the spirits of the canyon. We laughed, and then we let the silence and peace of this natural world enveloped us.

"Okay, we have about four hours before the sun rises and the march starts. Let's try to get a few hours of sleep," Elroy said, standing up and getting blankets from the truck bed.

Lake and I went back to our bags. Frankie got comfortable in the truck cab, and Savannah and Elroy wrapped themselves in blankets and settled on the desert floor like us.

"Goodnight, everyone," Lake said.

"Goodnight, goodnight, goodnight."

"Goodnight, earth," I said, grabbing Lake's hand and closing my eyes.

Frankie got us all up before dawn. Elroy had brought all the fixin's for a good breakfast. He even picked up some fake meat sausage patties for me and Lake. After a good; hot meal, we rolled out all our banners on the ground.

"You guys have outdone yourself!" Frankie said with a big laugh.

"Elroy helped make these," Lake added.

"I know. I see his design work on the borders. He couldn't stop talking about how blown away I was going to be."

"They're beautiful," Savannah said, shaking her head with a big smile.

"Time to go, guys. Let's get you two dressed, and we'll get these banners rolled up," Frankie said, throwing out the coffee in his cup.

"I've got to make one last call," I said, and stepped to the rim of the canyon.

"Is that to his rafting buddy down in the canyon?" Elroy asked.

"Yeah, it's crazy, plan B, but we may need it," Lake said

"Good time to be safe. Okay, dear, time to get you dressed," Elroy said, and he and Savannah helped Lake put on her outfit. Frankie rolled up the rest of the banners and loaded them into the truck. After I was outfitted, Lake and I climbed into the back of the truck with all our important stuff crammed into two large Duluth packs. We looked at the VW and said our good-byes.

"You're going to take care of her, right Elroy?" I said in a loud voice as Frankie started the truck.

"Jack, I will love her like she was your daughter!" Elroy shouted through the passenger window.

As we slowly drove away from the rim, the sun was just beginning to peak from the east of us on the hills surrounding Tuba City and the Hopi Mesas.

"Is he going to be down there?" Lake asked, watching the rim disappear as we traveled the dirt road toward highway where the march would begin.

"Yes. He said he canceled his trip down the canyon, but kept the permit. If we need to go to the river, he'll get us out of here."

"That's comforting."

"Yeah, it is."

Two big exhales, and we covered our heads with the costumes final piece. Two paper Mache helmets. I was a horned toad, and Lake got to be the colorful Gila monster.

Chapter Forty-Nine

HIGHWAY 89, just a few miles north of the turn-off to Tuba City, was lined with hundreds of people milling about, waiting to join the procession. Frankie, Elroy and Savannah were amazed with the mass of people assembled. Frankie pulled over on the shoulder.

"Oh Great Spirit, this is amazing." Lake spoke, looking up and down the highway.

"Lake?" I said and asked.

"Yeah?" she turned to look at me.

We looked at each other, smiled, held hands and looked back out at the scene before us.

A small group of Navajo and Hopi high school kids dressed in well-crafted animal costumes, lit up when they saw Savannah. She was a local celebrity. After Savannah had a short conversation with the group, she came back to the truck and held out her hand to help Lake out of the truck bed.

"I told them you're old friends from Flagstaff, the Petersons," Savannah whispered to Lake and they both laughed.

"You look good," Elroy said to me, with a big grin out the passenger window.

"I'm a horny toad, Elroy," I responded, looking at him through my cutout eyes.

"It's horned toad, but go with horny. It works." Now Elroy was laughing.

"You better have some cold water when I see you next."

"You're a horny toad!" Savannah played along. Elroy was now busting a gut and moved over to make room for her in the truck. Frankie did a one eighty back onto the blacktop. He paused.

"See ya soon, Horny Toad!" he yelled and sped off to Tuba City. I could hear the laughs spilling from the open windows.

"Nice to meet you Mr. and Mrs. Peterson," said a young girl dressed as a crow. None of the teens' costumes had the full-head helmet like Lake and I had. They had used feathers to create an eye mask with the color of their animal. Our heads were made of paper Mache. They weren't that hot, and gave us complete anonymity. Lake's looked good. The Gila monster is a beautiful animal, the largest lizard in the United States, and one of the few lizards in the world that is venomous. Beautiful and she will bite—that was Lake. Now, why was I a horned toad?

Tuba City is the tribal headquarters for the Navajo western nation. The hospital was here, the public schools were here, and 'Box-Mart' had been present for some time. Directly across the highway was Moenkopi, the largest Hopi pueblo, and the beginning of the road across the three Mesas of Hopi land. There was a rich and varied patina spread across this land, and Tuba City was where all the different shades would come together and decide to be with or without Frackzon.

"I love you guys!" Savannah said, giving both Frankie and Elroy a hug. They had pulled into a packed parking lot at the crossroads in Tuba City.

"We love you!" Frankie replied as Savannah hurried off to take her position at the front of the march. Elroy and Frankie slid the banners out from the back of the truck. The only plan for these banners was their positioning. There was an order to this message.

"Pass these out to the people behind the drummers. They're numbered on the corner. You don't need to say where you got them," Elroy said to his niece and Frankie's three sons.

"Go Green Jeans!" said the youngest of Frankie's sons.

"Don't say Green Jeans if there's a cop nearby. Okay?" Frankie stated looking at the four.

They all said they understood and took off carrying the eight banners over their shoulders.

Over five thousand people from twenty tribes, and people of all colors and status, were minutes away from starting the march out of Tuba City to the confluence. The parade was, ten rows deep, ten in a line. A hundred drummers beat their drums as one. Every few minutes, a drummer would announce a solo and all the other drummers would raise their sticks, allowing the voice to be heard. Then, the hundred-drum beat would continue. Behind the drum line, now a mile in length, was row after row of people walking in concert. The people of twenty tribes were represented with well over three thousand marchers wearing their tribes' ceremonial finest. Another three thousand or more were made up of non-natives from as far away as Maine. Many dressed in homemade costumes that reflected the flora and fauna of this country. Some with hand-painted signs voicing their disapproval of the project. There was a row of ten youths from Phoenix that had the canyon's confluence screen-painted in pieces across their T-shirts. When they stood close the puzzle became a picture of this sacred place. It went on and on. It was a parade of people that had a common purpose, a specific purpose today. Stop the absurdity!

As we waited on the side of highway 89 with our new animal friends, three Frackzon Corp. heavy-duty pickups sped past us and then turned up the dirt road to the confluence. A minute later, two more Frackzon trucks passed, turned onto the confluence road and stopped. The occupants hopped out and began removing fold up tables and chairs from the truck bed.

"What the hell are they doing here!?" said a teen dressed as a bald eagle.

"Making a presence," Lake answered.

"I should go knock that table down," Bald eagle announced.

"No, you do that, then that's what runs on the news," I said, pointing to the news crew positioning their camera on the Frackzon workers setting up their tables.

"Leave the stupid people alone, maybe someday they'll understand they're part *of* this world and not just *on* it. You turning a table over will only piss them off," said a girl dressed as a diamondback rattlesnake.

Lake and I looked at each other through our paper Mache eyes, and I could she was smiling, and she saw I was too. There was hope.

We could hear the drums. Both sides of highway 89 were packed with cars for miles above and below the turn-off to Tuba City. I swallowed hard. Another two thousand people! They were mostly non-native, standing ready to join the procession to the confluence. The collective energy was strong. Thousands of people coming together with one common purpose created an electricity that hummed through the desert. Being a sovereign territory was to the advantage of Tribal police, and the state highway to Tuba City, now cut off to traffic for the last hour and half, did not allow the state troopers to carry out the rules of the road. With the protest cresting a ridge and now visible to the awaiting crowds on 89, an eruption of shouts, hoots and applause gave the troopers another pause. The governor herself had issued a stand-down order to the troopers, unless there was an emergency that needed use of the road. Politics to some degree, but currently Arizona's governor was more enlightened than the dozen that had preceded her. Which wasn't saying much, as far as Arizona politics go.

Then, we saw them. Twelve leaders of twelve Indian nations riding bareback on twelve magnificent animals. They filled the roadway. These elders, from various tribes bordering the canyon as well others from the north and south, rode with pride and purpose on their steeds. Fully dressed in their ceremonial best, they were followed by the hundred drummers and then by over three thousand Native Americans, all dressed in the full regal of their cultural history. All the colors of the rainbow gleamed off their outfits in stark contrast to the lunar landscape that lined both sides of the road. The drummers responded to the applause and beat their drums with a heightened vigor. The crowd along 89 responded in kind with cacophony. The march was currently over a mile in length. In ten minutes, the procession would reach highway 89, and another half mile of marchers was joining the protest. Lake and

I looked at each other, raised our hands in the air, and gave each other a double hand high-five.

"Those signs are cool! Look at 'em Sheri!" Bald Eagle passed the binoculars to Crow.

All the signs had the red sandy color of the earth as a background. The first two were lettered in black. For the next two, we'd used bright, vibrant colors of the sun, the clouds, and the grass. On the fifth banner Frackzon was written in black and other words were bright colors. All the banners that followed were bright colors, and Elroy had used Hopi designs to border all the canvases. They were our best work to date.

> COAL * GAS * URANIUM * OIL
> THIS IS FRACKZON
> HOME * BIRTH * DEATH *LIFE
> THIS IS THE CONFLUENCE
> FRACKZON ONLY TAKES FROM THE EARTH
> THE CONFLUENCE ONLY GIVES
> SHE CANNOT BE REPLACED
> WE ARE THE STEWARDS
> WE ARE THE CARETAKERS OF THE EARTH
> IF WE DON'T KEEP HOUSE THEN
> WE WON'T HAVE A HOUSE
> MR. AND MRS. GREEN JEANS!!!!!

"They signed it Mr. and Mrs.! Cool!!!!" Bald Eagle yelled and pointed to signs.

"Do you think the Green Jeans people are here?" Crow asked Lake.

"I don't know, it's pretty dangerous right now for them," Lake answered.

"I know people who are here just to see if they can get the reward," Bald Eagle added.

"Your people?" Lake asked, looking at me.

"We have thieves just like you do," Crow answered.

Dozens of news crews, just like Gus had promised, walked off the road next to the marchers shooting as much footage as they could while trying to avoid walking into clumps of sage and cacti. All the major networks were represented. Even NPR was here doing a live feed of the march online.

As the march hit highway 89 and turned left, we saw something to give us pause.

Chapter Fifty

THE STATE TROOPERS alongside employees of Frackzon Corp., were walking up the road, passing out the flyers with our pictures, and the reward had increased to forty thousand dollars.

They hadn't reached us yet, but we noticed the people who wore a costume with headwear were being asked to remove it for a quick identity check.

"Do you see that, Jack?" Lake whispered after pulling me out of anyone's earshot.

"Yeah, don't use my name," I whispered back.

"Sorry. What are we going to do?"

I got out our phone and quickly put it together and dialed Frankie.

"We're in trouble here," I said softly into the phone.

"Okay, I can see you, walk up the road. I have an idea," Frankie said as he marched just behind the eight banners. He was at a higher elevation and had a good view of the Highway. We were standing at the north side of the intersection, the horses and drummers had just passed us. Frankie was just minutes from us.

"Okay." I hung up the phone.

"Let's go," I said to Lake, and grabbed her hand.

"Where are you guys going?" Crow asked as we started to walk up the road.

"We want to get a picture of you guys when you join in, from a distance, you know?"

"Oh, that's nice. Thank you."

We began walking on the desert side of the cars lining the road. We hadn't walked more than a few minutes when we a four-wheeler came across the desert directly at us: two officers motioning for us to halt. They stopped right beside us.

"Get in, please," the uniformed driver said

"Why?" Lake asked, thinking this was it. The end. Our worst fears took hold, no pension, no home, no family, just bars.

"This is not a question. Get in." said the officer in the passenger seat.

We got in the back seat, and the four-wheeler sped off into the desert away from the march.

"Where are we going?" Lake said loud enough to be heard over the drone of the engine. The driver turned around and smiled at us.

We hurdled through the desert, making a wide sweep and then crossing the highway a few miles north of the road to the confluence, where the procession would turn and make its final leg. We stopped in a shallow arroyo, and both uniformed men got out.

"Okay, we're just a mile from the confluence. As soon as we hear the drums, we'll drive you to the march, and you guys just blend in," officer Yazzie said, pouring us each a cold cup of water from a thermos.

"What!? You're not turning us in?" I said downing the water and holding my cup out for another pour. .

"If they catch you two, then the march will be remembered for that. It will also scare people who want to get involved in this fight, or any fight. You two cannot be caught," Yazzie said filling Lake's cup a second time.

"Can I get your autograph?" asked Officer Begay, the younger of the two. He hadn't said a word since we pulled off our paper Mache heads. He had just stood and stared at us.

"Begay, this is not…." Yazzie began.

"No, that's all right. We've never given an autograph. We'd be happy to!" Lake interrupted.

"Mise well, everyone knows our names now," I said, as officer Begay took a small spiral notepad from his back pocket.

"I want you to sign it Mr. and Mrs. Green Jeans, if that's all right?" Begay asked.

Back at the march, the procession was now over two miles long. All the people who had been waiting on highway 89 joined the march. They were halfway down the dirt road that ended at the confluence. The state troopers waited on the highway for the marchers to return, which would be a good two hours or more.

The table set up by the Frackzon Corp. at the start of the confluence road didn't get the attention they'd hoped for. They had attached a banner on the front of the table that read: 'Now Hiring'. A stack of applications sat unused, as not one person had left the march to inquire. Even though the project hadn't received a green light, Frackzon wanted to give the impression that the deal was as good as done. They were masters of the smoke-and-mirrors game. They had to be. If they told the truth about all their endeavors, they would have been shut down years ago. Only a few reporters had stopped for an interview, and their goal wasn't to give equal time to Frackzon. They wanted to know why Frackzon was offering employment when the development was still undecided. In the end, Frackzon had made a misstep with their presence. People were fed up with heavy-handed corporations, and the backdrop of the reservation and thousands of Native Americans as well thousands of non-natives was not a favorable press piece for them. Too late now.

Sitting in the shade on the east side of the arroyo, we heard the drums.

"Time to go," Yazzie said, getting on the four-wheeler. We put on our paper-Mache heads and climbed in.

"You guys are my heroes!!" Begay exclaimed as he got into the front passenger seat.

"You two are our heroes today!" Lake said patting both of them on the back. We took off through the desert, Yazzie was careful to not run over any plant life or hit a lizard. The sound of the drums got louder as we closed in on the march. There was also a chant. We couldn't make it out clearly until we climbed a small ridge.

"If we don't keep house, then we won't have a house!" was the chant—the last words Lake and I had written.

"Oh my gosh," Begay said, as Yazzie had paused at the ridge top to look down on the procession. The drop off into the confluence at the road's end could be seen. The procession was less than a quarter of a mile away. It was magnificent, in a word. Thousands of people, hundreds of colors and the backdrop of the amazing Colorado Plateau. This was a picture we had to have. I put the phone together and snapped ten pictures. There was one message on the phone. I listened to it.

"Frankie says there's a few bad ones in the march that have been looking for us. He has eyes on them."

"We will wait until they all reach the rim and drop you off in the crowd. I take it you know where you're going after the ceremony?" Yazzie asked, taking out a pair of binoculars.

"Yes. Down there." I pointed to the canyon leading down to the confluence. A trail dropped from the rim and snaked down to the convergence of these two life forces. At the top of the trail, only a few cacti lived. Otherwise it was sand and rock. As the trail dropped into the canyon, the green life of the canyon floor became visible. It would be a good thirty-minute hike down and where my old river buddy would be there to whisk us away.

"What? You'll be trapped," Begay said worried that we had lost our minds.

"We have a plan," Lake said, also worried that we had lost our minds.

We waited on the ridge for another thirty minutes. Yazzie handed us the binoculars, and we searched the march for Groundhog and Gus. We saw Groundhog first. He was wearing overalls, which he had covered from top to bottom with sage smudge sticks. He must have had a hundred of them hanging from him, front and back. Cactus Wren was next to him dressed as a cactus wren, she wore homemade, painted, cardboard wings and a beak cap. We saw Gus next. We'd never met his wife. She was tiny. She and Gus dressed all in green, were chanting along with everyone else, and smiling at each other as they walked. We were so glad they had made it. Frankie and Elroy were walking together and seemed to be preoccupied with a few marchers in front of them.

"I think those guys just in front of Frankie and Elroy are the ones looking for us," I said handing the binoculars to Yazzie. Yazzie peered through the glasses.

"That's one of our council members. He's a scavenger at best. He wants this project to go through. That's his nephew with him, who the Great Spirit forgot to give any common sense to."

"We can't let them see us drive down there, or we lose our jobs," Begay said turning to Yazzie.

"Just wait, Frankie knows the score. We'll get you down there," Yazzie said to us.

Chapter Fifty-One

THE CROWD HAD FORMED in a semi-circle around the rim. All the marchers looked out onto the canyon. At the lip of the canyon were the twelve horses, all at least sixteen hands tall. No matter how far back you stood in the crowd, you had a clear view of the elders on horseback facing the canyon. The chant had changed to: "We are the Stewards-We are the Caretakers of the Earth!" Officer Yazzie drove us down the ridge. He stopped just a few yards from the back of the circle.

Only a few people turned to see us arrive and then turned back quickly with no interest in two more people in costumes. We said our goodbyes, thanked them, and then blended in with the crowd. We both kept our eyes out for the two Yazzie had told us about. The chant continued as the twelve elders, sitting high, looked out over the canyon. One by one, they turned their beautiful animals around and faced the crowd. The elders all raised their hands, and the large gathering became silent. Dozens of TV cameras were rolling. A Navajo elder on one of the middle horses spoke.

"We gather here today on this sacred place where the lifeblood of this land flows quietly below. Part of her was taken years ago from above here and then again below. Two slabs of concrete placed in her path. She has been in pain ever since. She cannot endure anymore. This place is very important to my people, but this place is much more than that. It is the home to the animals of the ground, air and water, and all the flora that has been here long before we arrived. The decision to allow the project can be stopped with a simple vote of the tribal council, which I sit on. My vote is no.

The marchers erupted in applause.

But my vote alone cannot stop this. Your march today and your voice, and these TV reporters can all help to stop this.

The confluence is but one battle, I will fight before I die. This is one of many battles for our mother. This possible tragedy, with thousands of other poor decisions we have made across the planet, and continue to make, have created the climate change that is sure to take hold if we do not change our ways. We have weakened her voice because too many of us no longer understand how to listen. She still speaks, but we tread so heavily on her skin that she finds it hard to believe we know her anymore. I could say much more, but I would only be saying the same thing over and over again, just with different words. We have little time left. I want to thank all of you for being here today. I want to thank Mr. and Mrs. Green Jeans for their courage. (Loud applause.) I also want to thank Savannah for her tireless work. (Loud applause.) Their fight is the fight we must all fight. It is the fight to remember who we are and what we are. We are the children of the Earth. (Loud applause.) Now please, stand still and listen, and see if you can hear the mother speaking to you.

Over six thousand people became deadly quiet. The twelve elders on horses all closed their eyes, and one by one, a smile grew on their faces. They were listening. They were hearing. After a few more minutes of silence, the Navajo elder spoke for the last time.

"As you leave here today, meet someone new, make a connection. It is only in this way that we can win the battles before us. Then, we must win the war. Before you depart from this sacred place, blow a blessing into the canyon and let her know you are here for her. Bless you all!" He took the reins of his horse. The crowd parted, and he and the other elders began a slow trot back down the road followed by the hundred drummers, who beat their drums with a rhythm of a beating heart. It was over. A message had been sent. Today's event would run on all the major networks tonight.

"Hey, Horny Toad!" I turned and saw Frankie standing with Gus, Savannah and Groundhog. They all had a good laugh.

"I'm glad you guys got to meet," I said, looking around for anyone who might seem suspicious.

"This was incredible today," Gus said, getting a big hug from Lake.

"Really over the top," Groundhog said with his arm around his lady, Cactus Wren.

"It was magical! Thank you all for making this happen," Lake said as nervous as I was about getting caught.

"Where are the people looking for us?" I asked looking at Frankie.

"Still here. Keep your costume on, and we'll get you out of here," Elroy said also looking around.

"We're going down to the confluence, I have a friend meeting us with a raft."

"Maybe some other time, Jack. It's two miles down there and if they want you, a helicopter is at their disposal," Frankie said taking out his phone.

"What's your plan?" I asked, now getting very worried that we were sitting ducks out here on the plateau. He put up his hand, motioning for me to wait until he finished the call he just started.

Where the confluence road met highway 89, the state troopers, and the Frackzon employees had stationed themselves ready to apprehend us. They didn't know if we were here, but suspected with all the costumes, we might have slipped by them. The news crews had been busy editing their footage in TV vans along the highway, and sending off pieces to local and national channels. Frackzon was already getting some very bad press, and when the markets re-opened tomorrow, it was likely their stock price would fall. If they could arrest us, it might ease their stockholders' minds, except the ones that were already considering divesting and now would have more reason to do so.

Most of the crowd was making the walk back down the dirt road to the highway. We continued to scan the hundreds still milling about. Then, we saw them. They approached us having a hunch that we might be the Green Jeans' people.

"That's them, isn't it!" shouted the council member, as he walked to within a few feet of us. We stood next to Elroy and Frankie, still in full costume, not knowing what to do.

"Let's go," Elroy said, grabbing my arm, and Frankie escorted Lake, taking us away from the confrontation. I looked back and Groundhog was detaining the council member and his nephew.

"Get your hands off me!" The tribal council member yelled. The people who hadn't started the walk back all turned and watched as Groundhog and a few of his desert crew, physically held him and his nephew.

"Do you know who I am?!" The council member shouted. Groundhog didn't reply and held him tight. The nephew was much smaller, but made more noise than a pack of coyotes.

"You're in so much trouble! My uncle's on the council and you're on our land. If you don't let me goo….!!!" The nephew screamed until Cactus Wren came up from behind him and put a strip of duct tape across his mouth. Cactus Wren always carried duct tape with her.

The remaining people from the march all looked on and some had their phones out and were videoing the scene unfolding before them. This was not the plan. Gus and his wife stood and watched, wanting to help, but there was nothing they could do. Fortunately, all the reporters had left as soon as the ceremony ended. They all wanted to get their story out first and had made a beeline for their TV vans.

"Walk south," Frankie said and pointed to the barren hills in the distance.

"Where Frankie? It's just desert," I replied, looking south and seeing no escape. They'd be on us in minutes once word was out that Mr. and Mrs. Green Jeans were here. And word was out. The council member's nephew had been able to get a text off that we were here. He sent it to a number he'd been given by one of the Frackzon people. Back at the junction of the confluence road and highway 89, two four-wheelers with four riders had already left, ripping through the desert towards the confluence. They were just five minutes away.

"Go!" Frankie said and pointed again toward the desert hills. Lake and I shed our costumes' paper Mache headgear and began to run across the sandy soil. Where we were actually going, we didn't know, just away from here.

I turned and shouted back, "Tell Groundhog to go the confluence and look for a guy named Hoot," not stopping, as Lake and I kept running and jumping over any cacti in our path. Frankie waved, and he and Elroy walked back to where the council member and his nephew were now on the ground, with duct tape around their ankles and hands. Each had a piece over his mouth and eyes. They were immobile, blind and speechless.

Frankie relayed my message, and Groundhog, Cactus Wren and a few other diehards waved to Frankie and Elroy and disappeared over the rim and down into the canyon. Gus and his wife, on the advice of Frankie, were on their way back down the dirt road. There were only a few dozen people still at the gathering spot, when the four wheelers skidded to a stop next to the duct-taped council member and his nephew, who were now wriggling on the ground like fish out of water.

"What the hell is going on here!?" yelled one of the Frackzon guys, jumping off his machine.

"There was a scuffle," Elroy said with his hands in the air.

"Where are the Green Jeans people?" he asked, scanning the desert.

"Who?" Frankie asked.

"You know exactly who I'm talking about. Call the troopers. We have a possible federal crime, and they now have jurisdiction to be back here," the muscle-bound Frackzon employee said to his subordinate, still sitting in the passenger seat of the four wheeler.

Less than a minute later, the sirens of three state trooper cars could be heard barreling down the dirt track from the highway. Two of the Frackzon employees began removing the tape from council member and his nephew.

"Ooowwww. They went that way!" yelled the council member as the tape on his mouth was pulled off.

"Go get them!" cried the nephew still on the ground as the tape was ripped from his mouth. "That reward is ours too! Look, there are their tracks," he screamed and pointed at sandy ground, as he got to his feet.

"Okay, let's go!" The four Frackzon employees jumped back on the four wheelers and peeled off, ripping up more of the untouched desert. Following our tracks for a half a mile, they reached a spot where our footprints vanished and were replaced with horse hooves.

"What? Horses! These tracks go off in four directions," the Frackzon guy in charge said, looking in every direction for any visual sign of us.

"Let's just pick two," said another one.

"I'm calling in a helicopter." He got on his sat phone and called Frackzon's closest office in Flagstaff.

Back at the rim above the confluence, Frankie, Elroy and Savannah were in handcuffs and being put into the trooper's vehicles. All three of them wore smiles as the doors closed. They were going to be detained for questioning and possible arrest.

"What about the ones who assaulted us. They went down there. Are you going to get them?" The council member was livid and directed his question to a state trooper.

"We called for a chopper, it should be here in a few minutes. It will be coming from South Rim, so it shouldn't take too long. I need to get their descriptions from you," the state trooper said, getting out a notepad.

"They were dirty Anglos. One was the size of a grizzly bear, and he's the one that almost broke my arm. Then, there was this little, smelly one that taped me up, and two or three others that helped," the Navajo council member said, brushing the dirt off his pants.

Back out in the desert, the two four-wheelers took off, each choosing a horse path. It wasn't long before they both reached embankments that their vehicles could not navigate. Returning to the start of the four paths and tracking the two remaining, the results were the same, finding themselves where either the tracks disappeared across a long stretch of sandstone or up and over a deep sand ridge that would certainly get their vehicle struck. They'd torn up a good bit of desert in the last hour and managed to kill four lizards and two-dozen native plants. Not one of them took any notice of this.

Frankie, Elroy and Savannah were on their way to a holding cell in Tuba City. Groundhog and his crew had made good time down the canyon, reached the confluence and began looking for a lone raft.

"I don't see anybody," Cactus Wren said, dipping her feet in the cold Colorado.

"Hoot! Hoot!" Groundhog shouted across the confluence of the two rivers.

"Hoooooottttt!" a shout from across the river came back.

From a stand of Tamarisk, an invasive species that lined many of rivers in the Southwest, a tall, lanky, clean-shaven man in his late sixties appeared.

"Where's Jack and Lake?" He shouted across the mild roar of the river.

"Plan B. I'm Groundhog."

"He told me about you. Give a minute, and I'll swing the raft over there."

Once Groundhog, Cactus Wren and his two loyal ground squirrels were aboard the raft, Hoot pushed off the bank, and they rounded a corner and entered the Grand Canyon. A helicopter could be heard in the distance.

On top of the canyon, Lake and I were resting inside a Hogan, eating fry bread and beans. An old Navajo woman sat on a chair in the corner of Hogan, staring at us with no discernable expression. We both smiled, but she just stared at us. Fifteen minutes ago, we had been dropped off here by two young Native American men and told to wait till someone came for us.

"Well, we're still free, I think," I said looking at Lake.

"Seems that way," Lake said, glancing over at the Navajo woman who wore the most beautiful squash-blossom, turquoise necklace she'd ever seen.

"Green Jeans?" The woman asked, breaking the silence, but still with no expression.

We nodded.

She smiled.

Chapter Fifty-Two

IT HAD BEEN THREE HOURS NOW, and checking our phone in the first hour, we realized we didn't have a signal. We were deep into the reservation. Since we'd been here, we had heard a helicopter pass over us six times. If they didn't spot us from the air, we imagined the few dwellings that dotted this backcountry would be searched.

"We need to move, Jack," Lake said

"Frankie will come," I reassured her, not knowing Frankie, Elroy and Savannah were in a holding cell in Tuba City.

"Not if he can't," Lake said and noticed a photo of Savannah in small frame made from cactus bones.

"Savannah?" Lake pointed to the photo while looking at the old woman.

"Ot," The old woman replied, saying, "Yes," in Navajo.

Lake pretended she was cradling a baby in her arms. The woman smiled and mirrored Lake's acting, and then ran her hand down between her legs and swept them up in the air above her head.

Then she motioned for us to come into the other room, the only other room in the small Hogan. A standard-size bed sat against the wall of the small room and an exquisite Navajo rug covered part of the floor. There was nothing else in the room. She laid on the rug facing away from us and opened her legs and did the sweeping motion with her hands again. Then she turned her head and pointed to the spot on the floor between her legs where Savannah must have born. She had a big smile on her face and got to her feet. I gave her my best 'wow' expression, but Lake with tears of love starting to sprout, went and gave her a big hug, which the woman embraced in kind. Lake's heart led her, even though we had a forty-thousand dollar bounty on our heads, and were now hidden in a Hogan with only the clothes on our back. Savannah's mother grabbed Lake's hand, led her back into the main room, and sat her down at the table. She placed a big wooden bowl, a pitcher of water, a container of salt and a bag of flour on the table and began to teach Lake how to make fry bread. I found a comfortable spot on the floor and tried to close my eyes and meditate on a positive outcome. I had experienced a few panic attacks in my life, and this would certainly qualify as a good time.

I must have fallen asleep, because Lake was shaking me with unusual vigor.

"Jack, someone's here!" she whispered to me wide-eyed. I snapped out of 'my dead-to-the-world sleep' and heard the knocking on the door.

Savannah's mother was softly saying something in Navajo and gesturing for us to come into the other room. Lot of good that would do, if whoever was out there wanted to search the place. This could very well the end.

We followed her and she pulled back the rug to expose a pine trap door that had been hinged into the dirt floor with long pieces of wrought iron. I opened it and a blast of cool air hit my face. She hurriedly gestured for us to go down. A five-rung kiva ladder was set just below the lip of the passage. We didn't hesitate. Once down, she closed the door and pulled the rug back. We could still hear the knocking, as it must have gotten louder. We were in complete darkness. A tunnel stretched before us, but it was completely black now with the door closed. The next ten minutes were unquestionably the longest ten minutes either of us had ever experienced. We had heard whoever it was above, walking around the house and over the trap door. They spoke English, but we couldn't make out what they were saying. They didn't sound like cops.

A few minutes of silence passed and the trap door opened, and we saw Savannah's mother with a finger to her lips. She handed us a lantern and box of matches and indicated that we needed to follow the tunnel. She smiled again, and then she closed the door on us.

Outside the Hogan, two of Frackzon's finest sat in an air-conditioned truck. They'd seen the horse tracks and fresh droppings at the front of the Hogan, but the old woman didn't speak English, and there was no sign of us.

"Let's just sit here and wait for a while. I got a feeling they're somewhere around here," said the driver turning up the air-conditioning.

"Man, we are way back in here. We got no cell signal, and it's going to be dark soon. Let's just go eat," said the other Frackzon security officer.

"Forty grand. We wait just a bit. Keep your eyes on the hills around here. I'm thinking they might be looking at us right now."

"Okay," replied the other Frackzon guy, who was overweight and loading rubber bullets into his gun.

Down in the tunnel, we had the lantern lit. Before us was a natural slot canyon. The Hogan had been built over one of the ends of the narrow crack in the sandstone. Not only was it an awesome escape route, but provided natural air-conditioning during the summer months when Savannah's mother would open the trap door to let the cool air blow into her home.

"Jack, this is wild. It's a mini slot canyon."

"I know. How cool is this?"

"Shall we?" Lake said, holding the lantern out in front of her.

"We shall. Lead the way, Bonnie."

We had to go single file, rubbing against the red sandstone walls as we made our down the water-sculpted tunnel. The walls of the slot grew higher and our path became wider. Then we saw the first ray of light forty feet above, peeking through a small crack in the ceiling. Another twenty minutes, and we had reached the end of the canyon and found ourselves entering onto the desert floor. Looking back at where we exited the slot canyon, we viewed a hundred-foot, sandstone wall that ran as far as we could see in either direction. In front of us was nothing but high desert for miles and miles. The sun was beginning its descent.

"What do we do now?" Lake asked.

"I think we stay here," I replied, sitting down at the entrance to the slot canyon.

"We don't even have any water."

"We don't have anything, baby, but hope. Try to close your eyes for a while, I'll take the first watch."

"First watch? What are we in some western movie right now?"

"Yes, we are. Close your eyes, baby."

Lake complied. She was as exhausted as I was. In the last few days, really months, sleep had been anything but regular. Lake sat on the ground, leaned her back up against the sandstone cliff at the entrance to our escape route, and closed her eyes. I sat, staring off into the distance of the black night, listening for any sound that was not connected to this place. There was something moving out there and it was getting closer. I heard what sounded like a rock rolling down a slope. A branch snapped. Whatever it was, was coming right toward us.

"Lake, wake up!"

She rose quickly, and we took shelter inside the entrance to the slot canyon. It was something large, not a coyote or a fox. This was something much larger.

"Green Jeans?" called a voice, not far off from where Lake and I now squatted.

"Green Jeans, its Begay." Now we could see the outline of two horses. One held Begay, and the other was empty of a rider.

"Begay!" Lake said, exiting the slot and lighting the lantern.

"Turn off the light!" Begay said as he dismounted.

"Where's Frankie?" I asked, hoping something bad hadn't happened.

"Frankie, Elroy and Savannah are behind bars for the moment. A high-powered lawyer from one of those big environmental organizations is trying to get them out."

"Why are they in jail? They didn't do anything," Lake responded in an angry tone.

"I don't know. But there's some Frackzon suits walking around Tuba right now. We can talk later. Now I need to get you out of here."

"How did you know we were here?" Lake asked.

"I went to Savannah's mother's home to get you and a Frackzon pickup was sitting outside with a couple of men in it. I told them they were trespassing and had no right to be there. They left after a few choice expletives. She told me you went into the slot. Now, we have to go." Begay pulled Lake onto his horse and positioned the other horse next to a boulder, so I could easily mount him. He headed off through the desert, leading the horse I was riding.

"We cannot talk now. They have been searching all day for you, and not just Frackzon. There are some natives eager to claim the money, and they know this country. So from here on out, silence."

We rode for hours up over ridges, down in arroyos and across long flat stretches of desert. Occasionally we would spy a light off in the distance from someone's home. Otherwise the only sign of life was the sound of a rattler letting us know she was there, or the hoot of an owl or the eyes of a coyote reflecting the moonlight.

When we finally stopped, Begay got out his phone.

"Oh good... Yes, I have them... Sunrise gulch. Okay, Okay. Hahaha....*Ot.*" Begay put away his phone.

"We wait here. Good news. They have all been released from jail," Begay said, getting off his horse and helping Lake down.

"Oh, good," Lake said relieved.

"Where are we going, Begay?" I asked, climbing off the horse.

"I do not know. Frankie is coming to get you now."

We waited for another two hours and drank all the water Begay had brought with him. Headlights seemed to appear out of nowhere. They shined down in the arroyo where we'd been waiting.

"Yah teh hey," Frankie said, walking down into the arroyo.

"Frankie?" Lake asked, hoping it wasn't someone looking to turn us in.

"The one and only! Even might have a criminal record soon."

"For what?" I asked as he and Lake hugged.

"For organizing an unlawful assembly on state land."

"State land? We were on Dinah land," Lake exclaimed, while Frankie and I gave each other a long, two-handed shake and then a hug.

"Highway 89," Begay answered.

"That's crazy," I said, looking at Begay.

"It's to be expected. There is a lot at stake for those whose see the money. Begay, you be careful riding home. Thank you."

"Frankie, keep that radio going. Someday I want to read some poetry on it." Frankie laughed and began walking back up the path.

"Begay, bless you! I wish we had something to give you," Lake said as we both started to follow Frankie.

"You two are the gift. Don't stop." We waved as we trudged up the steep embankment to find Frankie's truck idling in the desert above the wash.

Back on the blacktop, we drove south onto Zuni land. Frankie pulled off onto a dirt track, and several bumps later, we reached a corral with horses. There was nothing else in sight.

"We're not getting on horses again, are we?" I asked, as I already had a sore butt amongst other lower sore areas.

"Come on, ya big wuss!" Lake said, as she watched Frankie go into the corral to pick out the horses.

"Did you just say 'wuss' to me?"

"I think I might have," Lake replied, starting a smile.

"That horse I rode had no blanket."

"Begay was leading you, and ours didn't have a blanket either."

"All right, you guys need nap time," Frankie said coming out of the corral leading three horses. He roped them together, pulled our packs from the truck, and secured them on the third horse.

"Where are we going?" I asked, using the cedar posts of the corral to climb onto a Pinto that looked at me as I mounted her bare back.

"We don't want you to get into any more trouble," Lake added as Frankie helped her onto another horse.

"As I don't want you two to get in any more trouble. You're our great white hope." Frankie let out a laugh that echoed off of a nearby canyon wall. "But trouble is here, and I will not walk away from it till I take my last breath. Trouble is what gave birth to Green Jeans, isn't it? And who's telling who about getting in trouble?"

After crossing miles of virgin desert, we arrived at the entrance to a shallow, red stone canyon. The three of us dismounted, and Frankie removed our Duluth packs from the horse.

"Follow the canyon for a mile or so, and on your right you will see a door above you. Here is a flashlight."

"Frankie, where are we going?" I asked again, as Lake put on her pack.

"I'll see you in three days. You have much to think about. You'll be safe there," Frankie said, getting back on his horse and taking off across the desert leading the other two horses behind him.

"Frankie!" I called out, but he didn't turn. He and the three horses vanished over a dune.

We stood at the entrance to the canyon. My pack was on the ground.

"Let's get going, mister," Lake said beginning down the canyon.

"What's going on? How come you're so cool about all this?"

"One of us has to be. Next time it'll be your turn."

"Okay, that makes sense. I mean what can we do about it now, right?" I stated, hefting up my pack as my anxiety began to wane. The desert for me is a place of peace, and it was working its juju like it always had.

"Right. We're in spirit hands now. So let's get going. I sure hope there's food behind the mystery door up here," Lake replied.

Buckling my pack's waist belt, we walked into the canyon. We were both spent, not just from today, it went all the way back to 'VASECTOMY REVERSAL' and 'BOX-MART'. It went all the way back to the decades of awareness that something just didn't match up. For an hour, we trudged down the canyon, shining the flashlight on the right wall, which had grown to at least a hundred feet in height. The dawn was now exposing the top lip of the wall, but it would be hours before the floor of this canyon saw any light.

"Do you think we missed it?" Lake asked, shining the flashlight on the red rock wall as we continued to make forward progress.

"I sure hope not," I replied, wishing it was just around the next bend. I dropped ten yards behind her.

"I found it!" Lake yelled minutes later.

The flashlight exposed a three-foot-tall, red, wooden door bolted ten feet up into the face of the cliff wall. To the right of the door, an ancient man-made, stone wall covered what had once been a large opening in the cliff. It ran for twenty feet from the door and was as high as five feet in spots. A wood ladder lay at the base of the cliff. I positioned the ladder and held it as Lake climbed up the pine rungs to the door. Turning the knob, she left the ladder and squeezed through the opening. A few seconds later, light shot out the doorway, and Lake's head appeared.

"You're not going to believe this!"

I climbed the ladder and poked my head through the portal.

"Oh my God!" I said, slithering through the door into huge cavern with two tunnels leading off into the rock on the back wall. There was furniture, a kitchen with a stove and fridge, a bed with fresh linens. Shelves had been carved into the stone. Some had books, but most had food. On the floor was a Zuni rug and GREEN JEANS had been woven in the center.

"I bet this was once a home to the Anasazi," I said, now standing and running my hand across the curvature of the rock wall and looking at the ceiling, which was still black in places from ancient cooking fires.

"But updated. Talk about a house flip!" Lake responded, making her way to a small refrigerator.

"There's a ginormous salad in here!" Lake shouted, taking out a large glass bowl brimming with greens. "Oh, there's green chili too! Turn on the stove, Jack!"

After stuffing ourselves, we both lay on the queen-sized mattress with fresh linens and were dead to the world within seconds.

The ancient ones had used this as a place of refuge and protection from unknown danger, and now, 800 years later, this cavity was harboring us from the same thing.

The next day, we explored the tunnels. The first one just went a few yards and ended in a small, cavity that was maybe five-by-six feet with a low ceiling. Two shelves of rechargeable solar batteries were networked off an electrical line that ran up into a bored hole in the rock ceiling. We imagined the solar panels that must be on the top of the canyon. The other tunnel off the back wall was a different story. Light bulbs hung every ten feet from the ceiling so we didn't need our flashlight. It was very much like a slot canyon. We had to walk single-file, duck in a few spots and after a few minutes we reached another small door. This one was locked. In a carved-out shelf next to the door was an envelope with our names on it. Lake opened it. There was a handwritten letter and a key. Lake read the letter out loud:

> Mr. and Mrs. Green Jeans, the key is for the door in front of you. If you decide to open it, which I imagine you will, you will see something to give you pause. I will come and see you in a few days. Your decision will be respected either way. I suppose it's time to open the door?
> Frankie

"Frankie, what have got up your sleeve?" Lake said holding the key.

"Go ahead," I said, looking at the key in her hand.

Lake opened the door.

We looked out at a horseshoe canyon. A small, adobe house sat in the center of a green acre, surrounded by canyon walls, except for a narrow outlet on the far side where a clear stream flowed through, following the base of the canyon. Next to the house was an old Chevy pickup with a small retro camper attached to its hitch. Rolls of canvas filled the truck bed. Gallon cans of paint were stacked on the front porch of the adobe house. We were speechless, absolutely dumbfounded. We were also thirty feet up on the canyon wall. There was no way down. Even if we used the ladder for the front door, it would be twenty feet shy of the canyon floor.

"He wants us to give this some thought," I said, as we both imagined ourselves below.

"Yes, he does," Lake said, staring down into the valley.

"Well?"

Lake took a seat in the doorway and let her legs dangle over the edge.

"Have a seat, Clyde."

I cautiously nudged myself next to her in the small doorway and let my legs hang with hers against the canyon wall. I put a hand on her knee, which she covered with hers, and used my other hand to hold onto the doorframe. We gazed out over the valley and what could be our future. Our lives had become surreal, and our current situation was far better than what we ever imagined might have happened. We could turn ourselves in, probably face jail time. We'd definitely lose our teaching certificates, and with that maybe our house. Brien had told us he'd be able to cover the mortgage and we'd square at a later date. It was doubtful that could access our retirement or use any credit or debit card. Our funds amounted to what we had in our pockets. A few hundred dollars.

"You okay?" I asked.

"We're stardust, baby. Just like everything else."

"I wish everyone knew that."

"Wha-Ooouuuuuuuuu!" Lake cried out over the valley.

"Wha-Ooouuuuuuuuu!" I followed, as her call bounced off the far canyon wall and met my cry in the middle of the valley, over the cabin and all the fixins' for the next phase.

Sometimes, once you get something started, it can be very hard to stop.

Epilogue

ANNE BREWER GOT HER TALK SHOW. Her rich boyfriend and now fiancé was crazy in love. Anne's web channel and regionally aired talked show featured guests with alternative ideas about health, economics, food, energy and many other topics. It was called 'Tread Softly'. For Anne, it was a business decision, and just into the first year, her viewership was steadily increasing each month. Anne didn't live too many of the ideas she presented, but slowly she was changing. She now recycled. She'd never done that. Maybe in ten years, she'll be composting!

In Dodge City, Vincent ran the story the next day. It didn't get the front page. The newspaper owner was too beholden to the cattle industry. They were a third of the papers advertising revenue. Vincent sent the story off to Gus, and Gus sent it out to his contacts across the country. In San Francisco, it got a three-page spread in Sunday's lifestyle section. In New York, Chicago, Portland, Los Angeles, and many places in between, newspapers ran the story. If it had just been the seventh page of the Dodge Globe, it would have faded as a fluke, stupid, hippie incident. But that's not what happened. The national coverage promoted more inspections of the animal industry at the federal level. As Vincent made his way about Dodge City, going to the grocery store, gas station, local hardware store or just being in the presence of the population, it was obvious things had changed. He was not liked here. He began his departure by listing his sequestered cabin and searching the web for prospective landing grounds. He also decided to get back in the game, the one he'd left so many years ago. The journalism of truth. He just couldn't do that here.

Elroy kept good care of the VW and used it to ferry his customers on his exclusive outings. It was a big hit. He and Frankie kept in close contact. They both prayed Lake and I, still had another round in us.

Ham made it to Guatemala. He stored his plane at small, single-strip, grass airfield in the mountains, owned by another veteran who had expiated two decades ago. Ham put on his pack and traveled the country by foot, train and bus, in search of his Nirvana location. Shortly into his journey, he realized what he'd done in his last hours in Phoenix were some of the most meaningful hours he had spent on this planet. He focused his attention on finding a farm. He was going organic, maybe even bananas. He was going to do his part, and with that, a peacefulness enveloped him.

Gus quit the local news channel in Manchester, took on some freelance camera work ten hours a week. He was done. He and his wife had a comfortable living on social security and some meager investments. They were content. They were also fired up. With caution to the wind, Gus and his wife began to print Mr. Green Jeans banner images to raise money for a dot org Gus had set up to support the environment. He was looking into seeing how some of the proceeds could be funneled to us.

Lillian was a local star. People dropped off fresh flowers on her doorstep at least three times a week. She was invited to many progressive lectures on campus, always with a driver and an escort. We talked on a disposable cell. She'd ask us to stop, then would tell us she loved us very much, and then would ask us to stop again, but was quite proud of what we had done. She was going to be all right. Her kids hadn't hurt anyone, and being the mother and mother-in-law of these two was proving to elevate her status in Manchester.

Brien had replaced us on 'pizza night' with Lillian, and he and my mother got along famously. He had outlined his sci-fi novel, and was now in a quandary about what the first sentence should say. The house was being watched, and we only talked with him when he called. He never called from the house. He would drive to a trail and go hiking, put his phone together and call us from the woods. On his last call, he informed us that two homeland guys had a warrant and searched the house. There was nothing to find, except the chainsaws, and they were still hidden in the dry cave. We always asked about Barney, Pearl and Smokey Joe. Everyone was doing well. Brien always kept a generous supply of dog bones and cat treats, that and lots of love. We had no concern about their welfare. We planned to make a clandestine visit soon. If just for a few days.

Frankie was a celebrity in Zuni. He was also tailed every time he left the reservation by homeland security and sometimes a Frackzon vehicle. Purely intimidation tactics. Both of these forces were currently trying to recruit someone within the reservation to befriend Frankie. Frankie knew the score and was planning accordingly.

Frackzon Corp. found themselves in a nightmare of bad PR. They were used to it. Protests might be escalating here in Arizona and other places across the globe recently, but the Frackzon Corp. wasn't worried. It was the price of big profits. For Frackzon, Green Jeans had proved to be quite a thorn. A small reward equated to just a few seconds in profit. The Confluence development had been put on an extended hold for more environmental studies. It could be years before anything would be decided. They were used to this, too, and they were confident their project would eventually go through. They were too big to stop.

Lake and I? We had a great ride. We felt we'd made a difference. After three days of peace in the cave, there was a knock on the back door. We made our way down the tunnel and with a big exhale, Lake opened the small weathered door. Frankie stood atop the thirty-foot ladder with a ribbon of climbing rope wrapped around his torso. He had a big smile. Elroy stood on the valley floor holding the ladder secure, also with a big smile. We had made our decision three days ago, moments after opening this door for the first time. Green Jeans was going a second tour.

More books from Harvard Square Editions:

Augments of Change, Kelvin Christopher James
Gates of Eden, Charles Degelman
Love's Affliction, Fidelis Mkparu
Transoceanic Lights, S. Li
Close, Erika Raskin
Anomie, Jeff Lockwood
Living Treasures, Yang Huang
Nature's Confession, J.L. Morin
A Face in the Sky, Greg Jenkins
Dark Lady of Hollywood, Diane Haithman
Fugue for the Right Hand, Michele Tolela Myers
Growing Up White, James P. Stobaugh
The Beard, Alan Swyer
Parallel, Sharon Erby

CPSIA information can be obtained at www.ICGtesting.com
Printed in the USA
LVOW11s2337190416

484293LV00002B/11/P